"HAVE YOU EVER REALLY KILLED ANYBODY, LEW?"

"Yes," I said. "Eleven or twelve years ago, I killed a man named Puddler who tried to kill me."

She leaned toward me confidentially. Her head gravitated towards my shoulder. "I'm being killed, too."

"How?"

"Little by little, a piece at a time. First he ruined my soul, then he ruined my body, then he ruined my face." She removed her dark glasses. Both of her eyes were blacked.

"Who did that to you?"

"I'll tell you when the time comes." Her head subsided on my shoulder like a frowzy bird coming home to roost. She reached across my chest and touched the shape of the gun. Her fingers caressed it through the cloth of my jacket. "I want you to kill him for me," she said.

THE WYCHERLY WOMAN

Ross Macdonald

BANTAM BOOKS
TORONTO • NEW YORK • LONDON • SYDNEY

The characters and incidents in this novel
are all fictitious, and have no reference
to any actual people or events.

*This low-priced Bantam Book
has been completely reset in a type face
designed for easy reading, and was printed
from new plates. It contains the complete
text of the original hard-cover edition.*
NOT ONE WORD HAS BEEN OMITTED.

THE WYCHERLY WOMAN
*A Bantam Book / published by arrangement with
Alfred A. Knopf, Inc.*

PRINTING HISTORY
Knopf edition published February 1961

*A condensed version of this novel prepared by
the author appeared in* COSMOPOLITAN *under the
title of* TAKE MY DAUGHTER HOME

Bantam edition / October 1963

2nd printing ...... July 1968	5th printing .. December 1973
3rd printing .... March 1972	6th printing ...... May 1974
4th printing .... March 1973	7th printing ...... June 1978
	8th printing ... February 1984	

ISBN 0-553-23855-8

Published simultaneously in the United States and Canada

Bantam Books are published by Bantam Books, Inc. Its trademark, consisting of the words "Bantam Books" and the por-
trayal of a rooster, is Registered in U.S. Patent and Trademark
Office and in other countries. Marca Registrada. Bantam
Books, Inc. 666 Fifth Avenue, New York, New York 10103.

PRINTED IN THE UNITED STATES OF AMERICA

H   17 16 15 14 13 12 11 10 9 8

chapter 1

COMING OVER THE PASS you can see the whole valley spread out below. On a clear morning, when it lies broad and colored under a white sky, with the mountains standing far back on either side, you can imagine it's the promised land.

Maybe it is for a few. But for every air-conditioned ranch-house with its swimming pool and private landing strip, there are dozens of tin-sided shacks and broken-down trailers where the lost tribes of the migrant workers live. And when you leave the irrigated areas you find yourself in gray desert where nobody lives at all. Only the oil derricks grow there, an abstract forest casting no shade. The steady pumps at their bases nod their heads like clockwork animals.

Meadow Farms lay on the edge of this rich and ugly desert. From a distance it was a typical lost valley city thrown down helter-skelter at the foot of barren-looking mountains and garnished with a little alkali dust. When I drove into it past the euphoric sign at the city limits, Fastest-Growing City in the Valley, I could see some differences. The main street was clean and freshly paved; the buildings along it included substantial new ones, and others going up; the people on the street had a hustling, prosperous look.

I stopped at a downtown corner for gas and information. When the leather-faced attendant had filled the tank of my car, I asked him the way to Homer Wycherly's house. He pointed along the main street to the outskirts where oil tanks gleamed like stacks of minted silver in the sun:

"Straight on through town, you can't miss it. It's the big stone house on the side of the hill. I heard Mr. Wycherly just got back last night."

"Back from where?"

"He took one of them luxury cruises to Australia and the South Seas. Been gone over two months. Myself, I got enough South Seas when I was in the Marines. You a friend of his?"

"I never met him."

"I know him well, knew his old man before him." He gave me and my car a quick once-over. It wasn't a recent

1

model, and neither was I. "If you're selling, don't waste your time on Mr. Wycherly. He's a hard man to sell to."

"Maybe I'll buy something from him."

The man grinned. "You just did. I'm one of the outlets for Wycherly gas. That will be four-forty."

I paid him and drove out of town past the silver tanks and a cracking station whose Disney towers smelled faintly of rotten eggs. The house stood high above the road at the top of a winding private drive. Its stone face was forbidding, like a castle built to dominate a countryside. From the old-fashioned verandah I could look down into the town and out across the valley.

A big man with wavy brown hair and a stomach answered the door. His hair was too uniformly brown for a man of his age: he probably had it dyed. He had a strong nose and a weak chin and a sort of in-between mouth. He wore imported-looking tweeds buttoned over his stomach. On his face he wore a home-grown expression of dismay.

"I'm Homer Wycherly. You must be Mr. Archer."

I acknowledged that I was. His expression didn't change much; it crinkled a bit around the mouth and eyes. It was the smile of a man who wanted to be liked and hadn't always been.

"You made good time from Los Angeles. I wasn't expecting you so soon."

"I started out before dawn. You said on the phone the matter was urgent."

"Very urgent indeed. But do come in." He led me along a dim hallway under old deer heads into a sitting room, keeping up a stream of half-apologetic chatter: "I'm afraid I can't offer anything much in the way of hospitality. I've just reopened the house, there isn't a servant in the place. The fact is, I didn't intend to come back here at all. I only did so on the off-chance that Phoebe might have come home." He sniffed. "But Phoebe hasn't."

The sitting room had the closed musty atmosphere of a Victorian parlor. Some of the furniture was sheeted; the heavy drapes were closed against the morning. Wycherly turned on an overhead light, looked around at the effect with disapproval, and went to the windows. I was struck by the violent way he jerked at the draw-cord of the drapes. Like a man hanging a cat.

Sunlight poured in, migrating across the room to a small picture on the wall above the marble fireplace. Composed of blobs and splashes of raw color, it was one of those paintings which are either very advanced or very backward, I never can tell which. Wycherly looked at the painting as if it was a Rorschach test, and he had failed it.

"Some of my wife's work." He added to himself, "I'm going to have it taken down."

"Is your wife the one who's missing?"

"Heavens, no. It's Phoebe. My only daughter. Sit down, Mr. Archer, let me explain the situation, if I can." He subsided into a chair and waved me into another. "I found out yesterday when I returned to this country—I've been on a cruise—I found out that Phoebe had dropped out of school away back in November. No one seems to have seen her since that time. Naturally I'm worried sick."

"What school?"

"Boulder Beach College. You've got to get her back for me, Mr. Archer. A girl of her tender years, with her protected upbringing—"

"How old is she?"

"Twenty-one, but she's a complete innocent."

"Has she ever done this before—gone away without telling you where she was going?"

"She has not. Phoebe's always been a well-conducted girl. She's had her problems, of course, but there have been no problems between her and me. She's always confided in me. We get along beautifully."

"Who did she have problems with?"

"Her mother." He glanced at the Rorschach painting over the mantel. His face became heavier and duller. "But we won't go into the subject of that."

"I'd like to talk to Phoebe's mother, if she's available."

"She isn't," he said flatly. "I don't know where Catherine is and I'll be frank to tell you I don't care. She and I decided to go our separate ways last spring. There's no point in rehashing the glory details. Our divorce had nothing to do with Phoebe's disappearance."

"There's no chance that she's with her mother?"

"No. After the spectacle Catherine made of herself—" He compressed his mouth over the rest of the sentence. I waited, but he didn't finish it.

"Exactly how long has Phoebe been gone? This is January the eighth. You say she left college in November. What time in November?"

"Early November. I haven't been able to pin it down precisely. That's your job. I did get Phoebe's roommate on the phone last night—her ex-roommate. But she's a rattlebrain."

"Two months is a long time," I said. "Is this your first attempt to have your daughter traced?"

"It's not my fault. I'm not responsible."

He rose in an angry pouncing movement, came up against magnetic lines of force which seemed to web the room and hem him in invisibly. He began to pace back and forth like a caged animal remembering jungle:

"You've got to understand, I've been out of the country. I didn't even know about it till yesterday. I've been cruising around the Pacific while God knows what has been going on behind my back."

"When did you see her last?"

"The day I sailed. She came up to San Francisco to bid me bon voyage. If I can trust what her roommate says, she never went back to Boulder Beach." He stopped in his tracks, and turned to me with murky eyes. "I'm desperately afraid that something has happened to her. And I blame myself," he added. "It really is my fault. I was thinking exclusively of myself when I embarked on that cruise. I was trying to put the whole wretched family trouble behind me. I deserted Phoebe in her hour of need."

Whenever he mentioned her name, it came out soggy with emotion. I tried to dehydrate it a little:

"You're melodramatizing a little bit, I think. When girls disappear, it's generally for some good reason of their own. Every year thousands of young women leave their families, or their schools, or whatever they happen to be doing—"

"Without telling anyone of their plans?"

"That's right. You've been out of the country, anyway. You wouldn't know if she had tried to contact you."

"I could always be reached in an emergency."

"But maybe it wasn't an emergency, to your daughter."

"Let's hope that's the case." He sat down heavily, as if his bout of emotion had exhausted him. "But what good reason could she possibly have for going away? A girl with her opportunities?"

"Opportunity is where you find it." I looked around the mortuary room, and out the window to the little city and the wide empty valley. "Was Phoebe happy at home?"

He said defensively: "She spent very little time here in recent years. We always went to Tahoe for the summer, and of course she's been going to school the rest of the year."

"How was she doing at school?"

"Adequately, so far as I know. She had a little academic trouble last year, but that was resolved."

"Tell me about it."

"She had to leave Stanford. She didn't flunk out, exactly, but it was suggested to us that she'd be more comfortable in a less competitive atmosphere. Which is why she transferred last fall to Boulder Beach. I wasn't too happy about the transfer, since Stanford's my alma mater."

"How did your daughter feel about it?"

"Phoebe seemed to be keen on the change. I gathered that she'd found herself a boy friend at the new place."

"What's the boy friend's name?"

"She called him Bobby, I think. Feminine psychology is not my forte, but she seemed to have quite a crush on this boy."

"A fellow-student?"

"Yes. I know nothing about him, but I wasn't displeased at the idea. She'd never taken much to boys in the past."

Girls fall hard, I thought, when they fall for the first time at twenty-one. "Is she attractive?"

"I'd say so. Of course I'm a fond father."

He produced an alligator wallet and flipped it open. Phoebe looked up at me through transparent plastic. She was attractive, but not in any ordinary fashion. Careless light-brown hair swirled around her head. She had great blue lamps of eyes. Her mouth was wide and straight, passionate in a kind of ingrown way. She looked like one of those sensitive girls who could grow up into beauty or into hard-faced spinsterhood. If she grew up at all.

"May I have this picture?"

"No," her father said flatly. "It's the best I have of her. I can let you have some others if you like."

"I'll probably need them."

"I might as well look them up now, while we think of it."

He left the room abruptly. I heard him going up the stairs two at a time, then banging around on the second floor. Something crashed and shook the ceiling.

Wycherly bothered me. He was a gentleman of the old school, as such things went in the sixties, but there was a violence in him that kept breaking out. He pounded down the stairs and flung the door open so that it rebounded against the wall. His face was an uneven crimson:

"Damn the woman, she's taken all my pictures. She hasn't left me a single one of Phoebe."

"Who?"

"My wife. My ex-wife."

"She must be quite fond of the girl after all."

"Don't you believe it. Catherine was never what you'd call a devoted mother. She took the pictures because she knew I valued them."

"When did she take them?"

"I presume when she went to Reno. That was last April. I haven't seen her but once since then. She shook the dust of Meadow Farms from her feet—"

"Is she still in Reno?"

"No. She simply went there for her precious divorce. I believe she's living somewhere in the Bay area, I have no idea where."

"You must have some idea. Aren't you supporting her?"

"That's handled by the lawyers."

"Okay, give me the name of a lawyer who knows her address."

"I will not." He breathed at me like a bull, or at least a good fat steer. "I don't want you making any attempt to contact Mrs. Wycherly. She'd simple confuse the issue, give you a completely false impression of Phoebe. Of both of us, for that matter. Catherine has a vile tongue." His elastic lips bulged over a mouthful of words. To judge by his expression, they tasted bitter. "She said the most dreadful things."

"When was this?"

"She came aboard the ship the day I sailed—forced her way into my cabin and attacked me. I had to have her removed."

"Attacked you?"

"Verbally, she attacked me. And most unfairly. She accused me of leaving her penniless. Actually I was most generous with her—a hundred-thousand-dollar settlement, and ample alimony."

"You say the divorce was in April?"

"It became final at the end of May."

"Has Phoebe been seeing her mother since the divorce?"

"Absolutely not. Pheboe considered that Catherine had done us both a great wrong."

"The divorce was Catherine's idea, then?"

"Entirely. She hated me. She hated Meadow Farms. She had no regard for her own daughter, even. I know for a fact that after Catherine left here the two of them never met, except for that ugly moment in my cabin."

"Phoebe was on the ship at the same time as her mother?"

"Yes, unfortunately."

"Why 'unfortunately'?"

"Phoebe was naturally shocked and horrified by the things my wife said. She did her best to calm her down, of course. She was really very good to her, I thought. Better than she deserved," he added prissily.

"Did they leave the ship together?"

"Certainly not. I didn't see them leave—frankly I was

feeling under the weather after Catherine's attack, and I didn't venture out of the cabin again. But it's unthinkable that Phoebe should have gone off with her mother. Quite unthinkable."

"Did Phoebe have funds of her own? Could she have taken a plane or a train?"

"She could have, yes. As a matter of fact, I gave her quite a large amount that very day." He went on in a self-justifying tone: "Her expenses at school had been running higher than she'd expected. She'd had to buy a car, and that put quite a dent in her allowance. I gave her an extra thousand to tide her over."

"In cash, or by check?"

"Cash. I happened to be carrying a good deal of cash."

"Where was she planning to go when she left the ship?"

"Back to the hotel. I had a suite at the St. Francis. I left it paid up a night in advance for her."

"Was she driving her own car?"

"No. Her car was in the Union Square garage. She wanted to drive me to the dock herself, but I was afraid of getting caught in a traffic jam. I insisted we take a taxi."

"Did she take the same taxi back to the hotel?"

"I presume so. She asked the driver to wait. Whether he did or not I can't say."

"Can you describe him?"

"He was a darkish fellow. That's all I can remember. A small darkish fellow."

"Negro?"

"No. More Mediterranean in type."

"What kind of a taxi was it?"

Wycherly uncrossed and recrossed his thick tweeded thighs. "I'm afraid I don't remember. I'm not a noticer."

"Can you describe Phoebe's car, or give me the license number?"

"I never actually saw her car. It's some sort of a small imported model, I believe. She bought it secondhand in Boulder Beach."

"I'll find out there. Now what was Phoebe wearing?"

His gaze went up over my head, focusing on the plaster cornice just below the high ceiling. "A skirt and a sweater, both brown. A tan coat, kind of a polo coat. High-heeled brown shoes. Brown leather bag. Phoebe always dresses simply. No hat."

I took out my pen and a little black leather notebook, turned to the first clean page, wrote 'Phoebe Wycherly' at the top of it, and under the name, 'mother—Catherine,' and 'boy friend—Bobby,' with a question mark. I listed her clothes.

"What are you writing?" Wycherly leaned towards me suspiciously. "Why have you written down Catherine's name?"

"I'm practicing penmanship."

The words slipped out. He was getting on my nerves.

"What do you mean by that?"

"Nothing in particular."

"How dare you speak to me like that?"

"Sorry, but you've been crowding me, Mr. Wycherly. I can't very well take on a case where whole lines of investigation are blocked off by the whim of my principal. I have to be free to follow the facts where they lead me."

"But you're working for me."

"I haven't taken your money yet."

"Here." He reached inside his coat, grinning at me fiercely, as if he felt a twinge of angina there. He slapped his hand with the alligator wallet. "How much?"

"It depends on how much of an effort you want. I usually work alone, but there are other people I can call in—men and organizations all over the country."

"No. We'll wait and see if that is indicated."

"It's your money. And your daughter. Have you considered using the police?"

"I talked it over last night with our local Sheriff. Hooper's an old personal friend, he used to work for Father. It's his opinion that we wouldn't get much cooperation by simply filing a missing report. You have to have a crime, it appears, before you can stir up the animals." His voice was bleak, and it didn't change perceptibly when he added: "Sheriff Hooper recommended you."

"That was nice of him."

"He said you had a reputation for discretion. I hope it's justified. I don't want any publicity in this thing, and I've had a bad experience with private detectives so-called."

"What happened?"

"We won't go into it. It has nothing to do with the present matter." He was holding his wallet like a poultice against his stomach. "How much do you want for a start?"

"Five hundred," I said, doubling the usual amount.

Without any argument, he dealt ten fifties into my hand.

"This doesn't buy me, you know. I consider myself free to follow the facts."

He managed to smile in a lopsided way. "Within the bounds of discretion, certainly. I simply don't want Catherine spreading poisonous lies about—well, about me, and Phoebe."

"What sort of lies does she tell?"

"Please." He raised his hand. "Catherine has taken up enough of our time. It's Phoebe we're interested in, after all."

"All right, you say she came to the boat to see you off, and that's the last you know of her whereabouts. What was the date?"

"The *President Jackson* sailed November the second. It brought me back to San Francisco yesterday. I tried to telephone Phoebe as soon as we docked. I'd been concerned at having no mail from her, though not so deeply concerned as I should have been. She's always been a poor correspondent. You can imagine the shock I experienced when her roommate told me on the phone that she hadn't been there for two months."

"Wasn't the roommate alarmed?"

"I believe she was. But she'd managed to convince herself, or been convinced, that Phoebe was with me. She thought, or said she thought, that Phoebe had decided at the last minute to go along on the cruise."

"Had you discussed that possibility with Phoebe?"

"Yes, I had. I wanted her to come along. But she was just beginning her senior year at a new school, and she was eager to stay with it. Phoebe is a very serious girl."

"And there was the boy friend."

"Yes. I'm sure he entered into the picture."

"What did Phoebe have to say about him?"

"Not very much. Presumably she'd known him less than two months. She only started at Boulder Beach in September."

"I should be able to find out who he is from the roommate. Can you give me her name?"

"It's Dolly Lang. I talked on the phone to both her and the landlady. They're a pair of typical addlepated females who couldn't seem to grasp the realities—"

"Landlady's name?"

"I never did get it. No doubt you'll find her on the premises. The address in Boulder Beach is 221 Oceano Avenue. I understand it's near the campus. And while you're out that way, you'll probably want to talk to some of the people on campus who knew Phoebe—her teachers and advisers. I presume you'll be going over to Boulder Beach today, there's a good road through the mountains . . ."

He went on talking in a slightly frantic rhythm. I waited

for him to run down. He was one of the managing sort
who are better at telling other people what to do than
doing anything for themselves.

I said when he had finished: "Why don't you talk to the
college people yourself? You'd probably get further with
them than I could."

"But I wasn't planning to go over there today."

"Why not?"

"I don't drive. I detest driving. I simply don't trust myself
to do all the right things."

"I don't trust anybody else to do them."

There was a silence between us, with a kind of stuffy in-
timacy involved in it. I realized dimly that we might just
have exchanged our outlooks on life.

"Ride along with me if you like," I said.

chapter 2

BOULDER BEACH COLLEGE stood on the
edge of the resort town that gave it its name, in a green belt
between some housing tracts and the intractable sea. It was
one of those sudden institutions of learning that had been
springing up all over California to handle the products of the
wartime population explosion. Its buildings were stone and
glass, so geometric and so spanking new that they hadn't begun to merge with the landscape. The palms and other plant-
ings around them appeared artificial; they fluttered like
ladies' fans in the fresh breeze from the sea.

Even the young people sitting around on the grass or saun-
tering with their books from building to building, didn't look
indigenous to me. They looked like extras assembled on a
set for a college musical with a peasant subplot.

A very young man who resembled Robinson Crusoe directed us to the administration building. I left Homer Wycherly standing on the steps in front of it, goggling around
with a lost expression on his face.

I'd have laid odds that he was a lost man in almost any
environment. On our way over from the valley, he'd told me
something about himself and his family. He and his sister
Helen were the third generation of the old valley family
which had founded Meadow Farms: the town stood on his
grandfather's original homestead. The old man's pioneer
energies had dwindled in his descendants, though Wycherly

didn't put it that way to me. His grandfather had made a farm out of semi-desert; his father had struck oil and incorporated; Homer was nominal head of the corporation, but most of its business was done in the San Francisco office, which was managed by Helen's husband, Carl Trevor. When I stopped the car in front of Phoebe's apartment, I made a note of Trevor's name and address for future reference. He lived on the Peninsula in Woodside.

Oceano Avenue was a realtor's dream or a city-planner's nightmare. Apartment houses were stacked like upended boxes along its slope; new buildings were going up in the vacant lots. The street had a heady air of profits and slums in the making.

221 had a discreet sign painted on a board: Oceano Palms. It was a three-storied stucco building girdled by tiers of balconies on which the individual apartments opened. I knocked on the door of number one.

It opened slightly. A woman with iron-gray hair looked out at me as if she was expecting bill-collectors.

"Are you the landlady, ma'am?"

"I'm the manager of these apartments," she said in a tone of correction. "We're all filled up for the spring semester."

"I'm not looking for living space. Mr. Wycherly sent me."

She said after a pause: "The young lady's father?"

"Yes. We were hoping you could tell me something more about her. May I come in?"

She looked me up and down with eyes that had seen them all and found most of them wanting.

"I very seldom have trouble with my girls. Practically never, you might say. Are you a policeman?"

"A private investigator. My name is Archer. I'm sure you don't object to telling me what you know about Phoebe Wycherly."

"I hardly knew her. *My* conscience is clear." But her thick figure blocked the doorway. "I think you should take it up with the college authorities. When a girl drops out of school like that, it's their headache, not mine. Wandering off heaven knows where with heaven knows who. Whom. She only lived here for less than two months."

"Was she a good tenant?"

"As good as most, I guess. I'm not sure I ought to be talking to you. Why don't you go over and talk to the college people?"

"Mr. Wycherly is doing that. It will be nice if he can tell them that you co-operated with our investigation."

She considered this proposition, biting her upper lip and

then remembering not to. A tuft of black hairs on her heavy chins quivered at me like displaced antennae.

"Come in then."

Her living room smelled faintly of incense and widowhood. A square-faced man with an oblong moustache smiled from a black frame propped up on top of a closed upright piano. The walls were hung with mottoes, one of which said: "The smoke ascends as lightly from the cottage hearth as from the haughty palace." A radio murmured through the ceiling like a mild threat of modernity.

"I'm Mrs. Doncaster," my hostess said. "Sit down if you can find a place."

There was nothing on any of the chairs, nothing out of place in the small stuffy room. Except me. I took a platform rocker which creaked when I moved, so I sat rigidly still. Mrs. Doncaster sat down about eight feet away.

"It's a blow to me, losing a girl like this. I practically never have trouble with my girls. If they do get into trouble —I don't mean serious trouble, we don't have that—they come to me for help. I give them good advice, at least I try to make it good. Mr. Doncaster was a minister in the Church of Christ."

She bowed towards the picture on the piano. The movement seemed to dislodge her stuck feelings:

"Poor Phoebe, I wonder what happened to her?"

"What do you think happened?"

"She didn't like it here, that's my opinion. She was used to a different style of living entirely. So she simply picked herself up and went away, to someplace she liked better. She had the money and the freedom to do it. Her parents gave her too much freedom, if you want to know what I think. And I don't know what Mr. Wycherly thought he was doing —traipsing off around the globe and leaving his young daughter to fend for herself. It isn't *natural*."

"Did Phoebe take her things with her when she left?"

"No, but she had plenty of things, and she could always buy more. She took her car."

"Can you tell me the make and model?"

"It was a little green car, one of these German imports, Volkswagen? Anyway, she bought it here in town, and you should be able to find out all about it. Most of my girls don't have cars of their own, and they're better off without them."

"I take it you disapproved of Phoebe Wycherly."

"I didn't say that." She gave me a hard defensive look, as if I'd accused her of wishing the girl into limbo. "I never really got a chance to know her. She was in and out, and back and forth in that little green car of hers. She had better things to do than talk to me."

"How was she doing in her studies?"

"I don't know. The college could tell you that. I never knew of her opening a book, but maybe she was so brilliant she didn't have to."

"Was she—is she brilliant?"

"The other girls seemed to think so. You can talk to her roommate Dolly Lang about that, and other things. Dolly's a good girl, you can count on her to tell you the truth as far as she understands it."

"Is Dolly in the building?"

"I think so. Would you like me to call her?" She started to get up.

"In a minute, thanks. What does Dolly have to say about her?"

Mrs. Doncaster hesitated. "I think I'll let Dolly speak for herself. We don't entirely agree."

"What's the point of disagreement?"

"Dolly thinks she meant to come back. I don't. If she meant to come back, why didn't she come back? Because she didn't want to, that's my opinion. This place wasn't good enough for Miss Wycherly. She was constantly complaining about the facilities, objecting to perfectly sensible regulations. She wanted something fancier and freer."

"Did she say so?"

"Not in so many words, perhaps. But I know the type. The first thing she did when she moved in was tear out all my good drapes, and put in her own. Without even asking permission."

"That sounds as if she meant to stay, and to come back."

"That isn't what it means to me. It means that she was thoughtless—a spoiled rich brat who cared for nobody!"

The ugly phrase hung in the room. A vaguely appalled expression crept over Mrs. Doncaster's face, changing the hard mouth and transforming the eyes. They went to the pictured face on the piano with something approaching shame, or even fear. She said to the smiling oblong moustache, not to me:

"I'm sorry. I'm all upset, I'm not fit to talk to man nor beast." She got up and moved to the door. "I'll call Dolly down for you."

"I'd just as soon go up. I want to see the apartment, anyway. What number is it?"

"Seven, on the second floor."

I faced her in the narrow doorway. "Is there anything important you haven't told me about Phoebe? About her relations with men, for example?"

"I hardly knew the girl. She didn't confide in me."

Her mouth closed like a mousetrap, not the kind that would ever cause the world to beat a path to her door.

I went up the outside stairs to the second floor. Behind the door of number seven, a typewriter was stuttering. I knocked, and a girl's voice answered wearily:

"Come in."

She was sitting at a desk by the window, with the heavy drapes closed and the reading-lamp on. A small rabbit-shaped girl in a bulky white Orlon sweater and blue slacks. Her eyes were blurred with what was probably thought, and her legs were twisted around the legs of her chair. She didn't bother to disentangle them.

"Miss Lang? I'd like to speak to you. Are you busy?"

"I'm horribly busy." She tugged at her short dark bangs, miming advanced despair, and gave me a quick little ghastly smile. "I have this Socio paper due at three o'clock this afternoon and my semester grade depends on it and I can't concentrate my quote mind unquote. Do you know anything about the causes of juvenile delinquency?"

"Enough to write a book, I think."

She brightened. "Really? Are you a sociologist?"

"A kind of poor-man's sociologist. I'm a detective."

"Isn't that fabulous? Maybe you can tell me. Is it the parents or the children who are responsible for j.d.? I can't make up my quote mind unquote."

"I wish you'd stop saying that about your quote mind unquote."

"Is it boring? My apologies. Do you blame the parents or the children?"

"I don't blame anybody, if you want an honest answer. I think blame is one of the things we have to get rid of. When children blame their parents for what's happened to them, or parents blame their children for what they've done, it's part of the problem, and it makes the problem worse. People should take a close look at themselves. Blaming is the opposite of doing that."

"That's good," she said enthusiastically. "If I can only get it into the right language." She twisted her mouth around. " 'The punitive attitudes of the familial group'—how does that sound?"

"Lousy. I hate sociological jargon. But I didn't come here to talk to you about that, Miss Lang. Mr. Wycherly asked me to come and see you."

Her mouth formed a round O, and then pronounced it. A grey clayey color showed itself under her skin. It made her look years older.

"It's no wonder I can't concentrate my mind," she said. "When you think of that silly girl going off by herself. I haven't thought of anything else, *really*, for two months. I wake up in the middle of the night in a cold sweat, imagining what's happened."

"What do you imagine happened?"

"Terrible things. The things you think about in the middle of the night. Like in that Eliot play about Sweeney Agonistes." She grimaced. "I had to read it for English 31. 'Everybody's got to do a girl in.'"

She looked up at me as if I was Sweeney himself, about to do her in. Disentangling her legs from the chair she trotted across the room, a small bouncing white and blue blob. She flung herself on a studio couch where she ended up immobile, back against the wall, knees up, chin on her knees, watching me over them. Her eyes reflected the lamplight like new dimes.

I turned the chair around and sat down with my back to the lamp: "Do you have any reason to think she was done in?"

"No," she said in a squeaky voice. "It's just what I'm afraid of. Mrs. Doncaster and everybody else thinks Phoebe went away deliberately. I thought so too for a while. But now I think she meant to come back. I'm practically sure of it."

"What makes you sure?"

"A lot of things. She only took her overnight bag, with enough clothes for the weekend."

"Did she plan to stay in San Francisco for the weekend?"

"I think so. She told me she'd see me Monday, anyway. She had a nine o'clock class on Monday morning, and she was planning to be there. She mentioned it."

"Did she confide in you, Miss Lang?"

She nodded her head. Its movement was restricted by her knees. Her eyes changed from silver to black in the changing reflection of the lamplight, and back again to silver.

"I didn't know Phoebe long," she said, "just since she moved here in September. But we got close in a hurry. She was—she's a good head, and she helped me with some of my courses. She was a senior"—the past tense kept slipping in—"and I'm only a sophomore. Besides, we had some of the same experiences in our background."

"What experiences?"

"Parent trouble. I won't go into mine—it's between me and them—but Phoebe had a ghastly family background, perfectly ghastly. Her mother and father didn't get along, and finally they got divorced, last summer I think it was. Phoebe felt pretty bitter about the divorce. She felt she had no home to go home to, you know?"

"Whose side was she on, in the divorce?"

"Her father's. Apparently her mother took him for a lot of money. But she blamed both of them, for acting like children." She caught herself up short. "There's that blame idea again—maybe you have something, Mister—? I don't think you told me your name."

I told her my name. "Did she talk about her mother very much?"

"No, she hardly even mentioned her."

"Did she ever hear from her mother?"

"Not that I know of. I doubt it."

"Did she know where her mother lives, at the present time?"

"If she did, she never told me."

"So there's no indication that she may be with her mother?"

"It doesn't seem very likely. She had a real down on her mother. She had good reason."

"Did she ever discuss the reason with you?"

"Not right out." Dolly screwed up her mouth again, as if she was searching for the right words. "She hinted around about it. I remember one night, when we were talking in the dark, she told me about some letters that came to her house. Crank letters. They came last year before the divorce, when Phoebe was home from Stanford for Easter vac. She opened the first one herself. It said some awful thing about her mother."

"What things?"

The girl said solemnly: "That she had committed adultery. The way Phee talked, she seemed to believe what the letters said. She said another thing that I didn't understand. She said the letters were her fault, and they were what broke up her parents' marriage."

"She didn't mean that she wrote them herself?"

"She couldn't have meant that. I don't know what she meant. I tried to get her to talk about it some more, but she went into a tizzy. I brought up the subject again in the morning, and she pretended that she hadn't said *any*thing." A queer expression crossed her face. "I don't know if I should be telling you all this."

"If you don't, Dolly, who will? When did this conversation occur?"

"The week before she took off. I remember she was talking about her father's trip the same night."

"How did she feel about her father's trip?"

"She resented it. She wanted to go along, but not with him."

"I don't get it."

"It's simple enough. She wanted to take a slow boat to China, all by herself alone. But she didn't."

"How do you know she didn't?"

"Because she planned to come back and finish her senior year. It was very important to her, to get a degree and get a job and stand on her own two feet and not have to take money from anybody."

"Anybody like her father, you mean?"

"Yes. Besides, a girl doesn't go away for a long trip and leave all her best clothes behind—her formals, and her Italian sweaters and simply piles of shoes and bags and coats. She even left her blond sheared beaver coat, and it's worth a fortune.'"

"Where is it?"

"With the rest of her things, in the basement. I didn't want them put there, but Mrs. Doncaster said it would be all right." Dolly twisted uncomfortably, wrestling with her knees. "It seemed so heartless, moving her things out. But what could I do? After Phoebe's rent ran out, I couldn't afford to pay the rent for both of us. I had to find myself another roommate. And Mrs. Doncaster had me convinced for a while that Phoebe had simply pulled up stakes and gone away with her father. I didn't really know different until yesterday."

"Where did Mrs. Doncaster get that idea?"

The girl hesitated. "She just had it, I guess."

"It must have come from somewhere."

After further hesitation, she said: "I suppose it was wish-fulfillment. She didn't really want Phoebe to— No," Dolly broke in on herself. "I don't mean that the way it sounds."

"You don't mean that Mrs. Doncaster didn't want Phoebe to come back?"

"No. I mean, she didn't want anything to *happen* to her. But she was just as satisfied when she *didn't* come back. She wanted to think that Phoebe had gone for good. I mean, she kept telling me that one of these days we'd hear from Phoebe. She'd send for her things, from New Zealand or Hong Kong or who knows where, and that would be that. But it isn't, is it?"

"I don't understand Mrs. Doncaster's motive. Does she dislike your roommate?"

"She hates her. It's nothing personal. I'm not trying to say that Mrs. Doncaster had anything to do with it."

"It?"

"Whatever happened to Phoebe. She isn't dead, is she?"

"I don't know. We still haven't got to the bottom of Mrs. Doncaster."

"It's simple enough." To Dolly, everything was very simple or very complicated. "I didn't want to drag his name into it —he's a nice boy—but Bobby Doncaster had a crush on Phoebe. A heavy crush. He used to hang around with his tongue hanging out a yard, panting. Mrs. Doncaster didn't like the idea at all."

"Was it a two-way crush?"

"I guess so. Phee didn't wave her torch around the way Bobby did. But as a matter of fact—" She caught herself up short, blinking her dimey eyes.

"You were going to say?"

"Nothing."

"It must have been something."

"But I hate gossip. And I'm not a snooper, really."

"I am. This is a serious matter, Dolly. You know it. The more you can tell me about Phoebe's life, the better chance I'll have of finding her. So what were you going to say?"

She twisted her legs, untwisted them, and ended up sitting on them in a kind of yogi position. "I think Phoebe came here, to this college, on account of Bobby. She never actually admitted it. But it slipped out one time when we were talking about him. She met him last summer at some beach up north, and he talked her into registering here."

"And renting an apartment from his mother?"

"Mrs. Doncaster doesn't know that. And I don't know it for certain." Dolly gave me a worried look. "You mustn't think there was anything going *on*. Phoebe isn't that kind of a girl. Neither is Bobby that kind of boy. He wanted to marry her."

"I'd like to talk to him."

"That shouldn't be hard. I heard him down in the basement when I got home from class. He's working on a surfboard."

"How old is Bobby?"

"Twenty-one. The same age as Phoebe. But he can't tell you anything much about her. He didn't *know* her. I was the only one who knew her, and I didn't *really* know her. Phoebe was—Phoebe is *deep*."

"Just what does that mean?"

"*Deep*. She never let on what she was really thinking. She could put up a perfectly good front, chatting along with the rest of us, but her mind would be on other things. Don't ask me what things, I don't know. Maybe her parents. Maybe other people."

"Did she have other friends besides you?"

"Nobody really close. She was only here a little over seven weeks. *I* ran into her in the housing office. We were both looking for roommates, and I needed an upperclassman to live with so I could live off-campus. Besides, I liked Phoebe, very much. She was a bit of an odd-ball, and I am, too. We hit it off together, right away."

"In what way was she an odd-ball?"

"That's hard for me to say. Psych is not my line. I mean, Phee had two or three personalities, one of them was a *poisonality*. She could be *black,* and frankly I'm not so highly integrated, either. So we sort of matched up."

"Was she depressed?"

"Sometimes. She'd get so depressed she could hardly crawl around. Then other times she was the life of the party."

"What was she depressed about?"

"Life," Dolly Lang said earnestly.

"Did suicide ever enter the picture?"

"Sure, we talked about suicide. Ways and means and all. I remember once, we were talking about suicide as an expression of the personality. I'm the Golden Gate Bridge type, the jump-off, highly dramatic."

"What about Phoebe?"

"She said she'd shoot herself in the head. That was the quickest."

"Did she have a gun?"

"Not that I know of. Her father had, though, plenty of them, back home in Meadow Farms. Phee thought it was ghastly, having guns around the house. She'd never shoot herself. It was just talk. Actually, she was afraid of guns. Very neurotic, like all nice people."

Never argue with a witness.

I got up and turned the chair back toward the typewriter. It held a half-filled sheet of typescript, headed "The Psychic Origins of Juvenile Delinquency," by Dorothea S. Lang, and ending in a half-finished sentence: "Many authorities say that socio-economic factors are predominate in the origins of anti-social behavior, but others are of the opinion that lack of love" . . .

The e's were out of alignment. Maybe it was a clue.

chapter 3

THE SLOPE FELL AWAY towards the rear of the building, so that the entrance to the basement was at ground level. A few cars were parked in the yard behind it. Inside, there were noises resembling groans and shrieks of anguish, which came from a room at the back of the basement. I made my way towards it among packing cases and cleaning equipment, and looked into a windowless workshop lit by an overhead bulb.

Under it a young man with broad shoulders was planing a piece of board clamped in a vise. Sawdust dusted his reddish crewcut. Curled shavings crackled under his feet. I stood and watched him make a number of passes with the plane. His back was to me, and the muscles in it shifted heavily and rhythmically under his T shirt.

He didn't know I was there until I spoke: "Bobby?"

He glanced up sharply. He had bright green eyes. His heavy, slightly stupid mouth and chin reminded me of his mother. Otherwise he was a good-looking boy. His upper lip sported a fresh pink moustache.

"You want something, sir?"

I told him who I was and why I was there. He backed against a pegboard wall studded with tools and looked around his cubicle as if I had deliberately trapped him in it. The plane glittered like a weapon in his hand.

"I hope you don't think I had anything to do with it."

He tried to surround this remark with a smile, but his smile was stiff and frightened. I couldn't tell if this was his reaction to detectives and disappearance or if the fright was chronic in him, waiting for occasions to break out.

"You hope I don't think you had anything to do with what?"

"The fact that Phoebe hasn't come back."

"If you had anything to do with it, now's the time to say so."

His green eyes clouded. He looked at me in confusion. He did his best to convert it into anger: "For God's sake!" But he wasn't quite man enough. He was mimicking anger, safely: "Where did you get the idea that I did anything?"

"You brought the subject up."

He tried to reach his moustache with his lower teeth. It

20

was his mother's mannerism; I had the impression that he hadn't decided whether he was his mother's boy or his father's.

"But let's not play word-games, Bobby. You were close to Phoebe. It's natural I should want to question you."

"Who have you been talking to?"

"That's unimportant. You were close to her, weren't you?"

He noticed the plane in his hand and set it down on the workbench. With his eyes still averted from mine, he said:

"I was crazy about her. Is that a crime?"

"It's been known to lead to crime."

His head came up slowly. "Why don't you lay off me? I was crazy about her, I told you. I still am. It's been rough enough, these last two months, waiting to hear from her."

"You didn't have to sit and wait."

"I don't know what you mean." He spread his hands, saw that they were dirty, wiped them on the dirty front of his T shirt. "What do you mean?"

"You could have gone to the authorities."

"I wanted to." His mouth did the mousetrap trick.

"But your mother wouldn't let you."

"I didn't say that."

"I did."

"Who's been telling lies about us? Who have you been talking to?"

"Your mother, and one or two of the tenants."

"You have no right to come bothering my mother. She only did what she thought was right. She believed that Phoebe had gone off on a trip with her father. We both did," he added as an afterthought. "We kept expecting to hear from her. It isn't our fault she didn't write. You'd think she'd send a postcard at least, to tell us what to do with her things."

"Why do you think she didn't?"

"I don't know, honestly. I don't know anything about it."

He was painfully defensive. Perhaps he was simply too scared to co-operate. I realized that I hadn't been handling him with any tact, and I changed my line of questioning:

"I'm interested in the things she left behind. Can you tell me where they are?"

"Yes. They're in the storage room. I'll show you."

He seemed glad to have a chance to move. He led me around a big gas furnace, ducking under its vents, and unlocked a door in the corner of the basement. Dust-laden sunlight slanted from a high window in the concrete wall. Bobby switched on a hanging bulb. Half-a-dozen suitcases and hatboxes were piled beside a large steamer trunk. The trunk was plastered with hotel labels, American and foreign.

Bobby Doncaster had the key to the trunk on his key ring. He unlocked and opened it. The contents smelled faintly of lavender and of girl. They included masses of dresses and skirts, sweaters, and blouses, an expensive beaver coat. Bobby watched me finger the coat with something like jealousy in his eyes.

"Are the suitcases hers?"

"Yes."

"What's in them?"

"All kinds of things. Clothes and shoes and hats and books and jewelry and doodads. Cosmetics."

"How do you know what's in them?"

"I packed them myself. I kept expecting to hear from Phoebe, so that I could send her her things."

"Why didn't you send them home?"

"I guess I didn't want to. It seemed so—well, so final. Besides, she told me her father had closed—was closing their house. I thought her stuff would be safer here. I kept it under lock and key."

"She left a lot of stuff behind," I said. "What did she take with her?"

"Just a weekend bag, I think."

"And you believed she went off on a two-months' cruise with nothing more than a weekend bag?"

"I didn't know what to believe. If *you* believe I know where she is, you're wrong. You couldn't be wronger." He added in a gentler tone: "I only hope you find her."

"You may be able to help me find her."

This startled him: he was easily startled. "How?"

"By telling me what you know about her. First I'd better have a look at the suitcases."

I went through their contents in a hurry and found nothing that seemed significant. No letters, no photographs, no diary, no address book. It occurred to me that Bobby might have combed them out.

"Is everything here?"

"I think so. I packed everything I could find of hers. Dolly Lang helped me. She's—she was Phoebe's roommate."

"You didn't put anything aside, as a keepsake perhaps?"

"No." He seemed embarrassed. "I don't go in for that sort of thing."

"Do you have a picture of her?"

"I'm sorry, I haven't. We never exchanged pictures."

"You mentioned some books of hers. Where are they?"

He pulled a heavy cardboard carton from behind the trunk. The books inside were mostly textbooks and reference books: a French grammar and a Larousse dictionary which was dog-eared with use, an anthology of English Romantic poets, a complete Shakespeare, some novels including Dostoevsky in translation, a number of quality paperbacks on psychology and existentialist philosophy. The name inscribed on the flyleaf, 'Phoebe Wycherly,' was in a small, distinctive hand—the kind that is supposed to indicate intelligence and sensitivity.

"What kind of a girl is she, Bobby?"

"Phoebe's a wonderful person." As if I'd questioned this.

"Describe her, will you."

"I can try. She's fairly tall for a girl, about five foot seven and a half, but slender. She wears size twelve clothes. She has a very good figure, and nice hair, cut medium short."

"What color?"

"Light brown, almost blonde. Some people wouldn't call her pretty, but I would. Actually, she was beautiful when she felt good—I mean when she was happy. She has those deep dark eyes. Blue eyes. And a wonderful smile."

"I take it she wasn't always happy."

"No. She had her problems."

"Did she talk about them to you?"

"Not really. I knew she had them. Her family had broken up, as you probably know. But she didn't like to talk about that."

"Did she ever mention some letters that came last spring?"

"Letters?"

"Attacking her mother."

He shook his head. "She never said anything about them to me. In fact she never spoke about her mother at all. It was one of those closed subjects."

"Did she have many closed subjects?"

"Quite a few. She didn't like to go into the past, or talk about herself. She had a rocky childhood. Her parents were always quarreling over her, and it left its mark on Phoebe."

"In what way?"

"Well, she didn't know if she wanted to have any children, for one thing. She didn't know if she'd make a fit mother."

"You talked about having children?"

"Of course. We were going to get married."

"When?"

He hesitated, and glanced up at the hanging bulb. The

light held his eyes. "This year, after we graduated. I was going on to graduate school. It would have worked out, too." He pulled his eyes down from the hypnotic bulb. "I don't know what I'm going to do now."

"It's strange your mother didn't mention this. Does she know about your marriage plans?"

"She ought to. We argued about it enough. She thought I was too young to think about getting married. And she didn't understand Phoebe, or like her."

"Why?"

A wry, sideways smile made his mouth ugly. "Mother probably would have felt that way about any girl that I was interested in. Anyway, she's always hated people with money."

"But you don't."

"It makes no difference to me, one way or the other. I can make my own way, I'm an all-A student. At least I was until this semester, and I still have a couple of weeks to pull it out."

"What happened this semester?"

"You know what happened." He looked down at Phoebe's abandoned belongings, green eyes half-shut, lower lip thrust out. He shook his head tautly. "Let's get out of here."

"This is as good a place to talk as any."

"I don't want to talk any more. I'm getting pretty sick of your insinuations. You keep hinting that I'm lying."

"I think you're holding back on me, Bobby—suppressing some of the facts. I want them all."

"We can't stand here all day."

"Sit down then."

He didn't move. "What else do you want to know?"

I picked a fairly neutral subject. "How was she doing in school?"

"Pretty well. She knocked off mostly B's at the mid-terms. She was majoring in French, and she has a knack for languages. She told me she was doing a lot better than last year at Stanford—didn't have so many emotional problems."

The wry and ugly smile took hold of his mouth again. He straightened it out, but it left the impression that he was mocking himself.

"What about her emotional problems?" I was wondering about his.

He shrugged his muscle-packed shoulders, awkwardly. "I'm no psychiatrist. But anybody could see that she had her moods. She was up one day and down the next. I

thought she ought to go to a psychiatrist. She told me she'd
tried that."

"When?"

"Last spring in Palo Alto. She didn't give it much of a try,
though. She only saw the doctor a couple of times."

"What was his name?"

"I wouldn't know. Her aunt might be able to tell you. Mrs.
Trevor. She lives on the Peninsula near Palo Alto."

"Do you know the Trevors?"

"No."

"Or the rest of the family?"

"No."

"How long have you known Phoebe?"

He thought about his answer. "Just since she came here,
in September. About two months altogether. Less than two
months."

"In less than two months you decided to get married?"

"*I* decided right away. Something clicked," he said, "the
first time I saw her."

"When was that?"

"In September. She came to look at the apartment. I was
painting the kitchenette."

"I understood you met her before that."

"You understood wrong."

"You didn't meet her at a beach last summer, and talk
her into coming to college here?"

He went into deep thought, which left his face inert and
his eyes blind. I thought for an instant that this case was
going to be short and successful and bitter: the girl
dead, killed by the boy, who was getting ready to crack.

"Yeah," he said painfully. "As a matter of fact I did."

"Why lie about it?"

"I didn't want my mother to find out."

"I'm not your mother."

"No, but you've been talking to her. You'll probably be
talking to her again."

"Why is it so important that she shouldn't know?"

"I guess it really isn't. It's just that I didn't tell her. She
wouldn't have liked the idea of Phoebe taking one of our
apartments. She has a suspicious mind."

"So have I. Were you and Phoebe having an affair?"

"No. We weren't. It would't be any business of yours if
we were. We're both adults."

"Legally, anyway. *Were* you having an affair?"

"I said we weren't. You don't fool around with the girl
you want to marry. I don't."

I almost believed him.

"Where did you meet her?"

"A place called Medicine Stone, north of Carmel. I went up there for a week in August. They have a good reef for surfing—better than anything around here. Phoebe was staying there with the Trevors and I got to know her on the beach."

"You picked her up?"

"That's twisting what I said. She wanted to try surfing, I let her. She was looking for a school to shift to, and I told her about this one. She'd been considering it, anyway."

"And while you were at it you rented her an apartment."

"She asked me to find an apartment for her," he said, flushing.

"So you had a cozy two months."

His fists tightened; the muscles stood out like brown wood in his arms. I thought he was going to hit me, and I sort of wished he would. Give me a chance to shake out the truth that I felt I wasn't getting from him.

But he held himself under rigid control. "Crack wise if you like. We had a *good* two months. Followed by the worst two months of my life."

"When did you see her last?"

He seemed ready for the question: "On the morning of November the second, that was a Friday—early in the morning. She was going to drive up to San Francisco to see her father off. She asked me to check her oil and tires, which I did. My own car wasn't running, and on the way out to the highway she dropped me at the corner of the campus. That was the last time I saw her." He said it without emotion.

"What kind of a car was she driving?"

"1957 green Volkswagen two-door."

"Do you know the license number?"

"No, but you can get it from the dealer. She bought it secondhand at Imported Motors, in town here. I helped her to pick it out."

"How long before she left?"

"A month, or more. She found out she needed one here, to get around. The bus service to town is pretty chancy."

"Was she in good spirits when she left?"

"I think so. You never could tell about Phoebe. Her moods were always changing, as I said."

"Did she tell you what her plans were for the weekend?"

"No. She didn't."

"Or when she was coming back?"

"She didn't say."

"Why not?"

"I don't think I asked her. I took it for granted that she would be back Sunday night or Monday morning."

"Did she mention anyone that she was going to see, besides her father?"

"No."

"And you didn't ask her what she was going to do all weekend?"

"No."

"What do you think she did, after she said goodbye to her father and left the ship?"

"I have no ideas on the subject." But he had ideas. They flickered darkly at the back of his green eyes like fish in water too deep for identification.

Suddenly he looked sick. He lowered his head. The color of his eyes seemed to have run and tinged his cheeks greenish.

"Did you by any chance go along to San Francisco with her?"

He waggled his hanging head.

"Where did you spend that weekend, Bobby?"

He looked at his hands as if they fascinated him. "Nowhere."

"Nowhere?"

"I mean here. At home."

Mrs. Doncaster said behind me: "Bobby was here with his mother, where he should be. He came down with a touch of the flu that Friday. I kept him home in bed all weekend."

I moved sideways along the wall, and looked from the son to the mother. Her face was grim. His eyes were intent on it. He nodded almost imperceptibly. He was very much his mother's boy at the moment.

"Is that true, Bobby?" I said.

"Yes. Of course."

"Are you calling me a liar?" the woman said. "Because if you are I want to know about it so that I can take legal recourse. My son and I are respectable citizens. We don't have to put up with any guff from people like you."

"Have you ever been in trouble, Bobby?"

He looked to his mother for an answer. She was boiling with answers:

"My son is an upright young man. He's never been in trouble, and he's not going to start now. You're not going to drag him into something like this, just because he had the misfortune to go out a few times with a foolish girl. You go and peddle your dirt someplace else. And I warn you, if you besmirch our good name, you'll find yourself at the receiving end of legal action."

She moved on him in a kind of possessive fury and put her arm around his waist. I left them looking at each other.

Outside, the offshore wind was rising. The choppy sea at the foot of the street reflected crumpled light.

chapter 4

I DROVE BACK to the college and picked up Homer Wycherly. He was angry and frustrated. Most of the college people were out to lunch; the only person he'd been able to contact who even knew Phoebe by name was an assistant counsellor in the Dean of Women's office. She knew of no particular reason why Phoebe had dropped out of school, and showed no particular excitement about it. Students were leaving without notice all the time.

Wycherly had an appointment with the Dean for later in the day. He asked me to drive him to the Boulder Beach Inn and when we got there invited me to have lunch with him. I hadn't eaten since breakfast at 3 A.M., and I was glad to.

It was a big old-fashioned resort hotel, Spanish Mission in style, which stood in extensive gardens on the sea at the edge of town. The furnishings in Wycherly's bungalow were like his life, heavy, expensive, and uncomfortable. The waiter who took our orders had a Swiss-German accent; the menu was in restaurant French.

"You haven't told me what *you* found out," Wycherly said when the waiter had left the room. "I presume you found out something."

I told him in general what my three witnesses had said, suppressing the doubts I had about Bobby Doncaster. There was no point in turning an angry father loose on him. I wanted Bobby to stay in one place.

"The indications are," I concluded, "that your daughter intended to come back here after a weekend in San Francisco. Something happened to change her mind."

We were sitting in a window embrasure facing each other. Wycherly leaned forward and grasped my knee, letting me feel his weight. His hand was thick, with sun-bleached hairs sprouting like straw on the back of it. His leaning body gave an impression of heavy blind force which went strangely with the anxiety in his face:

"You suspect foul play, don't you? Be honest with me now."

"I can't rule it out. Phoebe was last seen in a section of San Francisco where people have been killed for carfare. She was carrying a large amount of cash. I think you should get in touch directly with the San Francisco police."

"I can't. I simply can't endure any more publicity. You don't know what the papers did to us last spring when Catherine divorced me. Besides, I can't believe that she's been killed." He removed his hand from my knee and applied it to his chest. "I feel, here, that my daughter is alive. I don't know where she is, or what she's doing, but I'm certain she's alive."

"The chances are she is. Still, it's better to think and act as if she isn't."

"You expect me to abandon all hope?"

"I didn't say that, Mr. Wycherly. I've barely started on the case. If you want me to carry on by myself, I'm willing."

"That's what I want. Definitely."

The waiter knocked gently at the door. He brought in a loaded cart and set a table for us. Wycherly went to work on the food as if he hadn't eaten for a week. He sweated as he ate.

I looked out the window, munching my steak. The grounds of the hotel, green as any oasis, sloped down to a sea wall against which the water seemed to brim. A pair of black-suited skin divers were braving the January sea, kicking up their fins like mating seals. Farther out, a few sails slanted in the wind.

I tried to imagine Wycherly's voyage to the islands and countries that hung below the curve of the horizon. The South Pacific I remembered smelled of cordite and flame throwers; and Wycherly was a hard man to imagine anything about. He blabbed out his feelings freely but kept his essential self hidden—as hidden as his daughter was below the curve of time.

"Something else came up," I said, "when I was talking to the roommate, Dolly Lang. Your daughter told her about some letters that were delivered at your house last spring. She was very disturbed about them, according to Dolly."

He gave me a guarded look across the table. "What did the girl say?"

"I can't reproduce it exactly. She was talking a blue streak and I didn't take notes. I gather that these letters slandered your wife."

"Yes. They made some unpleasant allegations."

"Were they threatening letters?"

"I'd say so, in an indirect way."

"Did they threaten Mrs. Wycherly?"

"They were a threat to all of us. They were addressed to the whole family—which is how Phoebe happened to see the first one."

"How many of them were there?"

"Just the two. They came a day apart."

"Why didn't you bring them up before?"

"I didn't think they were relevant, to the present situation." But the thought of them pressed more sweat out on his forehead. He wiped it off with his napkin. "I didn't know that Phoebe was especially upset about them."

"She was. Her roommate said she blamed herself for them in some way."

"How could that be?"

"I'm asking you."

"I have no idea what she meant. Of course she was rather shocked when the first one came. She was home for the Easter break, and she happened to bring the mail up to the house that morning. The letter was addressed to The Wycherly Family, and naturally she opened it herself. Then she showed it to me. I tried to keep it from Catherine, but my sister Helen saw it and mentioned it at the breakfast table—"

I cut in on his anxious explanations: "Exactly what was in the letters?"

"They both said very much the same thing. I won't smell up the air with it."

"Did they accuse your wife of having an affair with another man?"

Wycherly picked up his knife and fork and brandished them over his clean plate. "Yes."

"Did you take the accusation seriously?"

"I didn't know what to think. The letters had a wild note to them. I suspected they were the work of a psychopathic mind. But I had to take them seriously."

"Why?"

"They were just about the last straw in my marriage. Catherine blamed me for doing nothing about them. She was always blaming me for sins of omission. When actually I did everything possible to find out who was sending them and put a stop to it. I even hired a—" He compressed his lips.

"A detective?"

"Yes," he admitted unwillingly. "A man named William Mackey, from San Francisco."

"I know him slightly. What were his conclusions?"

"He didn't come to any. Sheriff Hooper thought it was probably a disgruntled employee, or ex-employee. That didn't shed much light. We have employees all over the valley, all over the state, and the employee turnover in our business is high."

"Was there any extortion involved?"

"No. Money was never mentioned. As far as I could see, the object was sheer malice."

"Was Phoebe singled out in them?"

"I don't believe she was. No, she wasn't. She wouldn't even have known about them if she hadn't happened to go to the mailbox that morning. I'm sure they had nothing to do with her disappearance."

"I'm not so sure. Were the letters locally mailed?"

"Yes, they were postmarked in Meadow Farms. That was one of the—well, alarming things about them. They were written by someone we knew—perhaps someone we saw every day. There was this vein of personal malice in them, which is why the Sheriff thought they came from an ex-employee."

"Do you have any thoughts on his identity?"

"Not a one."

"Who are your enemies?"

"I don't believe I have any."

He offered me his dismayed smile, which tried hard to be likable and wasn't. I gave up hoping for much realism from him. He was a weak sad man in a bind, ready to bandage his ego with any rag of vanity he could muster.

"Who was the man referred to in the letters?"

His hand flexed slowly on the tablecloth, like a beached starfish. "I have no idea. He wasn't named. He was probably sheer invention, anyway. Catherine and I had our differences, but—" He let the sentence expire, as if his heart wasn't in it.

"How were the letters signed?"

"'A Friend of the Family,' with an interrogation mark ahead of it."

"That's Spanish punctuation."

"So my sister Helen pointed out."

"Were they handwritten?"

"No, all typewritten, including the signature. This Mackey fellow said he could probably trace the typewriter if I wanted to spend a lot of time and money. His time, my money. But the letters stopped coming, and I hated to have him poking around in our private affairs, so I took him off the case."

"I'd like very much to see those letters. Where are they?"

"I got them back from Mackey and destroyed them. You can understand my feelings."

He was ready to explain them to me, but I didn't want to understand his feelings. I could end up baby-sitting with Wycherly instead of doing the job he'd hired me for. I stood up.

"Where are you going?"

"San Francisco, naturally."

"What are you going to do in San Francisco?"

"I'll find out when I arrive." I looked at my watch: it was nearly two. "I should be able to get there before dark. One other thing, Mr. Wycherly. In the light of what you've told me about those letters, do you want to reconsider about giving me your ex-wife's address?"

"I don't have it," he snapped. "In any case, I don't want you talking to her under any circumstances. Give me your word on that."

I gave him my word, with a mental reservation.

In the doorway I passed the waiter carrying a tray of French pastries. Wycherly looked at the tray with greedy, grief-stricken eyes.

I stopped in town at Imported Motors and got the license number of Phoebe's car before I headed north. GL3741.

chapter 5

THE SHIP ROSE like a chalk cliff over the dock. Gulls circled above it, flashing in the late afternoon sunlight. I climbed the forward gangway unchallenged. The main deck was practically deserted.

A man in white coveralls was cleaning the bottom of an empty swimming pool with a long-handled vacuum brush. Most of the officers were ashore, he told me above the whine of his machine. Maybe the purser was still aboard. He directed me to his office.

It was an artificially lighted cubicle below decks, occupied by a moon-faced bald man wearing a white shirt and blue uniform trousers. He remembered Mr. Wycherly very well. Mr. Wycherly had occupied one of their best staterooms on the voyage just completed. I told him that I represented Mr. Wycherly.

"In what capacity?"

"I'm a private detective."

He gave me a heavily insured look. "I'm sure Mr. Wycherly was satisfied with his accommodations. He shook my hand and thanked me before he left us yesterday."

"There's no beef about the ship," I said. "It has to do with Mr. Wycherly's daughter Phoebe. She came aboard to say goodbye the day you sailed. She hasn't been seen since."

He put his hand on top of his naked scalp as if I'd blown cold on him. "You're not suggesting she stowed away or anything like that? Or that we're in any way responsible?"

"It hardly seems likely. I'm trying to trace her, and this is the obvious place to start. I need your help."

"We'll be glad to help in any way we can, of course." He stood up and gave me his hand, adding in a more personal tone: "I have a daughter. My name is Clement."

"Archer." I took out my notebook. "Now what was the date you sailed?"

"November second. That is to say, November second was the scheduled sailing date. We had a little mechanical trouble and didn't actually get under way until early the following morning. But Mr. Wycherly came aboard on the afternoon of November second. His daughter was with him, as you say."

"You know that for a fact?"

"I remember the occasion very well," Clement said. "I have reason to."

"How so?"

"Well, there was quite a hullabaloo in Mr. Wycherly's stateroom. This woman—apparently she was Mr. Wycherly's divorced wife—was stirring up a dreadful fuss in front of some of the other passengers. The steward couldn't quiet her, so he sent down for me. I'm afraid I couldn't quite handle her, either. She was one of those big blonde furies, if you know what I mean. Bleached blonde," he added snidely. "And very much in her cups. Eventually I had to get our master-at-arms to persuade her to leave the ship. The way that woman talked!" He threw up his hands.

"What was she saying?"

"I'm afraid I can't remember her exact words. They wouldn't be repeatable, anyway. You can imagine how I felt. We like our sailings to be gay affairs, and there she was in the middle of the festivities howling out obscenities. She'd taken off her shoe, and was hammering with the heel at Mr. Wycherly's door. It left *welts* in the paint."

"You must have some idea of what she said."

"Well, she wanted in, of course. They wouldn't let

her in. She claimed that they were betraying her, turning their backs and leaving her in the lurch. She threatened to get back at them."

"Just who was she threatening?"

"The people in the stateroom—Mr. Wycherly and his daughter, and I believe a couple of other relatives who'd come to see him off. She said she'd ruin them all if they didn't let her in and talk to her."

"Who were the other relatives?"

"I really couldn't say. Quite a crowd had begun to gather round. When I remonstrated with the woman, she actually menaced me with the heel of her shoe. She looked at me like a basilisk, I mean it. Much as I hated to do it, I had no choice but to call in the master-at-arms. He managed to get her off the ship, with some help from the daughter."

"Did Phoebe leave the ship with her mother?"

"I believe so. Once things were under control, more or less, the girl came out of the stateroom and talked to the woman. Apparently she said the right things. They walked down the gangway with their arms around each other."

"Did the girl come back aboard?"

"I really didn't notice. I always have so many things on my mind, sailing day. Mr. McEachern may be able to tell you. He's our master-at-arms, and he kept a closer eye on the party than I did."

"Is McEachern on the ship now?"

"He should be. He's on duty." Clement picked up an intramural telephone.

I talked to McEachern on the upper deck. He leaned on the rail, a rawboned slab of man in a petty-officer's uniform. There was something nautical in his bearing, and something of the hotel dick.

"Sure I remember her," he said. "The lady was looped, if you want my opinion. I don't mean falling-down looped. She could probably walk a chalk-line and handle herself physically. But she had that varnished look they get when they've been drinking hard, maybe stayed up a couple of nights drinking. Some people it gives the fantods to."

"Did it her?"

He spat into the oily water forty feet below. "She wasn't making much sense there for a while. She called me every name in the book. The lady has a sensational vocabulary."

"Did she threaten anybody with bodily harm?"

"You mean Mr. Wycherly?"

"The husband or the daughter. Anybody."

"Not in my hearing. The purser said she made some

threats before I got there. She was going to castrate all the males in sight. You never can tell whether to take that stuff seriously—I see a lot of hysterical drunks in my work, male *and* female. She calmed down all right when the girl came out and talked to her."

"What did the girl say?"

"She said that she was sorry. They both said they were sorry." McEachern grinned, and the wrinkles fanned out from his eyes. "They didn't say what they were sorry about."

"But they had some kind of reconciliation?"

"That's right. They went ashore together. I followed along, just to make sure that everything was all right. The girl had a taxi waiting on the dock. I helped them into it—"

"Both of them?"

"Yeah, and they tooled away as though nothing had happened. So maybe," he added hopefully, "it wasn't such a bad split in the family after all. I wouldn't want to be judged myself by what I say and do when I'm plastered. By the way, would you like a short snort? I have some very fine Scotch which I picked up in Hong Kong."

"Thanks, I don't have time. I'm wondering where the two of them tooled away to."

"Let's see." He tipped back his peaked hat and tapped his forehead, listening to the repeated clunks with a certain amount of approval. "I *think* the girl said to take her back to the St. Francis."

"What kind of a cab was it?"

"Yellow."

"Can you describe the driver?"

"I can try. Heavy set, late thirties or so, black hair and dark eyes, large nose, heavy black beard—the kind you have to shave twice a day if you want to have a clean appearance." His hand rasped on his chin. "He looked like an Italian or maybe an Armenian—I didn't hear him say anything. Oh yeah, he had a triangular white scar on the side of his jaw, like a little arrowhead."

"Which side of his jaw?" I asked him with a smile.

He touched the side of his face with his right hand, then used it to point at my face. "My right, his left. The left side of his jaw, just below the corner of his mouth. And he had bad teeth."

"What was his mother's maiden name? You have a talent for faces."

"Faces are my bread and butter, chum. My main job is keeping the passengers in their own classes. Which means I learn two or three hundred faces every couple of months."

"Speaking of passengers, how did you size up Homer Wycherly?"

"I scarcely ever saw him. He stayed in his cabin most of the voyage—even had most of his meals there. I don't think he likes people. What gives with him and his family, anyway?"

"That's what I'm trying to find out. Incidentally, the purser tells me the ship didn't sail on schedule last November."

"No, one of the engines broke down. We were supposed to sail at four in the afternoon, but we didn't clear the harbor until the next morning."

"Did all the passengers stay aboard during the delay?"

"We asked them to. We didn't know how long the repairs were going to take. A few of them went out to the dockside bars."

"Did Wycherly?"

"I couldn't say."

"Who could?"

"Maybe his steward. Let's see, Sammy Green had that stateroom last trip. Sammy isn't aboard, though."

"Where is he?"

"Probably at home. I'll see if I can find his address for you."

McEachern disappeared into the bowels of the ship. I walked around the deck and imagined that I was taking a long sea voyage for my health. The presence of the city interfered with my fantasy. I could hear the traffic on the Embarcadero. Beyond it rose the peopled hills. Coit Tower was bright in the sunset. I turned my back on it and looked across the water, but Alcatraz floated there like a shabby piece of the city cut adrift.

McEachern came back with a slip of paper in his hand. "Sammy Green lives in East Palo Alto if you want to follow through on him." He handed me the slip. "I don't know what you're looking for."

"The girl," I said.

"She's long gone, isn't she?"

"Too long."

"You could try the cab-rank at the St. Francis. Some of those drivers follow the same routine month in and month out."

His suggestion was a good gone. The dispatcher in front of the St. Francis, an old man in an overcoat and a yellow cap marked "Agent," recognized my driver from the description.

"I don't know his name," he said. "All the boys they call him Garibaldi, but that ain't his name."

"Where's Garibaldi now?"

"I dunno. He isn't one of my regulars, I see him maybe every two-three days. Any cab in the city, 'cepting the radio cabs, can line up here any time——"

I interrupted his flow of information: "Do you know where he lives?"

"I believe he told me once." He tilted back his cap and scratched at his hairline. "Someplace down the Peninsula, South San Francisco maybe, or Daly City. Likely he's gone home for supper. You can try and catch him here tomorrow."

I said that I would do that, and left him my name and a dollar.

I took my car down the ramp into the underground garage. While I was there, I asked the cashier if they had any record of Phoebe's car. So far as he knew, no green Volkswagen had been abandoned there in the month of November.

I crossed the street, dodging a cable car, and went into the St. Francis. The lobby was full of conventioneers with name-cards pinned to their lapels. A man named Dr. Herman Grupp with Martinis on his breath offered me his hand, then saw that I had no name-card and withdrew the offer. From snatches of conversation I heard, all about spines and supersonic therapy, I gathered that it was a chiropractors' convention.

I had to stand in line at the black marble desk. One of four harassed clerks told me they were full up. It was hopeless to try to question him about Phoebe Wycherly.

I had to stand in line again at the telephone booths. Willie Mackey's office didn't answer. His answering service told me under compulsion that Willie was up in Marin on a case. He hadn't left any number to call and his home number was unlisted, even if I was a dear old friend of Willie's. I wasn't, exactly, but we had worked together two or three times.

I stepped out of the booth sweating and frustrated. A chiropractor elbowed in past me. His name was Dr. Ambrose Sylvan.

Just for fun, I did the obvious thing and looked up Mrs. Wycherly in the local telephone directories. Her name was in the second book I opened: Mrs. Catherine Wycherly, 507 Whiteoaks Drive, Atherton; with a Davenport number.

When Dr. Ambrose Sylvan had muscled his way out of the booth, I called the Davenport number. A zombie voice told me with recorded politeness that it had been disconnected.

chapter **6**

HIGHWAY 101 divides into two branches on the Peninsula. The western branch, Camino Real, doubles as the main street of a forty-mile-long city which stretches almost unbroken from San Francisco to San Jose. Its traffic movement is slow, braked by innumerable stop-lights. The name of the endless city changes as you go south and cross the invisible borders of municipalities: Daly City, Millbrae, San Mateo, San Carlos, Redwood City, Atherton, Menlo Park, Palo Alto, Los Altos.

The eastern branch of the highway, which I took, curves down past International Airport, roughly following the shoreline of the Bay. Mapmakers call it 101 Alternate; the natives of the region call it Bloody Bayshore.

A million people live here between the Bay and the ridge, in grubby tracts built on fills, in junior-executive ranchhouse developments, in senior-executive mansions, in Hillsborough palaces. I'd had some cases on the Peninsula: violence and passional crime are as much a part of the moral landscape as P.T.A. and Young Republican meetings and traffic accidents. The social and economic pressures make life in Los Angeles seem by comparison like playing marbles for keeps.

I turned off Bayshore, where the drivers drive for keeps, into the bosky twilight peace of Atherton. A sheriff's car with San Mateo County markings passed me cruising. I honked and got out and was told where Whiteoaks Drive was.

It paralleled Bayshore, about halfway between Bayshore and Camino Real: a quiet street of fairly large estates which was more like a country lane than a city street. Mrs. Wycherly's number, 507, was engraved in a stone gatepost set in an eight-foot stone wall. The moulded iron gates were chained and padlocked.

Wired to one of them was a metal sign which looked like a For Sale sign. I got a flashlight out of my car. For Sale, Ben Merriman, Realtor, with an Emerson telephone number and a Camino Real address.

The white front of the house glimmered through trees. I turned my light towards it. Oaks on either side of the driveway converted it into a rough green chasm whose gravel floor was drifted with brown leaves and yellowing newspapers. It was an impressive Colonial house but it had an abandoned air, as though the colonists had given up and gone back to the mother country. Blinds and drapes were drawn across all the windows, upstairs and down.

I focused on the newspapers in the gravel. There were twelve or fifteen of them scattered around inside the gates. Some of them were wrapped in waxed paper, against rainy weather; several of them had been trampled into mud.

I reached through the bars, the side of my face against cold iron, and got hold of the nearest one, a *San Francisco Chronicle* still trussed with a string for delivery. I broke the string and read the date at the top of the front page. It was November 5, three days after Phoebe disappeared.

I wanted to see what was inside the house. I put on driving gloves and chinned myself on the top of the stone wall. No spikes or broken glass: the escalade would be easy.

"Get down off there!" a man's voice said behind me.

I dropped to the ground and turned. He loomed large in the darkness, a dim grey figure in a snap-brim hat.

"What do you think you're doing?"

"Looking."

"You've had your look. So beat it, Tarzan."

I picked up my flashlight and turned the beam on him. He was a big man of about forty, handsome except for an upturned clown's nose and something about the eyes which reminded me of a Tanforan tout or a gambler on the Reno-Vegas circuit. He wore a sharp dark flannel suit and an indefinable air of failure pinned in place by a jauntily striped bow tie.

The nostrils in his upturned nose glared darkly at me. His teeth glittered in a downward grin:

"Take that light off me. You want me to smash it for you?"

"You could always try."

He took a couple of steps towards me, as if he was walking uphill, then stood back on his heels. I kept the light on him. His pointed shoes fidgeted in the dirt.

"Who do you think you are?"

"Just a citizen, trying to find an old acquaintance. Her name is Mrs. Catherine Wycherly."

"She doesn't live here any more."

"You know her?"

"I represent her."

"In what capacity?"

"I'm responsible for the security of these premises. We don't like prowlers and snoopers around here."

"Where can I get in touch with Mrs. Wycherly?"

"I'm not here to answer questions. I'm here to see that no-body vandalizes this property." There was a nasty little whine in his voice. He reached into his back pocket and matched it with a nasty little gun. "Now get."

My gun was in the back seat of my car; which was just as well. I got.

Crossing Bayshore on an overpass, I felt as if I was cross-ing a frontier between two countries. There were some white people on the streets of East Palo Alto, but most of the peo-ple were colored. The cheap tract houses laid out in rows between the salt flats and the highway had the faint pe-culiar atmosphere of a suburban ghetto.

Sammy Green earned Sailors' Union wages and lived in one of the better houses on one of the better streets, almost out of hearing of the highway and almost out of smelling of the Bay. His wife was a handsome young Negro woman wearing a party dress and a complicated hairdo, under which earrings sparkled.

She told me that her husband was in Gilroy for the night; he always visited his folks the second night of his vacation, and took the children with him. No, his parents had no telephone, but she'd be glad to give me their address.

I asked her instead how to get to Woodside, where Phoe-be's aunt and uncle lived.

chapter 7

IT WAS FIVE WINDING MILES across the hinterland of the Stanford campus. Eventually I found Carl Trevor's mailbox on the road that climbed towards the coastal ridge. His place had a name: Leafy Acres. A horse whickered at me from somewhere as I turned up the drive. I didn't whicker back.

I rounded a wooded curve and saw the long low redwood and stone house, many windowed, full of light. A maid in a black and white uniform answered the door. She turned on outside floodlights before she unhooked the screen.

"Is Mrs. Trevor at home?"

"She isn't back from Palo Alto yet."

"Mr. Trevor?"

"If she isn't back he isn't back," she said in an instructive tone. "She went to the station to meet his train. They ought to be here any time now, they're later than usual."

"I'll wait."

She looked me over, apparently trying to decide whether I belonged in the front part of the house or the kitchen. I assumed my most respectable expression and got bidden into the library, as she called it. It was a beautiful panelled room with actual books on its shelves. The Trevors went in heavily for history, particularly Western Americana.

I leafed through a copy of *American Heritage* until I heard a car engine in the drive. I went to the window and saw them get out of their Cadillac convertible. She climbed out on the driver's side, a thin woman of about fifty with a face like a silver hatchet. He was a heavy-shouldered man wearing a Homburg and carrying the inevitable brief case. He looked sick.

She offered him her arm as they started up the front steps. He pushed her away, without touching her, in a gesture that combined irritation and pride. He ran up the steps two at a time. She watched him go with naked fear on her face.

The fear was still in her eyes when she came into the library a few minutes later. She had on pearls and a simple dark gown which had probably cost a fortune. A wasted fortune. It accentuated the taut angularity of her body and left her frying-chicken shoulders bare.

"What do you want?"

"My name is Archer, I'm a private detective. Your brother Homer Wycherly hired me to look for your niece Phoebe. I don't know whether you've heard from him—"

"I've heard. My brother phoned me this afternoon. I don't know what to make of it." She wrung her hands so hard that they creaked. "What do you make of it? Is she a runaway?"

"I have no theories, Mrs. Trevor. Not yet. I've just been over in Atherton, where I found out that Phoebe isn't the only one on the missing list. Her mother's house is up for sale, and apparently empty. I was hoping you could tell me where Mrs. Wycherly is."

"Catherine?" She sat down suddenly, and let me sit down. "What has Catherine to do with this?"

"Phoebe was last seen in her mother's company. They left the ship together the day your brother sailed. Shortly after that, Mrs. Wycherly seems to have moved out of her house. Do you know anything about the move, or where she's gone?"

"I don't keep track of Catherine's comings and goings. By

her own choice, she's no longer a member of the family."
Good riddance, was the unspoken implication. "As Homer
may have told you, she divorced him last May. In Reno."

"Is that when she moved to Atherton?"

She nodded her thin grey angry head. "Why she chose to
come here and become our virtual neighbor!— Of course I
know why she did it. She hoped to trade on our standing in
the community. But my husband and I were not about to fall
in with her plans. Catherine made her bed and she can lie in
it." Her mouth was thin and cruel. "I'm not surprised she
gave up on Atherton and moved out."

"Do you have any idea where she moved to?"

"I told you I do not. I'm sure in any case that you're on the
wrong track. Phoebe couldn't conceivably be with her. They
don't get along."

"That may be so. I still have to talk to her."

"I'm afraid I can't help you with that." She cocked her
head, as if a moral hearing-aid had switched on and let her
hear the harshness in her voice. "You mustn't think me
un-Christian, Mr. Archer. Where my former sister-in-law is
concerned, we have *had* it, as the young people say. I really
did my best for her over the years. I took her into my own
house before she married my brother, and tried to teach her
the things a lady should know. I'm afraid the indoctrination
didn't take. As a matter of fact, the last time I saw her—"
She compressed her lips in a way that reminded me of her
brother.

"When did you last see her?"

"That same day. The famous day when Homer embarked
on his voyage of discovery. Or escape. Catherine must have
read about it in the paper, and saw a chance to get her talons
into him one more time. I'm surprised they let her aboard.
I've seen her drunk before, but never as loud and violent as
she was that afternoon."

"What was she after?"

"Money, or so she said. There Homer was with his
millions, sailing off to the South Seas, and there was poor
Catherine destitute and starving on the meager pittance that
he doled out to her. I felt like telling her that a starvation
regime would be good for her figure. But of course her
version of the facts was grossly exaggerated, as usual. I
happen to know that Homer gave her a hundred-thousand-
dollar settlement and pays her three thousand dollars a
month alimony in addition. And she spends every penny of
it."

"How?"

"Don't ask me how. She's always had expensive tastes, which is doubtless why she married my brother in the first place. I heard she paid seventy-five-thousand dollars cash for the Mandeville house—a ridiculous outlay for a woman in her position."

"The Mandeville house?"

"The one in Atherton—the one you tell me she's selling. She bought it from a Captain Mandeville."

"I see. Getting back to that shipboard scene, did you notice your niece's reaction?"

"Not specifically. She was appalled, I'm sure. We all were. My husband and I left before it was over. Mr. Trevor has heart trouble, and the doctor wants him to avoid that sort of tension. If Catherine aimed to spoil our leave-taking, she succeeded very well."

"You didn't see her leave the ship with Phoebe?"

"No, we'd already left ourselves. Are you sure that information is correct? It doesn't seem likely."

"I got it from one of the ship's officers. They left the dock together in a taxi. I don't know what happened after that."

She clasped her hands at her breast. "It's a horribly upsetting situation. My husband is almost prostrated by it. I should have waited to tell him until he'd had his rest—he comes home from the city so exhausted. But I had to go and blurt it out as soon as he stepped off the train."

"He's fond of Phoebe, your brother tells me."

"Deeply fond. She's been like a daughter to us, especially to Carl. I do hope you can get her back for him. For all of us, but especially for him." Her hands had climbed to her throat and were picking at her pearls. "I'm deeply concerned about how this shock will affect my husband's health. I've seldom known him to be so disturbed. And he blames me for what happened."

"Blames you?"

"When Phoebe didn't answer our Christmas invitation, he wanted to drive down to Boulder Beach and see that she was all right. I persuaded him not to—he's not supposed to drive. Besides, I felt she had a right to be on her own if she chose. I naturally believed that it was her choice, that she wanted to be free of family for once in her young life. Perhaps I was a little impatient with her, too, when she failed to acknowledge my letter. In any case, we didn't go. We should have. We should at least have phoned."

Her fingers were active at her throat. Her pearls broke, cascading down her body, rolling in all directions on the floor.

"Damn it!" she cried. "This is the day when everything happens to me."

Kicking pearls out from under her feet, she moved to the doorway and jabbed a bell push with her thumb. The maid came running, got down on her knees at once and began to pick up the pearls.

A middle-aged man in a plaid smoking jacket leaned in the doorway and watched the scene with barely repressed amusement. His balding head was large for his body, and rested like a pale cannonball on his shoulders without much intervention from his neck. His voice was deep, and seemed to take a certain pleasure in its own depth:

"What goes on, Helen?"

"I've broken my pearls." Her narrow look implied that in some obscure way he was responsible.

"It isn't the end of the world."

"No, but it's exasperating. Everything seems to be happening at once."

The kneeling maid gave her a quick glance, sideways and upward. She said nothing. Mrs. Trevor moved on her husband with a kind of furious maternality:

"You're supposed to be lying down. We don't want anything else to happen today." It sounded like a move in a complex verbal game which nobody ever won.

"Nothing will," he said. "I'm feeling much better." He looked inquiringly at me. His eyes were blue and intelligent.

"I'd like to talk to you, Mr. Trevor."

I started to tell him who I was, but Helen Trevor intervened:

"No, Mr. Archer. Please. I don't want my husband troubled with these affairs. I'll be glad to answer any other questions you—"

"Nonsense, Helen, let me talk to him. I'm perfectly all right now. Come with me, Mr.— Archer, is it?"

"Archer."

Trevor turned his back on his wife's protests and led me into a small study off the library. He closed the door with a small sigh of relief.

"Women," he said under his breath. "Let me get you a drink, Mr. Archer. Scotch or Bourbon?"

"Nothing, thanks. I'm driving, and Bayshore is murder."

"Is it not? I prefer to commute by Southern Pacific. Now sit down and tell me what all this is about Phoebe. The version I got came by way of my wife, and it's probably garbled."

He placed me in a leather armchair facing his and listened

to what I had to tell him. There was a silence when I'd finished. Trevor sat immobile. He gave the impression of mental or physical pain stoically endured.

"I blame myself," he said finally. "I should have looked out for her, if Homer wasn't willing to. Why he had to choose this winter to forsake his responsibilities and become a white shadow in the South Seas—" He punctuated the unfinished sentence with his fist on his knee. "But the real question is, what are we going to do about it?"

"Find her."

"If she's alive."

"They usually are," I said with more assurance than I felt. "They turn up counting change in Vegas, or waiting table in the Tenderloin, or setting up light housekeeping in a beat pad, or bucking the modelling racket in Hollywood."

Trevor's thick eyebrows came together and tangled like hostile caterpillars. "Why would a well-nurtured girl like Phoebe do any of those things?"

"The standard motives are drink or drugs or a man. They all add up to the same idea, rebellion. It's the fourth R they learn in school these days. Or someplace."

"But Phoebe wasn't particularly rebellious. Though Lord knows she had plenty of reason to be."

"I'm interested in the reasons. I couldn't get much out of Wycherly directly. As far as his daughter is concerned, he seems to be living in a dream. And he doesn't want to wake up."

"That's natural enough, he's one of the reasons."

I waited for him to go on. He didn't. I tried another tack: "I did learn that your niece went to see a psychiatrist last spring. Do you know anything about that?"

His eyebrows went up. "No. But I'm not surprised. She was an unhappy girl when she came back to Stanford after Easter. I know her studies were going downhill."

"What was she unhappy about?"

"She didn't confide in me. According to my wife, there was quite a family ruckus in Meadow Farms over the holiday. It had to do with some libellous letters."

"Did you ever see those letters?"

"I didn't, but Helen did. They were pretty vile, I gather. They set off the last of a long series of family explosions." He leaned towards me earnestly. "I try to avoid gossip, but I'll tell you this much. It wasn't a happy marriage the Wycherlys had. They should have divorced twenty years ago, or never married in the first place. I used to spend a good deal of time at their house, when Helen and I were still living in Meadow Farms, and I can tell you it wasn't a good place to raise a child. They fought continually."

"What about?"

"Anything. Catherine detested the place, Homer wouldn't leave it. They simply weren't meant to live together. He was well on in his thirties when they married, and she was still in her teens. It wasn't only a matter of age. They were as far apart as night and day, and Phoebe was caught in the middle until she finally got away to school. I don't mean that Homer isn't a gentle enough soul, but he has those generations of money behind him. It makes a man soft in some ways, hard in others." He smiled slightly. "I should know. He's been my titular boss for twenty-five years."

"What sort of a woman is Catherine? I've gotten some pretty fierce reports on her."

"No doubt." His half-smile changed to a half-grimace. "She's gone to pieces since her divorce, as women often do. She used to be quite a forceful woman, and quite a handsome one, if you like the big blatant blonde type. I used to get alone with Catherine fairly well. We understood each other to some extent. She came up the hard way, as I did. If marrying money at eighteen is coming up the hard way."

"What did she do before that?"

"I really don't know. Homer met her in the South and brought her to Meadow Farms to marry her. We put her up for a while before the wedding. She knew nothing about running a house; which is Helen's métier. I think the girl was originally some sort of a secretary."

"How old is she now?"

"She must be nearly forty." Trevor paused, and gave me a long look from under his eyebrows. "You seem to be excessively interested in Catherine Wycherly. Why?"

"Phoebe was last seen in her mother's company."

"She was? When?"

"The day Wycherly sailed. They left the ship together, drove away in a taxi. I'm doing my best to trace the taxi."

"Wouldn't it be simpler to take it up with Catherine?"

"I'd like to, but I don't know where she is. That's one reason I came to you."

"I haven't seen her since November second. She put on an act that day aboard the ship which I'd just as soon forget. I presume she's in the house she bought in Atherton."

"She isn't, though, and I don't think she's been there for the last two months. The house is up for sale."

"I didn't know that. Are you sure?"

"I was over there an hour or so ago. A sleazy character caught me trying to climb the wall and pulled a gun on me." I described the man in the bow tie. "Do you know who he is? He claimed to be in charge of the property."

Trevor shook his head. "I'm afraid I don't know the man. And I haven't the slightest idea where Catherine's gone to."

"Do you know people she knows?"

"Not on the Peninsula. I'll be frank with you, Mr. Archer. We didn't and don't move in the same circles as Catherine Wycherly. It was a matter of choice, on our part."

"What circles does she move in?"

"A downward spiral, I'm afraid. But I won't repeat gossip."

"I wish you would."

"No. I owe that much to Catherine. Or to myself." His broad cheeks colored faintly, and the brightness of his eyes intensified. He said with the irresistible smoothness of a steam roller: "We're getting rather far afield from the subject of my niece, and it's not getting any earlier. Tell me, what can I do to help?"

"You might talk to the local police. If I go to them cold I'll get no action. Also, there's the danger of publicity. Wycherly is dead set against publicity. But you could probably make a confidential inquiry, and get them rolling in a quiet way."

"By all means. Tomorrow morning."

"Tonight would be better."

"All right." Sick or not, Trevor showed the serviceability of a powerful man who didn't have to prove anything to himself. "What precise form should this inquiry take?"

"I'll leave that to you. The authorities in the entire San Francisco area should be on the lookout for her. Also they should check their backlog of unidentified bodies going back to early November."

Trevor's face lost its remaining color. "You said they usually turn up alive."

"They usually do. But we have to rule out the other possibilities. Do you have any pictures of her?"

"I took some last summer when she was staying with us. I'll get them."

He rose vigorously. The movement showed no trace of effort unless you were watching his eyes. The brightness in them dimmed down like a lamp-flame for an instant.

Trevor came back five minutes later with a sheaf of colored pictures in his hand. He sat down and dealt them to me one at a time. Phoebe smiled brightly among camellias in a white summer dress. She swung a tennis racquet in yellow linen. She sat and stood and reclined on beige sand beside an indigo sea. Some of the pictures had sea cliffs in the background.

The girl was almost beautiful in a poignant way of her own. Not beautiful enough, though; they never are. In the beach shots particularly, her smile was incandescent with self-consciousness. She thrust her sharp small breasts towards the voyeur eye of the color camera, agonized by the effort to be really beautiful for it.

Trevor was studying my face when I looked up.

"She's a valuable girl," he said. "A fine deep girl who has had a hard growing up. She deserved better parents than she got."

"She seems to be personally valuable to you."

"I love her like a daughter. We have no children of our own, and I should have kept in closer touch with her. But there's no use crying over spilt milk."

"These pictures were taken last summer?"

"Yes. I have earlier ones, of course, going all the way back to infancy. I tried to pick out the ones that look most like her present self. Phoebe's slimmed down since her teens."

"Did she spend the summer with you?"

"Just a few days of it, actually, a few days in August. We have a beach cottage near Medicine Stone, and she was supposed to stay longer. But she and my wife were tense with each other for some reason. She left by unspoken mutual agreement. Which didn't include me."

"Do you recall a boy she met in Medicine Stone? Good-looking college boy with reddish hair?"

"I saw him at a distance, I believe. In the surf. I'm forbidden the surf myself. Phoebe and he were cavorting with some other young people." There was a trace of envious sadness in his voice.

"But you never met him?"

"Phoebe didn't choose to introduce him to us. I think that was one of the sources of friction with Helen. Phoebe was seeing quite a lot of the young man while she was with us."

"Do you know anything about him?"

"No. He seemed like a healthy young animal. And Phoebe was pleased and flattered by his attentions. But as I said, I never had the privilege of meeting him. Do *you* know anything about him?"

"I talked to him this morning in Boulder Beach. He's a student there."

"Are—is he still interested in Phoebe?"

"He was, until she disappeared."

"Do you suspect him of having something to do with it?"

"No."

His eyes were penetrating. "You do, though."

"I suspect everybody. It's my occupational neurosis. But he has no motive, and an alibi."

"You're thorough. What's the boy's name? Bobby something, isn't it?"

"Bobby Doncaster." I changed the subject. "Which of these pictures is the closest likeness?"

He shuffled them with a poker-player's deftness, and picked out the one in the white dress. The one in tennis clothes was almost as good, he said. I asked for it, and got it.

"Now, is there anything else I can do, for you or Phoebe?"

"You might have some copies of her picture made. Fifty, or a hundred, just in case Wycherly decides to make a major effort."

"What form would a major effort take?"

"Use of a national detective agency, mass media publicity, all-out police dragnet, with FBI co-operation if possible. Wycherly's a wealthy man, he could swing a lot of weight."

Trevor clapped his hands together. "I can swing it for him if necessary. Do you recommend it, Archer?"

"Wait till tomorrow. If I can put a finger on Catherine Wycherly, she may give me some answers. Do you know a real-estate man named Ben Merriman, by the way?"

"I'm afraid I don't." His eyebrows came together in concentration. "I may have seen his sign on Camino Real. Why?"

"He's selling Mrs. Wycherly's house. Maybe he can give me her new address. I'll get in touch with you tomorrow. In the meantime, you'll talk to the local police tonight?"

"As soon as you leave," he said, rising.

It was an invitation to go. On my way out through the library, I stepped on a pearl.

chapter **8**

BEN MERRIMAN'S NAME was written in red neon across the cornice of a narrow pink stucco building. It was in a gap-toothed section of rundown houses and vacant lots and struggling businesses. A dog hospital stood next to Merriman's office. Diagonally across the street, a drive-in swarmed with cutdown cars and their owners.

I locked the door of my car: I had a seventy-five-dollar revolver in a brief case on the back seat and a contact microphone in the dash compartment. Dogs barked. I could smell pesticide.

A light outlined a closed door in a partition at the back of Merriman's place. The glass front door was locked. I tapped on the glass with my car keys, and the door in the partition opened. Spilled light made a faceless silhouette of the woman who came uncertainly towards me. She fumbled at the self-lock and got it open.

"Is Mr. Merriman here?"

"No, he isn't," she said in a monotone.

"Can you tell me where to find him?"

"I wish I knew. I've been waiting for him for the last hour-and-a-half." Resentment cracked her voice. She swallowed it. "Are you a client of Mr. Merriman's?"

"A prospective one, maybe. I'm interested in some property he's got listed."

"Oh. Fine."

She opened the door wide and turned on all the lights and urged me in. She was a thirtyish blonde in an imitation mink coat which had seen better days. So had she. One of those blondes who ripened early like California fruit, hung in full teen-age maturity for a few sweet months or years, then fall into the first high reaching hand. The memory of the sweet days stayed in them and fermented.

Closing the door she brushed against my back in a movement which was either erotic or alcoholic. The odor of gin which she wore instead of perfume suggested the latter possibility. But she opened up her minkless mink and gave me a dazzling smile across her figure. Touch me if you dare, the smile said: I dare you, but don't you dare. They never got over their grudging need of the reaching hands that violated their first fine careless narcissism.

"I don't really work for my husband any more, but I'm sure that I can help you with your needs, since he isn't here at the moment. We have many fine properties listed."

Coat and figure swinging in an interesting cross-rhythm, she pulled a straight chair out from a desk and offered it to me. I sat. A layer of dust powdered the formica desk-top. The daily calendar hadn't been changed for the new year.

In front of the calendar was a little pile of three-by-five business blotters decorated with a photographic cut. The cut showed the clown-nosed man wearing a polka-dot bow tie and a carnivorous grin. It was captioned: "Ben Merriman the Realtor—firstest with the mostest. An honest deal every time."

"Many fine," his wife said. She sat down in a businesslike way which her unbusinesslike body parodied. "How large a property are you interested in, Mr——?"

I got out my wallet and produced a card which a Santa Monica life insurance salesman had presented to me before he found out what I did for a living. The name on the card was William C. Wheeling, Jr. I gave it to her.

"Wheeling," I said. "I like a big house—something big and traditional-looking like that white Colonial I saw in Atherton today. It has your husband's sign on it."

"You must be thinking of the Mandeville house on White-oaks. Big stone wall around it?"

"That's the one."

"I'm sorry." She was really sorry. "It sold. Too bad. You could have gotten a terrific buy. The owner knocked off thousands from the price."

"Who was the owner?"

"A Mrs. Wycherly, a very fine woman, well-heeled. She told Ben she intends to travel."

"Where to?"

"I wouldn't know, I'm sure." She opened her eyes wide in dubious innocence: they were dull purple like Santa Clara plums. "If you're thinking of trying to contact her and make an offer, it's no use. I think it's even out of escrow already. The new owners are moving down from Oakland Heights any day now. Wonderful people. Ben said they paid cash out. But we have many other splendid buys."

"I'm interested in this one. The for-sale sign is still up."

"That doesn't mean a thing. Ben should have taken it down long ago. If he'd keep his mind on the business—"

The front door opened, blowing cold air on the back of my neck. I thought it was Merriman and rose turning to meet him. It was a younger man in a turtle-neck cashmere sweater, robin's-egg blue, the color of his eyes. His blonde good looks were spoiled by a small goatee which wagged on his chin like an unfinished piece of face.

"Where's Ben?" he said to the woman. "I mean it, doll."

"I don't know where he is. He stood me up here two hours ago, said he had an appointment."

"With Jessie?"

The woman's hand went to her mouth. Through the fair

skin on the back of it, I could see the branching veins climb like fine blue ivy. The tip of her middle finger slipped in between her teeth. She bit on it hard, unwincing.

"Jessie?" she said around it. "What's Jessie got to do with it?"

"He made a heavy pass at her today while I was at the store. I don't like it."

She took her finger out of her mouth. "I'm crazy about it. Are you sure that Jessie isn't making it up?"

"I know damn well she isn't."

He raised his fist and held silent communion with it. There were fresh marks on the knuckles, which looked like toothmarks. His blue eyes were mean. He brushed his goatee with his fist:

"It isn't the first time he made a pass at her. I didn't tell you before. I'm telling you now. If you can't stop him, I will. With what I've got on him—"

"You lay off Ben," she said.

"Then make him lay off Jessie. What's the matter? Aren't you getting along?"

"Oh, sure," she said with bitter irony. "Everything's coming up dandelions. Go away now, will you? I'm with a customer."

"Since when are you working nights for Ben?"

"I told you he left me waiting here. We were going to go out on the town for a change."

"When do you expect him back?"

"I don't, now. I guess he decided he'd have more fun by himself."

"Yeah. Well, he better keep his hands off my pig."

"Tell *her* to stop wiggling her fat little rump at him."

They grinned at each other like old enemies. He slammed out. She sat forgetful of me, her eyes focused on something between us, invisible in the air.

"The dirty son of a bitch," she said between her teeth. "Two can play at that game." Then she remembered me, and said in a more human voice: "Don't pay any attention to me. I'll be all right in a minute. Give me a minute, will you?"

It was the least I could give her. She went into the back room and closed the flimsy door. I heard the clink of a bottle on a glass, the distinct pouring sound which solitary drinkers imagine nobody can hear.

She came out wearing fresh lipstick on a muzzy gin smile. "I've been looking at the figures on the Mandeville house. If you're *really* interested, we might be able to work something out with the new owners. They got such a *terrific* buy, they could sell to you at a profit and still give you a bargain. Even at sixty thousand it's a steal. It was originally listed at eighty, and it would cost a hundred and twenty to replace at today's building costs."

I said with the necessary smile: "For a girl who doesn't work here, you put out a good spiel."

"Thank you, sir. I used to sell for Ben." She leaned across the desk, offering me her full white décolleté as a sort of bonus. "Seriously, are you interested in the property?"

"Very interested. Why don't you show it to me, then we'll talk about the deal?"

"Tonight?"

"Why not?"

She looked past me at the moving traffic in the street. "I better not leave, he might come back. Miracles can happen. If you can't wait till morning, I'll give you the keys. The electricity is on in the house, I think."

She went into the back room again and came out looking flustered. "Ben must have taken the keys. I'm sorry."

"That's all right. I'll come back in the morning."

Whiteoaks Avenue was less than a mile from Camino Real. I found the moulded iron gates standing open, the padlock gaping on its chain. I gathered up the rest of the scattered newspapers and looked at the date lines. The latest was November 17. The earliest was November 3, the day after Phoebe disappeared.

The bellying gray sky above the trees was expectant with moon. The house seemed to grow before me as I trudged up the driveway. Its façade returned the glare of my flashlight like a blank white sepulchre.

The ornate front door was closed but unlocked. I went in and found a light switch beside the door. The parquetry floor of the hallway was tracked with old mud and sprinkled with the cards of real-estate salesmen. From the rear of the hallway a white-banistered staircase curved gracefully upward into darkness.

I entered the main room to the right, and touched the switch. A yellowing crystal chandelier lit up incompletely. Most of the furnishings went with the chandelier: old striped English sofas facing each other from opposite ends of the room, a white marble fireplace containing a gas heater, over the mantel a bad oil painting of somebody's father, portly in a Prince Albert.

Mrs. Wycherly, or some other modern, had added a few touches of her own. The brash new multicolored drapes clashed like cymbals with the rest of the room. A blonde mahogany hi-fi console stood beside the fireplace. It was open, and it had a record on it: "Slow Boat to China." On the inside of the door a cork dartboard hung, surrounded by the scars which the darts had made in the white panelling.

I closed the door, pulled one of the darts out of the cork, walked back across the room to the fireplace, and threw the dart at the board, which it hit. I went through the other downstairs rooms humming "Slow Boat to China" to myself and thinking about a story I read in high school. It was called "The Vision of Mirza" and it had been cropping up in my memory for years.

Mirza had a vision of a bridge which a lot of people were crossing on foot: all the living people in the world. From time to time one of them would step on a kind of trap door and drop out of sight. The other pedestrians hardly noticed. Each of them went on walking across the bridge until he hit a trap door of his own, and fell through.

I hit mine, or something like it, at the top of the graceful stairs. It wasn't a trap door, exactly, and it wasn't exactly mine. It was a body, and it sighed when I stumbled over it. It sighed as if it had fallen the whole distance and lived.

I found the upturned face with my flashlight. It wasn't worth finding: a mask of blood behind which no life bubbled. The spattered striped bow tie and the sharp charcoal suit looked hickish and pathetic on a man so beaten and dead.

His jacket pockets were empty. I had to move him to get at his back pockets. He was heavy, as hard to lift as a cross made out of flesh. I found four one-dollar bills in his wallet, and a driver's license made out to Ben Merriman. His little gun was missing.

I put the wallet in the breast pocket of his jacket, so that I wouldn't have to move him again. Then I took it out and wiped it with my handkerchief and put it back. The flashlight on the floor watched me like a yellow suspicious eye. I picked it up and got out of there.

On my way back to Merriman's office I passed the Southern Pacific station. It was closed for the night, but there was a pay telephone on the outside platform. I used it to call the police.

Mrs. Merriman was still sitting at the desk in the front of the office. She looked up with her muzzy smile when I came in:

"I'm sorry, Ben didn't come back yet. I'm holding the fort all by my lonesome. Join me?" Then she saw the look on my face, and imitated it: "What's the matter?"

"I want Mrs. Wycherly's address."

"I don't have it."

"You must have, if you sold the house for her."

"Ben handled it. I told you I don't work for him, not on a regular basis. He does most of his business out of his hat."

"Let me see the listing."

"What for? You trying to work out a deal behind our backs or something?"

"Nothing like that. I want to know where Mrs. Wycherly is."

"The listing won't tell you. Look, I'll show you."

She rose unsteadily. I followed her into the little back room. A half-full bottle of Gordon's gin stood on a pile of papers on the desk. She riffled through the papers and came up with a mimeographed sheet. She was trying to read it with slightly blurred eyes when the telephone rang.

She picked it up and said yes and listened to it. Her face turned pearly young. Her eyes expanded. She thanked the telephone and put it down.

"Ben is dead. Somebody killed him, and I thought he stood me up."

She started out past me, walking like a woman in a trance. She collided heavily with the doorframe, leaned on the wallboard partition. The mimeographed sheet was crumpled in her hand. She dropped it and reached for the bottle.

I salvaged the piece of paper from the floor. The house on Whiteoaks Avenue had been listed at eighty thousand. The eighty thousand was crossed out and sixty thousand pencilled in. There were other pencillings, faint and half-erased, which I couldn't decipher. Mrs. Wycherly's address was given as 507 Whiteoaks Avenue.

The woman set the bottle down three-eighths full. Leaning on the desk, she lowered herself into the swivel chair that stood beside it. She twisted her hair in her fingers. It was dark at the roots, as if darkness had seeped up in capillary action from her mind.

"The crazy old bastard," she said. "I bet he did it to him. He came to our house last week and said he was going to do it. Unless Ben paid him off."

"Who?"

"Mandeville. Captain Mandeville. He walked right up to our front door with a forty-five revolver in his hand. Ben had to slip out through the patio and let me handle him. The old guy is as nutty as a fruitcake."

"What did Mandeville want?"

"What does everybody want? Money." She looked at me levelly. The quick one-two of grief and gin had stunned her into sobriety. "He claimed that Ben cheated him out of the money for his lousy house."

"Is that true?"

"How do I know? I lived five years with Ben, from pillar to post and back again. I never did find out what went on in his head, or where all the money went. I never even got a house of my own, and him in real estate. Call it real estate."

"What do you call it?"

"I gave up calling it anything. He'd work harder to turn a crooked buck—" She glanced up at me again, her mouth still open. She had lipstick on her teeth. "Why are you so interested in Ben? You don't even know him."

"No, I wish I had."

"What is this? What are you trying to pull on me?"

"Nothing on you, Mrs. Merriman. I'm sorry about what happened. By the way, who was the blond lad with the chinbeard?"

The fresh gin was rising in her eyes, disturbing their focus and dissolving their meaning. She used it as a kind of mask, letting her eyes go entirely dead:

"I dunno who you mean."

"You know who I mean. He came in here looking for your husband."

"Oh, him," she said with bleary cunning. "I never saw him before in my life."

"You're lying."

"I am not. Anyway, who are you to call me a liar? You said you were a prospect. You're no prospect."

"I'm a prospector. Who was he, Mrs. Merriman?"

"I dunno. Some jerk Ben bums around with—used to, I mean." The two tenses coming together cut her like scissors. Tears or gin exuded between her eyelids. "Go away and let me be. You were nice before. You're not nice any more." She added as if she was completing a syllogism: "I bet you're just a lousy cop."

"No."

For once I wished I was. The cops, the lousy cops, would be arriving any time now. I was far from home base and suitable for framing. I said good night to her and went out through the front office. On the way I picked up a blotter with Merriman's picture on it.

A sheriff's car with a dying siren drifted out of the traffic stream and took my place at the curb as I pulled away. Young heads at the drive-in across the road became aware of it, wondering if it had come for them. Some dogs in the kennels next door had begun to howl.

chapter 9

I FOUND Captain Theodore Mandeville's address in the telephone directory at the Atherton station. He lived in a large residential hotel on the main street of Palo Alto. It had a grandiose pillared portico, and a chintzy little lobby in which the smells of lavender and cigars waged a quiet battle of the sexes.

The woman behind the desk, who looked like the probable source of the lavender, told me that Captain Mandeville was in. She called him on a house phone and got permission from him to send me up.

He was waiting for me when I stepped out of the elevator —a lean brown old man with white hair and moustache and eyebrows like small auxiliary moustaches. He had on a grey flannel bathrobe over a boiled shirt and a black tie. His eyes were crackling black.

"I'm Captain Mandeville. What can I do for you, sir?"

I told him I was a private detective looking for a girl. "You may be able to give me some information about her family. The girl's name is Phoebe Wycherly."

"Mrs. Catherine Wycherly's daughter?"

"Yes. I understand you've had some business dealings with Mrs. Wycherly."

"I have, to my sorrow. But I don't know her personally, and I never met the daughter. Just what do you mean when you say that she is missing?"

"She left school over two months ago. The last word I have on her, she was leaving the San Francisco docks on the afternoon of November second. She was getting into a taxi with her mother. Any information that you can give me about the mother—"

He broke in: "You're not suggesting that she abducted her own daughter?"

"Hardly. But she may know where the girl is."

"I know where the mother is, at any rate. Is that any help to you?"

"It would be a lot of help."

"She's staying in a hotel in Sacramento—rather shabby quarters for a woman of her status. The name of the place seems to have slipped my mind for the moment. I believe I

57

have it written down somewhere. Come in and I'll look it up."

He led me down the hallway to his apartment and left me in the living room. Its narrow walls were hung with photographs. In one, a beautiful woman smiled dreamily from under a cloud of black hair. Most of the others were pictures of naval vessels, ranging from a World War One destroyer to a World War Two battleship. The battleship had been photographed from the air, and lay like a dark spearhead on crinkled metal sea.

Captain Mandeville came back into the room while I was looking at the battleship. "My last command," he said. "My son Lieutenant Mandeville took that picture a few days before he was shot down at Okinawa. Rather good, isn't it?"

"Very good. I was at Okinawa, on the ground."

"Were you now? How interesting." He didn't pursue the subject. He handed me a ruled page torn from a memo pad on which "Champion Hotel" was written in pencil. "I seem to have misplaced the street address but you should be able to find it, easily. I had no trouble finding it, and I'm no detective."

"You've seen Mrs. Wycherly recently?"

"No. I tried to, but she wouldn't see me. She's a stubborn woman, and I suspect a foolish one." His mouth quivered. His eyes sparkled like pieces of coal under his white eyebrows.

"Would you mind expanding on that? I don't want to pry, but I don't understand what Mrs. Wycherly has been up to. Or what's been going on about the sale of your property."

"It's a long story, and I'm afraid a sordid one. I don't pretend to understand it thoroughly myself, which is why I've hired a lawyer. I should have gone to a lawyer six months ago."

"When Mrs. Wycherly bought your house from you?"

"She didn't buy it from me. There's the rub. The fact that she didn't cost me twenty-five-thousand dollars. Which I could ill afford, let me assure you. A real-estate sharper named Merriman cheated me out of twenty-five-thousand dollars."

"Did Mrs. Wycherly have a hand in it?"

"No, I don't accuse the lady of that. No doubt she was just as much a victim as I. On the other hand, she hasn't been much help. I went to the trouble of getting her address from the escrow company, and I made a special trip to Sacramento to try to enlist her co-operation. She flatly refused to see me, as I said." His voice shook with controlled rage.

"But look. You don't want to go into all this. I have no wish to go into it, certainly. I made a bloody fool of myself, and at my age that can be painful."

"How were you cheated, Captain?"

"I'm not sure I can explain. My lawyer could. But the case is pending before the Real Estate Commission, and I doubt that he would be willing to discuss it with you. It's nothing to do with this missing girl of yours, in any case."

"I'm not too sure of that."

"Well, if you insist. Sit down, sir."

He picked up a *Yachting* magazine which lay open on a chair, waved me into the chair with it and sat down opposite me:

"Mrs. Mandeville died last spring and very shortly afterward my housekeeper left: it seems she couldn't stand my temper unalloyed by Mrs. Mandeville's presence. I decided to sell my house in Atherton and move into cozier quarters. This fellow Merriman got wind of my intention, I don't know how, and approached me. He offered to sell my house for me and give me a fifty per cent kickback on the commission. I'm not a businessman, and I didn't realize that the very offer was illegal. Merriman represented it as a favor from one old Navy man to another; he'd been in the Reserve during the last war.

"I don't know how he got in. The man's a rascal. I didn't know that at the time, of course. I've found out since, from a friend in the Bureau of Personnel, that he was asked to resign his commission in 1945. He was a supply officer stationed in the Eleventh District at the time, and he was using his position to sell San Diego building lots to enlisted men. In addition to which, he had unpaid gambling debts— the man's an inveterate gambler.

"Unfortunately for me, I knew nothing of all this when I gave him authority to sell my house for me. He came to the house at my invitation and looked the place over. He pretended not to be greatly impressed. In fact, he bore down heavily on its drawbacks—the old-fashioned plumbing, the need for repainting and decorating, that sort of thing. With the current tightness of money, he told me I would be lucky to sell the house and land for fifty thousand dollars.

"It sounded to me like a reasonable figure. When I had the place built, some thirty years ago, it cost me no more than twenty-five thousand, including the acreage. I'm no student of real-estate values, and a hundred per cent profit seemed a veritable bonanza.

"Besides," he added, "I was keen to get out of there. I built the house for Mrs. Mandeville, and after she went the place was a whispering gallery of memories. I sold it to the first man who made an offer. He offered me the full fifty thousand, and I took it gratefully."

"What man was that?"

"I'm afraid his name escapes me. He claimed to be a radio executive who was being transferred from Los Angeles. He was transferred, all right," the old man said grimly. "I've learned since that he was a disc jockey, so-called, on some minor radio station in the South. The station fired him for accepting payments from record companies. He'd been on the Peninsula for some time, looking for a job, and he'd often been seen in Merriman's company."

"How do you know all this?"

"I have friends," he said. "I asked my friends to make some discreet inquiries, belatedly. They discovered that a few days after this fellow bought my house from me for fifty thousand he turned around and resold it to Mrs. Wycherly for seventy-five. Merriman handled both deals, of course. He double-escrowed the property, as they say."

"Was your first buyer acting as a stand-in for Merriman?"

"That is what we strongly suspect. My lawyer and I have asked the Real Estate Commission to look into it. I've always hated litigation, but when a man's been defrauded of nearly a third of his capital—" Overcome with outrage, he couldn't finish the sentence.

"Who is your lawyer, Captain?"

"Chap named John Burns, completely dependable, I've known Burns at the Yacht Club for years. He tells me this isn't the first time that Merriman has been suspected of double dealing. I'm determined that it shall be the last."

"What does Mr. Burns think of your chances of getting your money back?"

"We have a fair chance, he believes, if the thieves still have the money. It's hard to deal with these fly-by-nights, but we intend to bring the utmost legal pressure on Merriman. Unless he refunds the difference to me, he's bound to lose his license. He may, anyway."

"Did Merriman know this?"

"Presumably. I told his wife. I went to his house last week and tried to talk to him, but he slipped out the back way. The woman tried to tell me that his skill in salesmanship was what made the difference in the price, that my house was only worth fifty thousand dollars after all. But I happen to know that they had it listed again last week, at eighty!" He pounded his knee with his veined fist. "God damn them to hell, they're nothing but sea-lawyers. Sea-lawyers, salesmen, paid liars, are taking over the country!"

The Captain's face had turned the color of cordovan. "I shouldn't attempt to talk about it. It's too hard on my coronaries. Let the law take care of Merriman and his cohorts."

"Have you ever thought of taking care of him yourself?"

His hot eyes turned frosty. "I don't understand you, sir."

"I heard you threatened Merriman with a gun."

"I don't deny it. I thought I could frighten him into honesty. But he wouldn't even talk to me face to face. He hid behind his wife's skirts—"

"Have you seen him today, Captain Mandeville?"

"No. I haven't seen him for some time. I take no pleasure in the sight of him, and my lawyer advised me not to approach him again."

"Did you?"

"Certainly not. What are you getting at, sir?"

"Merriman was beaten to death within the last three hours, in your old house on Whiteoaks Avenue."

His face went pale in patches. "Beaten to death? It's a dreadful thing to say about any man, but I can't say I'm sorry."

"Did you do it, Captain, or have it done?"

"I did not. The accusation is outrageous, outlandish."

"His widow is making it, though. You can expect a visit from the police before long. Can you account for the last three hours?"

"I resent the question."

"No matter. I have to ask it."

"But I don't have to answer it."

"No."

He rose trembling. "Then I'll ask you to leave. I'll be glad to explain myself to the duly constituted authorities."

I hoped he could.

chapter 10

THE HIGHWAY RAN across flatland, prairie-like under the moon, to the edge of the Sacramento River. In the queer pale light the abrupt bridge which spanned the river resembled the approach to an ancient fortified city. The slums on the other side of the river didn't do much to dispel the illusion. The night girls prowling the late streets, the furtive men in the doorways, looked sunk and lost forever in deep time.

The Champion Hotel was on the edge of the slums. It hadn't subsided into them yet, but it appeared to be slipping. It was a narrow six-story building with a grimy stone face, put up around the turn of the century, when it had probably been a good family hotel. Now it had the air of a place where you could get cheap lodging without amenities you couldn't afford: a place for one-night stands and last stands.

In a bar-and-grill next door people were singing "Auld Lang Syne." An old man wearing a faded maroon uniform and a stubble of beard was guarding the unbesieged door of the Champion. He crossed the sidewalk on mincing feet. His shoes had been cut across the toes to make room for bunions, and his voice rose through his withered body like the audible complaint of the bunions themselves:

"You can't park here, mister. Got to keep the curb clear. If you want to come into the hotel, you can leave your car in the parking lot around the corner. You planning to register?"

"I might as well."

"Okay, you go around the corner to the left. You can't go to the right, anyway, on account of they turned it into a one-way street five-six years ago." He seemed to resent this change. "Better lock up your car, and you can come back through the alley if you want. It's shorter that way. I'll turn on the light at the side door. You want me to take your luggage?"

"Thanks, I can carry it myself." Not having any.

The parking lot was a dark quadrangle hemmed in by the lightless walls of business buildings empty for the night. Carrying my brief case for appearance's sake, I walked along the alley to the side door where the old bellhop was waiting. The naked yellow insect-repellent bulb over the door splashed jaundice on his face. He accepted my brief case as if he didn't really expect a tip.

A woman with thyroid eyes and chins sat behind the desk in the deserted lobby. She offered me a room with bath for two-fifty, two dollars without. I didn't really want to stay there. The migrant years had flown through the place and left their droppings.

The Captain had made a mistake, I thought, perhaps a deliberate one. It didn't seem likely that Mrs. Wycherly had ever lived in the Champion. I decided to find out, before I contracted for a night-long date with depression.

The thyroid eyes were going over me, trying to decide if I was too choosy or too broke. "Well? You want the two-fifty with the bath, or the two-dollar one? I'll have to ask you to pay in advance," she added, with a glance at the worn brief case which the old bellhop was holding.

"I'll be glad to. But it just occurred to me, my wife may have taken a double room."

"Your wife a guest here?"

"She's supposed to be."

"What's her—what's your name?"

"Wycherly," I said.

The fat woman and the old man exchanged a look whose meaning I didn't catch. She said with something in her voice that was patronizing, almost pitying:

"Your wife *was* here for quite a bit. But she moved out tonight, less than an hour ago."

"Where did she move to?"

"I'm sorry, she left no forwarding address."

"Was she leaving town?"

"We have no way of knowing. I'm very sorry, sir." She sounded as if she meant it. "Do you still want a room? Or not?"

"I'll take the one with the bath. I haven't had a bath for a long time."

"Yessir," she said imperturbably. "I'll put you in 516. Would you sign the register please?"

I signed myself H. Wycherly. After all, he was paying for the room. I gave the woman a fifty-dollar bill, which she had a hard time making change for. The bellhop watched the transaction with great interest.

When he and I were alone in my room on the fifth floor, in the delicate interval between the window-raising and the tipping if any, he said:

"I might be able to help you put your hands on your lady."

"You know where she is?"

"I didn't say that. I said maybe. I hear things. I see things." He touched the corner of his bleared eye with the tip of his forefinger, and winked.

"What did you see and hear?"

"I wouldn't want to say it right out, you being her husband and all. I don't want to make more trouble for her. She's a troubled lady already. But you know that, you're married to her."

"I'm not working at it."

"That's good. Because if you was working at it you'd be getting pretty poor returns on your labor. I guess you know that, too, eh?"

"What I know doesn't matter. What do you know?"

"I don't like to make trouble for anybody." His old and slightly tangled gaze shifted from me to my brief case, which he had placed on a wicker luggage stand against the wall. "You wouldn't have a gun in that little case? I felt something in there that sure felt like a gun to me. And I don't want to be party to no shooting."

"There won't be any shooting. All I want to do is find Mrs. Wycherly and talk to her."

I was beginning to regret my impersonation of Wycherly. It had seemed like the quick way to get the facts, but it was involving me in too many facts.

"You don't need a gun for that," the old man said, edging towards the door. "Jerry Dingman's no trouble-maker."

"Look here, I carry the gun because I also carry a lot of money."

He stood still. "Is that so?"

"I'm willing to pay you for information, Jerry."

He looked down at his feet, which bulged like potatoes in his slit shoes. "I got this fifteen-dollar bill I owe Dr. Broch for my feet. I never get far enough ahead to pay it."

"I'll pay your doctor bill."

"That's real nice of you, son," he said sentimentally. "Let's see the color of your money."

"After I hear the color of your information. You know I have the money. Where did she go, Jerry?"

"From something she said when I was putting the luggage in the car, I *think* she was going to the Hacienda Inn. Anyway, she asked the guy if the Hacienda was a nice place. He said it was a big jump up from here, and that's no lie. It's a kind of a ritzy resort place out of town."

"She went there with a man?"

"I wasn't planning to tell you that. Shut my big mouth, eh?"

"Describe him."

"I didn't get a good look at him, either time I saw him. In the car, he kept his face turned away. He didn't want me to see him, me or anybody. Before that, when he went up to her room, he didn't take the elevator. He came in the side door and went up the back stairs. He didn't look like one of the guests, so I followed along behind to see what he was up to. He knocked on her door and she let him in and I heard him sing out her name. So I figured it was all right. Matter of fact, I thought *he* was her husband."

"Did you hear anything to that effect?"

"Just what I said. He called her Catherine when he went into her room—he sounded real glad to see her. Then they closed the door and that was all I heard. About twenty minutes later, she checked out and he was out front in the car waiting."

"What kind of a car?"

"I think it was a new Chevvie."

"Did she go with him willingly?"

"Sure. Matter of fact, it was about the first time I ever seen her reasonaly happy. Most of the time she dragged herself around here like she was expecting to hear the last trump any minute. I never seen a lady so blue in my life."

"How long was she here?"

"Two weeks and a little over. I thought it was sort of funny her checking in here in the first place. It's a decent enough place but not the kind of a place a lady would choose for herself. And she had good clothes, good luggage. You know that."

"What do you think she was doing here?"

"Hiding out from you, maybe," he said with a grizzled smirk. "No offense intended."

"None taken. Getting back to the man in the car, you should be able to give me a general description."

"Yeah. He was a fairly big man, not as big as you but a lot bigger'n me. He had on good clothes, dark coat and hat. He kept his hat turned down and his head turned away, like I said, and I never did get a good look at his face."

"Did he look anything like this?" I described Homer Wycherly.

"It could be him. I couldn't say for sure."

"How old a man was he?"

"Getting on, I'd say. Older'n you. But not as old as the old guy that came to see her last week. I can give you a good description of *him*."

"Thin old man with a white moustache?"

"Yeah. I guess you know him. I took him up to her room but she wouldn't let him in. She wouldn't even open the door. He was mad as blazes. He tipped me good, though," Jerry added reminiscently. "Speaking of tips, you promised me fifteen smackers."

"In a minute. Did Mrs. Wycherly have any other visitors?"

"Yeah, but listen, mister, I can't stand here jawing all

night, I got to put in an appearance down in the lobby.
That Mrs. Silvado on the desk, she watches me like a hawk
watches chickens."

"Who were the other visitors?"

"There was just the one that I remember. I'll tell you
about him, only right now I got to go down, let Mrs. Silvado
see that I'm on the job. I'll come right back up soon as I
can. Only pay me my money first."

I gave him a twenty-dollar bill. His gnarled hand closed
on it, burrowed with it under his faded jacket, and came
out empty.

"Thank you kindly. I'll bring you the change when I
come back up."

"You can keep the other five. There's something else I
want you to do for me. Which room did my wife occupy?"

"End of the hall on the third floor. Three-two-three, the
number is."

"Is there anybody in it now?"

"No, it's one of the ones we rent by the week. It ain't
even cleaned out yet."

"Let me into it, will you?"

"Not on your life, mister. I could lose my job. I been
working here nigh to forty years, ever since I got too big to
make jockey weight. They're just waiting for a chance to
retire me."

"Come on, Jerry. Nobody needs to know."

He shook his head so hard that his hair wisped out. "No,
sir. I don't unlock no doors for nobody but the rightful occupants."

"You could forget your passkey. Just leave it on my
dresser."

"No, sir. It ain't legal."

But he left it. Forty years as a bellhop hollows a man out
into a kind of receptacle for tips. Twenty years as a detective
works changes in a man, too.

I went down the firestairs to the third floor and let myself
into 323. It was a room with bath very much like my own,
containing the same bed and dresser, writing table and desk,
wicker luggage stand and standing lamp. And a sense of
heavy hours, of boxed and static time which refused to pass.

The dresser drawers gaped open, empty except for a
nylon stocking with a laddering run. The closet contained a
row of twisted wire hangers and dust-mice along the base-
boards. In the bathroom cabinet, I found spilled powder and
a green drugstore bottle with one lone aspirin tablet at the
bottom. The towels were damp.

I found the wastebasket behind the bed. It was full of crumpled newspapers and lipstick-stained pink Kleenex. A fifth bottle with a half-inch of whisky in it stood on the floor beside the wastebasket.

I pulled out the newspapers and looked them over: they were this week's *Sacramento Bees*. In the most recent, dated two days before, I found a pencilled check-mark beside an announcement in the shipping news. It stated that the *President Jackson* was due in San Francisco harbor the following day. Apparently Catherine Wycherly had been keeping track of her husband.

And thinking of her daughter, too, it seemed. When I stood up, the light caught the window and I could see writing on it. I crossed the room. The window overlooked an alley and faced a blank brick wall. Scrawled large in the dust that covered the pane was a single word, "Phoebe." Against the dark opposing wall it stood out like an inscription on a headstone.

Strangeness entered the room from the night outside. I could feel it entering me, and hear my heartbeat thudding in my ears. The sound of my heartbeat merged with the noise of the elevator throbbing like an embolism in the bowels of the building.

I closed the door of the ex-Mrs. Wycherly's ex-room and ran up the firestairs, keeping ahead of the noise of the elevator. It was ancient and slow, like its rider. I got back to my own room before Jerry Dingman did.

He had a bottle of beer in his hand.

"How are things down in the lobby?"

"Slow. I told Mrs. Silvado you wanted some beer so's I could get away again. I had to go next door for it, and that will cost you another fifty cents." He peered anxiously at my face, as if our whole deal might break down over this issue.

"All right," I said.

He let his breath out. "Aw hell, I'll throw it in. I'll throw the beer in." He set it on the dresser and surreptitiously picked up his key. "I hope you like beer."

"Sure. I'll split it with you."

"I couldn't do that."

"Why not? Sit down. I'll get a glass."

He edged nervously over to the bed and sat down sighing. I poured his half of the beer in a glass I got from the bathroom and drank mine out of the bottle.

The old man sucked foam from his bristles. "You wanted some more info. I kind of forget what it was."

"I'll make it quick. I want to get out to the Hacienda Inn before they hoist the drawbridge."

"Ain't no bridge there, Mr. Wycherly. It's nowheres near the river. It's golf course all around it—got its own golf course. Got its own flying field. Got its own everything. This is good beer." He smacked his lips, half drunk on the taste of it alone.

"You were going to tell me about Mrs. Wycherly's other visitors."

"Visitor," he corrected me. "There was just the one other, far as I know. He was here to see her a couple of times before."

"Before when?"

"Before last night, when they had the row. It sounded like he was slapping her around a little bit. I thought of calling the police, but Mrs. Silvado said no. She said if we called the police every time a guest had a private row, they'd be running in and out like Keystone cops. Anyway, it didn't go on very long."

"Who was the man?"

"I dunno his name." He scratched his thin hair. "He was a big man, sharp dresser. He smiled all the time. But I didn't like his eyes."

"What didn't you like about his eyes?"

"I dunno. He looked at me like a dog or something—a dirty dog in the gutter—and he was Jesus God personified. He had this turned-up nose like he was smelling something." Jerry used his forefinger to push up the drooping tip of his nose.

I produced the blotter I'd taken from Merriman's office, with Merriman's picture on it.

"Is this the man?"

He held up the blotter to the light. "It's him, yeah. Smiling all the time." Laboriously he spelled out the caption: "What does firstest with the mostest mean?"

"It's just a gag." A running gag that had run out. "What time was he here last night?"

"Along about nine—nine-thirty. He stayed about half-an-hour. He was still smiling when he came down. I noticed to-night she was wearing dark glasses. I think he blacked her eye."

"Do you keep watch on all the guests this way?"

"Just those I like. I was worried about your lady. I still am. You better get out to the Inn and get together with her, Mr. Wycherly. You appear to be the kind of man she needs."

"Did she ever talk about me?"

"No, she never talked about anybody, or *to* anybody. She spent all her time in her room, never went out."

"What did she do with her time?"

"Mostly she was eating, and drinking. She drank quite a bit this last week. I ought to know, I took the bottles up to her."

I played my last card, the picture of Phoebe in yellow. "Did this girl ever come to visit her? Don't give me a quick answer. Take a good long look and think about it."

He held the picture out at the full length of his arm. "She Mrs. Wycherly's daughter?"

"Yes. Have you seen her, Jerry?"

"Can't say that I have. 'Course I'm not on duty all the time. I can see the resemblance, though. Add on twenty years and twenty pounds—she's her mother's daughter all right. I got an eye for resemblances." The half-pint of beer had made him loquacious. His eyes came up to mine like an old hound's. "Your daughter took off on you, too, eh? You got family trouble for sure."

"I know it." I was glad I wasn't Wycherly. But I was beginning to feel his load of grief, as if I'd assumed it magically with his name. "You're certain you've never seen this girl?"

"Certain as I can be. The only people that come to see your lady was the two men—the old one she wouldn't let in, and Firstest with the Mostest."

"And the one she left with tonight?"

"Yeah. Him." He got up wagging his head. "Don't you go using that gun on him, mister. Take Jerry Dingman's advice."

"Thanks for the advice. And thanks for the beer."

When he had shuffled out, I got out the gun, which was in a shoulder holster, and put it on.

chapter 11

MONEY FLOWED THROUGH the state capital like an alluvial river, and the Hacienda Inn was one of the places where the golden silt was deposited. It lay off the highway to the north of the city, sprawled on its golf course like a separate village. A Potemkin village, maybe, or the kind the French kings built near Versailles so they could play at being peasants on sunny afternoons.

On this late night with its lowering moon, some of the paisanos who frequented the Inn were still awake. Light and laughter spilled from scattered massive bungalows, and from the big main building: a Spanish ranch-house with delusions of grandeur. I found a parking place in the dark lot beside it, and went in.

The elegant vacuous youth at the registration desk said that Mrs. Wycherly was not registered.

"She may be using her maiden name." I went on before he could ask me what it was: "She's a big platinum blonde wearing dark glasses, and she's supposed to have checked in here within the last couple of hours."

"You must mean Miss Smith—"

"That's right. Her maiden name is Smith. I have an important message from her family."

"It's pretty late to call her bungalow," he said doubtfully.

"She'd want you to. It's urgent."

"What did you say your name was?"

"Archer. I represent the family."

He made the call. No answer.

"I'm sure she's in the hotel." He glanced up at the electric clock on the wall: it was nearly one-thirty. "You may find her in the Cantina. She asked me where it was when she registered."

The Cantina was on the far side of a great flagstone courtyard. Twenty or so late-night revellers sat or leaned at the bar—an old carved mahogany monstrosity with a pitted brass rail which had probably been salvaged from some Mother Lode ghost town. Behind it a white-jacketed Filipino moved with speed and precision against a big mirror.

His customers were a mixed batch: a trio of beefy types wearing white Stetsons and Gower Gulch clothes; two men who looked like a legislator and a lobbyist sitting on either side of a redhead who looked like a bribe; a noisy party of businessmen and their wives; a pair of honeymooners gazing at each other with rapturous circles under their eyes. And beyond them, at the end of the bar, a blonde woman in dark glasses sitting alone with an empty stool beside her.

I slid onto the stool. She didn't seem to notice. She was staring into the glass in her fist like a fortuneteller studying her crystal. She rotated the glass in her fingers, and flakes of gold swirled in the colorless liquid.

I searched out the reflection of her face in the mirror. She was heavily made up. Under the paint, her flesh seemed swollen and bruised, not just by violence, but by the padded blows of sorrow and shame. Even so, I could see that she had once been attractive.

She was dressed and groomed like a woman who knew she wasn't attractive any more. Her hair, bleached the color of tin, was tangled as if her fingers had been busy in it. Her dark purple dress didn't go with her hair. She wasn't a thin woman, but the dress bagged on her as if she'd been losing weight.

The Filipino bartender broke in on my observations: "What will you have to drink, sir?"

"The stuff the lady's drinking looks interesting. With the gold in it."

"Goldwater? It's okay if you like a sweet drink. Isn't that right, ma'am?"

She grunted noncommittally. I said to her: "I've never tried goldwater. How does it taste?"

Her masked eyes swung towards me. "Lousy. But go ahead and try it. Everything tastes lousy to me." Her voice was fairly cultivated, but it had undertones of ugliness and despair.

One of the Stetsons rapped on the bar with a Reno dollar.

"Sir?" the bartender said impatiently. "You want the gold-water?"

I went on making a production out of it. "I don't know." I said to the woman: "Doesn't the gold get stuck in your throat?"

"It's very thin gold leaf. You don't even know it's there."

"All right, I'll try it," I said, as though she'd talked me into it. "Anything for kicks."

The bartender poured my drink from a bottle labelled "Danziger Goldwasser."

"That's what I used to think," the woman said.

"I'm sorry, I didn't catch that."

She leaned towards me, half in earnestness and half in the pull of gravity that exerts itself at the end of a long evening. I caught a glimpse of the eyes behind her glasses. In their depths was a lost and struggling spirit asking wordlessly for help.

"Anything for kicks," she said. "That used to be my philosophy of life. It doesn't work out the way you expect it to. Kicks include getting kicked in the head by a horse."

"Is that what happened to you?"

"You might say so. A horse of another color. A dark horse." Her heavy red mouth twisted mirthlessly.

She pulled herself upright and held herself that way. She wasn't drunk, or if she was she was able to carry it. Whatever was the matter with her went deeper than drink. She seemed to be holding herself still in the middle of vertigo; it tugged at my sympathy like the turning edge of a whirlpool.

I had a counterimpulse to walk out of the bar and away from the Hacienda and her. She was trouble looking for somebody to happen to.

And succeeding. I raised my drink and said with false cheer: "Luck to the gold drinkers."

She sipped at hers. "You didn't say what kind of luck, good or bad. Not that it matters, people don't get their wishes. Wishing-wells are to drown in. But I mustn't go on like that. I'm always pitying myself, and that's neurotic."

She made a visible effort, and focused her attention on me: "Speaking of luck, you don't look as if you had too much luck in your life. Some of those kicks you say you go for were kicks in the head, I bet."

"I've had my share."

"I knew it. I have a feeling for faces—people's faces. I always did have, since I was a young kid. Especially men."

"You're not so old now," I said. What I was hoping for was a personal relationship with Mrs. Wycherly, the kind of relationship in which she would talk freely without knowing she was being questioned. "How old are you?"

"I never tell my age. On account of I'm a hundred. Like Lord Byron when he was thirty-five or so and he was asked his age when he registered at some hotel, I think it was in Italy. He told them he was a hundred. *I* know how he felt. He died the following year at Missolonghi. Lovely story, isn't it, with a happy ending and all. You like my story?"

"It's a load of laughs."

"I have a million of them. Morbid tales for little people by the old lady of the sea. I think of myself as the old lady of the sea." Her mouth twisted. "I'm spooky, aren't I?"

I said she wasn't, in my chivalrous way, but spooky was the word for her. I drank the rest of my goldwater. It was sweet and strong.

"It's like drinking money," she said. "How does it taste to you?"

"I like the taste of money. But the drink is a little too sweet for me. I'm going to switch to Bourbon."

She looked past me along the bar. The honeymooners had drifted away.

"You'd better hurry up then. This place is going to close up any minute. While you're ordering, you might as well order me another." She added abruptly: "I'll pay for it."

I ordered for both of us, and insisted on paying. "I can

afford to buy you a drink. My name is Lew Archer, by the way."

"How do you do, Lew."

This time we clicked glasses.

"I'm Miss Smith."

"Not married?"

"No. Are you?"

"I was at one time. It didn't take."

"I know the problem," she said. "I've lived with it. Call it living. What do you do for a living?"

"I sort of live off the country."

"I don't get it. What do you *really* do? No, wait, let me guess. I'm good at guessing people's occupations." She sounded like a bored child looking for a game to play.

"Go ahead and guess."

Her gaze slipped down from my face to my shoulders, as if she was looking for a place to cry on. Tentatively, her hand came out and palped my left bicep. She had pretty hands, except for the tips of the fingers, which had been bitten.

"Are you a professional athlete? You seem to be in very good trim, for a middle-aged man."

It was a mixed compliment.

"Wrong. I'll give you two more guesses."

"What do I win if I guess right?"

"I'll carve you a plaque."

"Oh, fine. I need one for my grave."

Her heavy gaze went over me some more. I could feel it like a tangible pressure. I squirmed a little. My jacket gaped open. She said in a husky whisper:

"You're carrying a gun. Are you a policeman?"

"You have one more guess."

"Why are you wearing a gun?"

"That's a question, not a guess."

"You could give me a hint. You *did* say you lived off the country. Are you outside the law?"

There were possibilities in the role. "Keep your voice down," I said, and looked away from her along the bar in that sudden jerky movement I'd seen men make in other bars when I came in to put the arm on them.

The redhead and her escorts were on their way out. The Stetson brothers were talking in rapt religious voices about Aberdeen Angus bulls. The businessmen were persuading each other to have one for the road. As if the road needed it, their wives' expressions said.

The woman's hand touched my shoulder. Her breath tickled my ear. "Why do you carry a gun?"

"We won't talk about it."

"But I want to talk about it," she said in a wheedling tone. "I'm interested. Are you a gangster—a gunman?"

"This is the end of the guessing game. You wouldn't like the answers."

"Yes, I would. Maybe I would."

For the first time she seemed fully alive, but not with the kind of life I wanted to share. She circled her lips with the pale tip of her tongue:

"What do you use your gun for?"

"We won't talk about it here. Do you want to get me arrested?"

She whispered: "We could talk in my place. I have a bottle in my bungalow. They're about to close the Cantina anyway."

She picked up her lizardskin purse. I went along with her, across the courtyard, up a garden path where black moon-shadows crouched and pounced in the late wind blowing up from San Francisco Bay.

She fumbled in her purse for the key, fumbled at the lock. It was dark inside when she opened the door. She stood in the dark and let me walk into her. Her body trembled against me. It was softer and warmer than I'd supposed.

Her mind was harder and colder: "Have you ever killed anybody? I don't mean in the war. I mean in real life."

"This is real life?"

"Don't joke. I want to know. I have a reason."

"I have a better reason for keeping quiet."

"Come on," she wheedled. "Tell Mother."

She pressed herself against me. We were both aware of the gun in its harness between us. I felt as though I was being offered a large and dangerous gift I didn't want. Her pointed breasts were like soft bombs against me.

"I think you're exciting," she said in an unexcited way.

She was a crude and awkward operator, naïve for a woman of her alleged experience. No doubt her mind was running on one or two cylinders. I was beginning to wonder if she was disturbed. There were undertones and overtones in everything she said, like a steady growling and screaming below and above the range of my ears.

"You don't like me, do you?"

"I haven't had a chance to get to know you."

Against my neck, she hummed a few notes of a song about getting to know people. She got a grip on the back of my head. I felt her tongue on my lips, like a hot snail. I broke her masseuse grip:

"You promised me a drink."

"Don't you like women?" Coming from her, the question had a queer pathos. She leaned on me like a woman sliding down a wall. "I know I'm not so pretty any more."

"Neither am I, and I've had a long hard day."

"Working over a hot gun?"

"Not all day. I do all my killing before breakfast. I like to sprinkle a little human blood on my porridge."

"You're awful. We're two awful people."

She reached for the light switch, humming another song. Her singing voice was surprisingly light and girlish. A faint poignant regret went through me that I hadn't got to her sooner. Much sooner, in another place and time, on a different errand.

The room jumped up around us, colored and strange. She'd only had it a little while, but there were clothes on the bed and floor, as though she'd picked through every dress in her wardrobe looking for something becoming. The Navajo rugs on the floor were crumpled as if she'd been kicking at them.

A bottle of whisky and a smudged glass stood on the limed oak chest of drawers. She put down her purse beside the bottle, poured me a heavy slug in the glass and handed it to me slopping over the rim. She drank from the bottle herself, pouring the stuff down like a rank amateur or a far-gone alcoholic. It was a lovely party.

It got lovelier. She sprawled on the bed regardless of her clothes, hugging the bottle like a headless baby. Her skirt crept up above her knees. Her legs were remarkably good, but not for me. I watched her the way you watch an old late movie that you've seen before.

"Sit down." She patted the bed beside her. "Sit down and tell me about yourself, Lew. That's your name, isn't it—Lew?"

"Lew." I sat beside her, keeping a space between us. "I'd rather hear about you. Do you live alone?"

"I have been." She looked sideways at an inside door which led to another part of the bungalow.

"Divorced?"

"Divorced from reality." She grimaced. "True confession title: Mother went to Reno to get a divorce from reality."

"Do you have a family?"

"We won't go into that. Or anything else about me. You don't want to hear about me. I live in hell."

The words were melodramatic, but there was a throb of horror in her voice. She tilted up her damaged face. Behind the dark glasses under the inert and swollen flesh, I could see the fine bone structure. She had once been a handsome girl, as handsome as Phoebe. She seemed to read my thought, and the pity in it verging on contempt:

"Do we have to have that light? It *kills* me."

I turned on the bedlight and turned off the overhead light. When I came back to her, she had upended the bottle again like a crazy astronomer holding a telescope to her blind mouth. Her white throat shimmered as the whisky went down.

"Drink up," she said in a thickening voice. "You're making me drink alone, and that's not cricket."

"I have to drive. You'll be passing out if you keep drinking at this rate."

"Will I?" She raised herself and held the bottle upright between her knees. "It isn't as easy as you think. Passing out. Or even if you do make it, you wake up in the middle of the night with the boogies. The boogies are fun."

"You have a lot of fun."

"I'm a fun girl from way back. Drink up your drink, then I want to ask you something."

I took a swallow. "About killing people?"

"We'll come back to that. I want to know if you have underworld connections."

"Would I tell you if I had?"

"I mean it seriously. Alcohol doesn't work too well for me, I find. I've been thinking I ought to try drugs. They say it's the best way out there is."

"Way out of where?"

"Living in hell," she said quite casually. "I could use a little relief from all the thinking. And I've got some money, if that's what's bothering you. All I need is the right connections."

"You won't get it through me. Stick to whisky."

"But I don't *like* to drink. I really don't. I only use it to shut off the thinking at night."

"Thinking about what?"

"That's for me to know and you to find out." She looked down at her body, discovered her bare knees, covered them with her skirt. "I'm so ugly since I put on all this weight. Aren't I ugly?"

I didn't answer her.

"It's my ugly soul, it shows in my face. I'm an outlaw, just like you. I bet your soul is ugly, too."

"No doubt."

"Is that why you carry a gun?"

"I carry it for protection."

"Protection against who? Whom?" Her lips had trouble forming the word.

"People like you," I said with the best smile I could muster.

She wasn't fazed in the least. She nodded solemnly, as if we were coming to an understanding. A cold quick frisson went up my back.

"Have you ever really killed anybody, Lew?"

"Yes," I said, in the hope of unsticking the stuck record. "Eleven or twelve years ago, I killed a man named Puddler who tried to kill me."

She leaned towards me confidentially. Her head gravitated towards my shoulder. She raised it, grasping the bottle as if it presented her only handhold in space:

"I'm being killed, too."

"How?"

"Little by little, a piece at a time. First he ruined my soul, then he ruined my body, then he ruined my face." She set the bottle down on the bedside table and removed her dark glasses. "Look what he did to my face."

Both of her eyes were blacked. The bruises had been ineptly touched up with liquid make-up. She put on the glasses again.

"Who did that to you?"

"I'll tell you his name when the time comes."

Her head subsided on my shoulder like a frowzy bird coming home to roost. She reached across my chest and touched the shape of the gun. Her fingers caressed it through the cloth of my jacket.

"I want you to kill him for me," she said dreamily. "I can't go on like this. He'll push me over the edge."

"Who is he?"

"I'll tell you that when you promise to do it. I'll pay you well."

"Show me the money."

She got up with difficulty and started across the room towards the chest of drawers. She stopped in the middle of the floor, turned and went in a shambling run to the bathroom. I heard her retching through the open door.

I tried the other inner door. It was locked. I went to the chest of drawers and opened her lizardskin purse. It contained a clutter of make-up materials, lipstick, eye-shadow, liquid powder, tissues, a bottle of patent sleeping medicine, and a woman's wallet made of red leather and decorated with rhinestones. The wallet was thick with bills. It also held a driver's license issued the previous year to Mrs. Homer Wycherly, Rural Route Two, Meadow Farms; and a number of business cards. One of them was Ben Merriman's.

I put everything back in the purse and snapped the silver clasp shut before she came out of the bathroom. She was staggering, and clutching her heavy stomach. Her face had a greenish tinge under the paint.

"I guesh I dunno how to drink," she said, and collapsed on the bed.

I bent over her blind, deaf head. "Who is he?"

"Whoosh who?"

"The man you want me to kill."

Her head rolled back and forth among the crumpled clothes. "Funny. I can't remember 'shname. He shells real 'shtate on the Peninshula. He ruined me—ruined everything. I had to shpill everything."

"Ben Merriman?"

"Thash the man. Did I tell you 'shname before?"

"What did you spill to him, Mrs. Wycherly?"

"Wunyou like to know?"

Her eyes closed. She went out like a light. Her mouth was burned dry by neat whisky, and her breath came harshly through it. I felt more deeply than ever that blend of pity and shame which kept me at my trade among the lost, battered souls who lived in hell, as she did.

I couldn't rouse her again by ordinary means, talking or shaking her. I took the whisky bottle into the bathroom, emptied it in the sink and filled it with ice water; some of which I poured over her face. She woke and struggled up on her arms like Lazarus, looking at me out of underground eyes. Water dripped from her chin.

"What is this?" she said distinctly.

"You passed out. I was worried about you. I decided to bring you to."

"You had no right," she complained. "I've been trying all day to get to sleep. And all last night."

She dabbed at her wet face with a corner of the bedspread. Her eye-shadow ran like the paint on sad clowns' faces. I brought her a towel from the bathroom. She snatched it out of my hand, scrubbed her face and neck with it. With most of the make-up off she looked naked and younger. The bruises around her eyes stood out.

She blinked up at me. "What was I saying? What did I say before?"

"You hired me to kill a man."

"Who?" she said like a child listening to a story.

"Don't you remember?"

"I was awful drunk."

She still was, in spite of the cold douche. The whisky would be coming back on her soon.

"Ben Merriman?" she said. "Is that the one?"

"That's the one. Why do you want him killed, Mrs. Wycherly?"

She gave me a sly dull look. "You know my name."

"I've known your name for some time. Why do you want Ben Merriman killed?"

"I don't. I've changed my mind. Forget it." She wagged her disordered bright head slowly from side to side. "Forget the whole thing."

"That won't be easy. Merriman is already dead. He was beaten to death tonight in your house in Atherton."

"I don't believe you." But the horror that was in her like a chronic disease seeped into her eyes.

"You believe me."

She wagged her head some more; it swung loosely on her neck. "Why should I? You're just another liar. Why should I take the word of a cheap crook?"

"You'll be reading it in the papers, if they let you have the papers in your cell."

She got up unsteadily, looking at me with fear and loathing. "Nobody'sh gonna put me away. You get out of here."

"You invited me in."

"That wash the mistake of the week. Get out."

She pushed her hands against my chest. I caught her wrists and held her:

"Did you have something to do with Merriman's death?"

"I didn't know he was dead. Let me go."

"In a minute. I want you to tell me where Phoebe is."

"Phoebe?" The sly dull look came back into her eyes. "What about Phoebe?"

"Your husband Homer employed me to look for her. Your daughter's been missing for over two months. You probably know all this. I'm telling you anyway."

"Who are you?"

"A private detective. That's why I carry a gun."

I let go of her wrists. She slumped onto the bed, digging her fingers into her hair as if she could hold her thoughts steady:

"Why do you come sneaking around me? I never see Phoebe. I haven't seen her since the divorce."

"You're lying. Don't you care what's happened to her?"

"I don't even care what's happened to me."

"I think you care. You wrote her name on the window of your room."

She looked up in dull surprise. "What room?"

"In the Champion Hotel."

"Did I do that? I must have been crazy."

"I think you were lonely for your daughter. Where is she, Mrs. Wycherly? Is she dead?"

"How do I know? We haven't seen each other since the divorce."

"You have, though. On November second, the day your husband sailed, you left the ship with Phoebe—"

"Don't call him my husband. He ishn't—isn't my husband."

"Your ex-husband, then. The day he sailed, you drove away in a taxi with your daughter. Where did you go?"

She was a long time answering. Her face changed as she thought about the question. Her mouth moved, trying out words.

"I want the truth," I said. "If you ever cared for your daughter, or care for her now, you'll give it to me."

"I went to the station. I took the train home."

"To Atherton?"

She nodded.

"Did Phoebe go along with you?"

"No. I dropped her off at the St. Francis on the way to the station. She never came anywhere near the Atherton house."

"Why did you sell that house and hide out here in Sacramento?"

"That's my own business."

"Business with Ben Merriman?"

She kept her head down and her eyes hidden. "I'll take the Fifth on that." More than the cold water, the strain of the interview was sobering her.

"On grounds of self-incrimination?"

"If that's the way you want it."

"It isn't. I want Phoebe."

"I can't give her to you. I haven't seen her since that day in Union Square." She couldn't keep the feeling out of her voice, the sense of loss.

"You knew she was missing, didn't you?"

There was another long silence. At last she said:

"I knew she planned to go away somewhere. She told me in the taxi that she didn't want to return to Boulder Beach. She had a boy friend there, she wanted to get away from him. And other things," she concluded vaguely.

"What other things?"

"I don't remember. She wasn't happy at college. She wanted to go away somewhere and live by herself and work out her own salvation." She spoke in a steady monotone like a sleeptalker or a liar, yet there seemed to be truth in what she was saying, the truth of feeling. "That's what Phoebe said."

"What did you say?"

"Go ahead, I told her. People have a right to live their lives." She raised her eyes to mine. "So why don't you get out and leave me alone?"

"In a minute."

"That's what you said before. It's a long minute, and my head hurts."

"Too bad. Did she say where she was going?"

"No. Maybe she didn't know."

"She must have given you some indication."

"She didn't. She was going a long way, that's all I know." She might have been talking about her own long journey down. Grief pulled like wires at the corners of her mouth.

"All the way out of life?"

She shuddered. "Don't say that."

"I have to. She's long gone, and people are dying."

"You really believe Phoebe is dead?"

"It's possible. It's also possible that you know who killed her. I think you do, if she's dead."

"Think away, sonny boy. You're away off orbiting by yourself, in an *eccentric* orbit. Why don't you go away now, and be the first man in space?"

Her broken wit, her rapid shifts in mood and temper, disturbed me and made me angry. I said:

"You're a strange mother, Mrs. Wycherly. You don't seem to give a damn if your girl is dead or alive."

She laughed in my face. I almost hit her. The horror in her was infecting me. I turned on my heel and crossed the room to the door, followed by girlish laughter.

A man was waiting for me on the other side of the door. His face was like a shiny, lumpy sausage, bulbous and queer under a silk-stocking mask. He swung a tire-iron in his hand. It came over in a looping arc and reached the side of my head before my fingers touched my gun butt. I fell backwards into the room and darkness.

chapter 12

BEN MERRIMAN'S HEAD hung like a ruined planet in the darkness. I crawled away from it and woke up scrabbling at the door of the room. The room was empty. It was after three by my wrist watch, which I saw double. I had been out for some time.

My gun was still in its holster. I fingered the side of my head. It was wet and numb. My fingers got blood on them, dark as axle grease. I tried standing up. It worked.

The room was clean. The woman and her protector, if that is what he was, had left nothing but the empty bottle and my half-finished drink. I finished it.

I washed my cut head in the bathroom sink and improvised a bandage out of a clean towel. In the bathroom mirror, I looked like an Indian holy man who had run out of holiness and just about everything else.

"What happened to you?" the night clerk said when I walked into the Hacienda lobby.

"I had a little run-in with a friend of Miss Smith's."

"I see." His expression combined sympathy and a hotel-man's allergy to trouble. "Who did you say you had a run-in with?"

"Miss Smith's friend. Have they checked out?"

"Miss Smith has checked out," he said with great distinctness, as if I might have difficulty hearing him. "There was nobody with her when she checked out *or* when she checked in."

"Who carried her bags?"

"I did."

"How did she leave?"

"By car."

"What kind of a car?"

"I didn't notice."

Now I knew he was lying.

"How much did they pay you?"

He flushed up to the eyes, as if his trouble-allergy had brought on a sudden rash. "Listen, fellow, I don't like your allegations. I gave you civil answers. Now beat it, or I'll call the sheriff's office."

I was feeling weak. I beat it, on my fine new imitation rubber legs. He forgot to ask me for the towel.

I made my way to my car and drove on instruments into the city. The towers of the capital loomed in the pre-dawn sky. Guided by some perverted homing instinct I found myself going the wrong way on the one-way street that led past the parking lot of the Champion Hotel. I drove in.

Next thing I knew, Jerry Dingman's face came out of a yellow fog. We were in the alley under the insect-repellent light. All the insects in the world were buzzing in my ears. Through them the old man was saying:

"Take a sup of water, Mr. Wycherly. You'll feel better."

He squashed a paper cup against my mouth. His other hand was behind my head. I swallowed some water and spilled some. The buzzing began to fade. The yellow fog shrank to an aureole around the old man's head. The Good Sacramentan.

"What happened to you, Mr. Wycherly?"

"Accident."

"Traffic accident or people accident?"

"People."

"You want me to call the police?"

"No. I'm all right." I sat up.

"You're not as all right as you think. You got a nasty wound on the temple. I'll take you up to your room and you lie down. Then you better let me get you a doctor, you'll be needing stitches. I know one that makes night calls, and he don't charge too much."

Dr. Broch arrived in a few minutes, as if he sat up all night waiting for emergencies. His breath smelled of Sen-Sen, and the hands with which he opened his worn black bag trembled constantly. Behind horn-rimmed glasses his face had a washed and formless, almost marinated look. I was beginning to wonder if the Sacramento River ran alcohol instead of water.

The doctor spoke with a slight Middle European accent. "Mr. Wycherly, eh? There is or was a *Mrs.* Wycherly staying in this hotel. A relative, perhaps?"

"My wife. We've been divorced. You know my wife?"

"I can't say I know her, no. The manager Mr. Fillmore called me in to treat her one day last week. He was worried about her condition."

"What was the matter with her?"

He shrugged, turning up his hands over the open black bag. "It is not possible for me to say. She would not let me enter her room to examine her. Perhaps it was a physical illness, perhaps an illness of the psyche. Melancholia, perhaps."

"Melancholia is a form of depression, isn't it?"

"Yes. I believe she was depressed. She hadn't got up out of bed for several days. She wouldn't let the cleaning woman come into the room. That is why the manager was concerned. But I was unable to help her. All she let me see of her was the body under the bedclothes." His hand described shaky sinuosities in the air.

"How do you know she wasn't hurt, or physically sick?"

"She was eating well, very well indeed. Mr. Fillmore said she was eating a great deal—enough for two. She kept ordering food from the restaurant in the daytime and also at night—meats and pies and cakes and ice cream and beverages."

"Was she drinking hard?"

"Some, I believe. But alcoholics don't eat like that, you know." He smiled dimly, as if he had private sources of information. "Perhaps her problem is an eating problem. I suggest this to you so you can get her help, perhaps."

"Perhaps," I said. "Or there may have been someone with her in the room."

His eyebrows went up. "I had not thought of the possibility. Yes. It would explain her refusal to let me in, to let anyone in, wouldn't it?"

I left the question hanging. In spite of their alcoholic tremor, his hands worked on me quickly and efficiently, cleaning and stitching up the cut in my head. It took six stitches. When he had put away his sewing materials, he told me that I was indubitably concussed, and ought to go to bed for several days. I said I would, gave him the twelve dollars he asked for, and suggested that he make no police report. He didn't argue.

I went to bed for several hours, at least. Raw morning light at the window woke me out of raw black nightmare. I called the desk and after some negotiations got Jerry Dingman on the line.

"I'm just going off duty, Mr. Wycherly."

"Stay on a few minutes for me. Is the restaurant open next door?"

"I think so."

"Bring me three eggs, ham, hotcakes, a quart of black coffee, and a clothesbrush."

He said he would. I took a long hot bath. Jerry knocked while I was drying myself. I fastened a towel around my waist and let him in. He sat on the bed and brushed my clothes while I ate.

Over the rim of the coffee cup, the harsh light at the

window seemed to be softening down. The pulsing night-mare had dwindled to an all but forgotten blues with Phoebe's name running through it. I couldn't remember what I had dreamed about her.

"Feeling better?" Jerry said when I'd finishing eating.

"I feel fine." This was an exaggeration.

"Enjoy your breakfast?"

"Very much." I put a dollar on the tray for him. Then I added another dollar. "Those days when Mrs. Wycherly wouldn't get out of bed and had all the food sent up—who brought it up besides you?"

"Sam Todd, he's one of the day men. Sam was amazed by all the eats she guzzled. So was I, for that matter. For a while there she was ordering up a big steak every night around midnight. Sometimes two."

"Did she eat them herself?"

"She always licked the platter clean," he said. "With double orders of French fries and everything."

"Was there anybody in the room to help her eat them?"

"I never saw nobody, I told you that. I figured she just had a hearty appetite, or maybe she was feeding a cold, like."

"Could there have been someone in the room?"

"A man, you mean?"

"Or another woman."

He considered this. "Could be. When she was holed up like that, she never let me in. She made me set the tray outside the door, and then she'd take it in after I went away. I never even saw her for four-five days at a time. She telephoned her order down to the desk."

I picked up my jacket from the bed and brought out Phoebe's picture once again. "You never saw this—my daughter in the room?"

He took the colored photo to the window, and shook his head over it. "No siree, I never saw her anyplace around the hotel. I'd remember a pretty girl like her, too. I guess Mrs. Wycherly was pretty like her at one time. Before she started to eat so much?" He glanced up quickly. "No offense intended."

"None taken."

"Did you get to see her last night?"

"We won't go into it, Jerry."

"I was just wondering who clobbered you."

"So was I. Are the cleaning women on yet?"

"They ought to be by now."

He went away, looking slightly betrayed by my failure to

confide in him. I dressed and went downstairs to the third floor. A linen cart stood in the hallway outside the open door of 323. Inside the room a vacuum cleaner whined.

The brown-armed woman operating it jumped when I spoke to her back, and turned with one hand in her asphalt-colored hair.

"Yessir?"

"My wife has been in this room for the last couple of weeks. Are you the one who cleans here every day?"

"Every day when they let me in." She switched off the vacuum cleaner, looking at me somberly as if I was about to accuse her of a crime. "Is something missing?"

"Nothing like that. Jerry the bellhop says she wouldn't let anyone into the room for four or five days last week."

She inclined her head. "I remember. I was worried about her."

"Why?"

"I think she had a spell on her," the woman said with conviction. "My sister Consuela had a spell when we were living in Salinas. She put the bed against the bedroom door. She wouldn't talk or show her face. I had to sleep in the kitchen for a week. Then I found a *curandero* and brought him to Consuela. He lifted the spell, and she was my sister again."

I tried to keep the impatience out of my voice: "Was there anybody living in this room with her?"

"Nobody living." She crossed herself unobtrusively.

"What do you mean by that?"

My tone was wrong, and she didn't answer. I said more gently:

"Did you see anyone in the room, or anything out of the ordinary?"

"No. I see—I see nothing."

"Hear anything?"

"She cried. I heard her cry. I wanted to go in and comfort her, but I was afraid."

"No voices?"

"No voices. Only hers."

"I'm told she ordered up a great deal of food—enough for two people."

"Yes. I took the dirty dishes. She put them out in the hall every morning."

"What was she doing with all that food?"

"Feeding *them*," the woman said. Her eyes burned like candles in the niches of her brows. "They are hungry when they come back."

"Who are we talking about, Mrs.——?"

"Tonia. Everybody calls me Tonia. You know, I can see, you think I am a stupid woman. But I have had transactions with the spirits of the dead. They would not let Consuela sleep or eat or talk for seven days, until I fed them. The *curandero* reminded me to feed them, and she was my sister again."

She spoke in a whisper, so that the spirits would be less likely to hear her. She glanced furtively towards the window. Phoebe's name was still there, written large on the grimy pane. In spite of the bright morning, I was almost ready to believe in Tonia's theories.

"You believe that she was feeding the spirits of the dead?"

"I know she was."

"How do you know it, Tonia?"

She pulled at the small gold ring in her left ear lobe. "I have ears. I heard her crying for the dead. I do not listen at doors but I could hear her from the hallway, crying."

"What did she say?"

"She called on the murdered one to come back to her."

"The murdered one? She used those words?"

"Yes. She spoke of murder, of death and murder and blood, and other things I didn't understand."

"Try to remember."

"I can't. I didn't hear much. I was afraid. When the dead come back they attach themselves to anyone who is waiting. I ran and shut myself up in the linen room."

"When was this?"

"Six days ago, or seven." She counted on her fingers. "Six. It was the day before the Feast of the Three Kings—a bad time to call the dead."

"Did she say who was dead?"

"No, but the grief in her voice was very bad. Perhaps a member of the family? A son, or daughter?" Her look was sympathetic and inquiring.

I showed her Phoebe's picture. "This is her daughter— her daughter and mine." For some reason, it was hard to tell her the lie.

"She is beautiful." Tonia smiled. "I have one blue-eyed daughter who is almost as beautiful. Her father, who was my husband at that time, was also blue-eyed."

I brought her back to the point. "Have you ever seen this girl?"

She studied the picture for a long time. "I think so. I can't be sure. I think I have seen her face before now. Where would I have seen her?"

"In this room, maybe."

"No," she said flatly. "There was nobody in the room with
your wife. She slept alone, I can tell by the bedclothes. I
watch the bedclothes, see. When they try to double up in a
single, I tell Mr. Fillmore."

"You may have seen her on the street."

"Maybe." She handed the picture back to me. "I'm sorry I
do not remember. I can only say I have seen her."

"Recently?"

"I think so." She wrinkled her brow in concentration;
nothing came. "I'm sorry, I don't know where. I see so many.
But she is beautiful."

I thanked her and went to the widow, tearing a leaf from
my notebook. The paper was too opaque to make a tracing.
I made a copy instead, reproducing the slanting characters
as closely as possible.

"Caray!" Tonia whispered at my shoulder. "What is that?"

"A name."

"An evil name?"

"A good name."

"I cannot read," she said. "It frightens me."

"It's my daughter's name, Tonia. There's no need to be
frightened."

But she was crossing herself when I left her.

Mr. Fillmore, the manager, was in his office behind the
main desk. He was one of those slightly confused middle-
aged men who needed someone to remind him that his
dark suit could use a pressing and that his lank hair stuck up
like weeds at the back. I introduced myself as Homer
Wycherly. I was stuck with the name and the tragicomic
role as long as I stayed around the Champion Hotel.

The name seemed to impress Fillmore. He rose up out of
his early-morning doldrums and offered me his hand and a
chair. "Delighted to meet you, sir. What can I do for you?"

"I'm concerned about my wife, Catherine. She occupied
Room 323 until she checked out last night. I don't know
where she is now."

"I'm sorry." His face fell into doleful grooves, left by the
harrows of circumstance. "I hate to say this, but I believe
you have reason to be concerned. Your wife is a very sad
woman, Mr. Wycherly. I've seen a lot of them, and I never
saw a sadder."

"Did you talk to her?"

"I did, yes. I happened to be on the desk when she
checked in. That was a day or two before Christmas. I remember particularly because frankly I was a little surprised

that a lady like her would choose to stay at the Champion."

"Why shouldn't she?"

He leaned across the desk, so close I could count his pores. He had a lot of pores. "Please don't misunderstand me. I'm proud of my little hotel, for what it is, but I've worked in better places, let me assure you. I recognize a lady when I see one. Their clothes, their manner of speech. And ladies like Mrs. Wycherly don't normally stay at the Champion."

"She may have been short of money."

"I doubt that very much. She was well provided for, as you know."

"How do *you* know it?"

"She showed me one of your alimony checks." He was startled by his own directness, and went on in a flustered tone: "I mean, I have no wish to pry into your personal affairs, but it was a certified check for three thousand dollars. She mentioned that she got one every month."

"I'm glad she felt free to confide in you," I said, with a hint of the needle in my voice.

"Oh, it wasn't that. She wanted me to cash it, and she was assuring me it was genuine. As I'm sure it was," he added hastily, "but I had to tell her I couldn't possibly cash it. It was New Year's Day, the banks were closed, I had no way of raising three thousand dollars. I offered to take it for collection, but Mrs. Wycherly said she couldn't wait."

"What did she do with the check?"

"I guess she cashed it at the bank. At any rate, she paid her bill next day."

"Where did the check come from? Do you remember?"

"I'm afraid not. She mentioned it was her home-town bank." He looked at me with a trace of doubt in his boiled-onion eyes. "You should know."

"Yes, but I was wondering how it reached her, on New Year's Day."

"It came by Special Delivery. She asked me to notify her when it arrived." The doubt in his eyes became more apparent. "Please don't misunderstand me—it wasn't a phony check?"

"The check was well-backed," I said stuffily.

"Of course. I knew it was." The thought of my imaginary bank account made him emotional. "I know a lady when I see one, and I'm sure you won't take it amiss if I offer you a piece of advice. Look to your lady, Mr. Wycherly. This can be a dangerous town for a lady going it alone with or without a purseful of money. Especially with. There are toughs and drifters galore in this town." Fillmore permitted himself to stare directly at the bandage on my head. "Maybe you found that out for yourself. Mrs. Silvado told me you were injured."

"I fell and hit my head on the curb."

"In our parking lot? I *hope* not."

"On the public street," I said. "The falling sickness runs in the family."

"I'm sorry to hear that."

His hand went to his head in a nervous gesture. He discovered the tuft of hair sticking up at the back, mechanically took out a comb and ran it through his thin locks. The tuft stayed where it was. He put the comb away in his breast pocket.

"While we're on the subject of sickness," I said, "I'm grateful to you for looking after my wife."

"I tried to. We do our best. But she refused to see the doctor." He went on apologetically: "Of course Dr. Broch isn't the best medical man in the world, but his office happens to be nearby and he's the one we call."

"I talked to the doctor last night. He thinks she's suffering from depression."

"So he told me. It agrees with my own observation."

"Did she mention any reason for being depressed?"

"Not a hint. Sheer loneliness, maybe." There was a catch in his voice, as though he had experienced the condition. "At any rate she locked herself in her room and wouldn't budge from it for four or five days."

"Exactly when was this?"

"At the beginning of the month. It started the day she paid her first week's bill, January second. It went on for nearly a week. I called the doctor in the middle of the week, but she wouldn't accept treatment. Eventually she came out of it on her own, but I could tell by looking at her that she had been through something. She looked ten years older, Mr. Wycherly. She had been through an ordeal."

"Physical or mental?"

"Physical or mental, who can tell. I don't understand the mysteries of the human heart, particularly the female heart. I said farewell to all that some time ago." His hand discovered the stubborn tuft of hair again and gave it a good hard wrench. "I'm a divorced man, too, you and I have something in common."

"Is there any chance that there was someone in the room with her?"

"Someone?"

"When she wouldn't let the servants in. Could there have been another person with her?"

"I don't see how. We don't permit doubling up in a single. It's a matter of revenue as well as morals."

"I'm not thinking of a man, necessarily." I produced Phoebe's picture. "Have you ever seen this girl in the hotel?"

"No. I never have. She's your daughter, isn't she? I can see the family likeness."

"Yes, she's my daughter."

A repeated lie can do strange things to the mind. What you say often enough becomes a provisional truth. I caught myself half-believing that Phoebe was my daughter. If she was dead, I would share Wycherly's loss. I already shared his feelings about his wife.

chapter 13

I WENT BACK to San Francisco. It was a high clear January morning, one of those fogless winter days when the gods on Mount Diablo let the city tower in the sun, moated by wide blue water. I left the Skyway and drove down Market to Powell.

I parked under Union Square and bought a soft hat to conceal my bandage and talked a second time to the old dispatcher in the yellow cap. The driver he called Garibaldi hadn't shown up on his line yet. If he did, the old man promised to hold him for me. I gave him a five-dollar bill to nail it down.

The St. Francis lobbby was comparatively deserted. The clerk on duty at the desk had time to look up November's records for me. Homer Wycherly had taken a two-room suite on November 1, and had paid in advance for a second day when he checked out on November 2. His daughter could have used the suite the night of November 2. The clerk had no way of knowing if she had.

I went back to the telephone booths and made a couple of calls. Willie Mackey was busy with a client for the next hour, but he agreed to meet me for early lunch. Carl Trevor would see me right away.

The offices of the Wycherly Land and Development Company were on the tenth floor of a ten-story stone-faced building south of Market Street. A girl who hadn't quite made air-

line hostess took me up in an express elevator and let me out
in a reception room decorated with hunting scenes.

I passed through several echelons of secretaries into
Trevor's private office. It had a picture window with a seg-
ment of red bridge showing between two buildings in the
upper lefthand corner. It contained a lot of brown leather
furniture, a conference table surrounded by a dozen chairs,
a contour model of the Central Valley studded like a golf
course with red flags, a desk which dwarfed the man sitting
behind it. He had a telephone perched like a black bird
against his short neck. Between remarks about Consolidated
something and Mutual something else, Trevor told me to sit
down.

I sat and looked him over carefully, trying to decide how
far my client and I could trust him. Pretty far, I thought.
Wycherly obviously trusted him. He seemed genuinely fond
of Wycherly's daughter, maybe too fond for his own comfort.
His face showed blue puffiness under the eyes and other
signs of a bad night.

He hung up. "Sorry to make you wait, Mr. Archer. The
market's been acting like a yo-yo lately." He gave me a stern
bright look which pulled his face together. "Judging by your
appearance, you had a rough night."

"I was just thinking the same about you."

"It wasn't much fun, to be perfectly frank. I spent a part
of the night studying the photographs of unidentified women
and girls. Some of them had been dead for months." He
grimaced. "I don't envy you your business."

"It has its compensations, when they turn up alive."

He hunched forward eagerly. "Have you found some trace
of my niece?"

"Just this." I produced the copy of her name I had made
from the hotel window and explained it to him. "It isn't a
perfect copy, but I tried to imitate the characteristics as well
as I could. Would you say it's Phoebe's handwriting?"

He frowned over the page. "I couldn't say for certain. I'm
not too familiar with her signature."

"Do you have any samples of it?"

"Not here. Perhaps at home. You think Phoebe was in her
mother's hotel room?"

"Possibly. Or else her mother wrote the name herself.
Could this be Catherine Wycherly's writing?"

"It could be. I don't really know her writing." He pushed
the sheet across the desk to me. His eyebrows were still
knotted, and the eyes in the blue cavities under them were

puzzled. "What on earth was Catherine doing in a cheap Sacramento hotel?"

"Eating and drinking and crying."

"She's always been a great eater and drinker," he said, "at least in recent years. But the crying part doesn't sound like Catherine. She's more the gay-divorcee type."

"You didn't see her last night."

His head came up. "You mean to say you did?"

"I had quite a long conversation with her at the Hacienda Inn. It ended kind of suddenly. Some goon she's travelling with hit me with a tire-iron." I touched my bandage.

"What sort of people is she involved with?"

"Not the best."

"This thing is getting complicated, Archer. Complicated and nasty. While I was in the sheriff's office in Redwood City last night, a call came in from Atherton. A body had been found in Catherine's empty house. It was the real-estate man that she'd been dealing with—a chap by the name of Merriman."

"I know. I found his body."

"*You* found it?"

"I phoned in an anonymous tip because I didn't want to spend the night answering questions. I'd just as soon you didn't mention that to your friends in Redwood City. What's their theory on Merriman's death, by the way?"

"They think he ran into a pack of vandals. There's been an unconscionable lot of vandalism in unoccupied houses on the Peninsula. You know, Archer, whole strata of society seem to be breaking loose and running wild in this civilization—if civilization is the right word. It's Ortega's 'revolt of the masses,' with a vengeance."

"Is that all part of the police theory? You must have some highly educated police."

"Oh, we do. Of course they're not confining their efforts to the wolf-pack line. I happen to know they want to talk to Catherine."

"That sounds like a good idea. Her dealings with Merriman went further than the sale of her house. He beat her up in her room the night before last. It may have been a lover's quarrel, but I doubt it. More likely it was thieves falling out."

"I don't understand you. Are you accusing my sister-in-law of being a thief?"

"She's been running with thieves, or worse. Tell me this, Mr. Trevor. Assuming for the sake of argument that Phoebe is dead—"

"That's a pretty stark assumption, isn't it?"

"It doesn't change the facts, whatever they are. Assuming she's dead, who stands to benefit from her death?"

"Nobody would benefit," he said with angry force. "It would be an unalloyed tragedy and waste."

"I wonder. There's money in the family."

His forehead puckered. Under its overhang his eyes changed color, like blue water freezing into blue ice. "I see what you're getting at. But you're on the wrong track. Phoebe has no money of her own."

"No trust fund that might revert to a relative?"

"No, I'm quite sure there's nothing like that. If there was, my wife and I would know of it."

"Does she carry any life insurance?"

Trevor sat in dubious silence. "There is a policy Homer took out when he—when Phoebe was born."

"How much is the principal?"

"A hundred thousand or so."

"Who's the beneficiary?"

"Her parents. That's usual." He shook himself irritably. "You're doing some pretty rough assuming."

"It's my job."

"Let me get this straight. You can't be suggesting that Catherine did away with her own daughter in order to get her hands on her insurance. That's insane."

"So is Catherine, I think. Not being a head-shrinker, I don't know how far gone she is. She was flying last night, on broken wings."

Trevor took a mottled green cigar out of a glass tube and lit it. He said through swirling blue smoke: "I'm not surprised, she's been on the verge for some time. It doesn't mean she's capable of murder."

"She's capable of wanting murder done."

"Is that another of your assumptions?"

"It's a statement of fact."

"You'd better explain yourself."

"Let me ask you a question first—a personal question. How good a friend are you to the Wycherlys?"

"I'm trying to be a real friend," he said in a real way. "I owe a good deal to Homer, and more to his father before him. And as you know, I married into the family. What is this all about?"

I took a breath, and a plunge on his integrity: "Catherine Wycherly tried to hire me to kill Ben Merriman last night."

"Seriously?"

"She was serious. I wasn't. I was simply letting her talk."

"What time did this conversation take place?"

"Around two A.M."

"But Merriman was already dead. The police think he died around dinnertime."

"She didn't know that, or she'd forgotten it."

"What do you mean?"

"She may have killed him, or hired someone else to kill him, then blanked out on it. She'd been drinking heavily."

"This is incredible," Trevor said. "You mean she actually approached you and offered you money to murder the fellow?"

"I approached her, in the Hacienda bar. She noticed that I was carrying a gun. It brought out the worst in her, and her worst is no picnic."

"I know that. She raised a hell of a fuss the day Homer sailed. But that's still a long way from murder. What possible motive could she have for wanting Merriman dead?"

"He was asking for it. He beat her up the other night. I think he did more than that to her."

Trevor's cigar had gone out. He removed it from his mouth and looked at it with distaste. "What do you have in mind?"

"Blackmail. That's only a hunch, but it fits the picture. She's a woman with a load of grief and guilt. A lot of money's been running through her fingers, with no visible outlet. You ought to see the hotel she's been living in. The Champion's about one short step from hunger."

Trevor shook his large head. "It doesn't sound like Catherine. What's happened to her?"

"I can think of better questions. What happened to Phoebe, and what did Ben Merriman have on Phoebe's mother?"

"You're assuming again, aren't you?"

"I have to. I don't know the facts."

"Neither do I, but I'm morally certain you're wrong. Parents don't kill their own children, outside of Greek tragedy."

"Don't they? Read the papers. I admit they don't usually wait until the children grow up."

Trevor regarded me with loathing. "Do you know what you're saying, man?"

"I know what I'm saying. It isn't pretty. Murder never is."

"You're seriously accusing Catherine of murdering her own daughter?"

"I'm bringing it up as a possibility that should be looked into."

"Why bring it to me?"

"Because you're in a position to help me. Catherine Wycherly is running loose around the countryside with murder on her mind. I think we should try to get to her before something else happens, or before the police pick her up. But I can't drop my other leads and go on concentrating on her, as I've been doing. I was hired to search for Phoebe."

"But you think Phoebe's dead."

"It's not proven, one way or the other. Until it is, I'm sticking to her trail."

"What do you want me to do?"

"Use your influence with Homer Wycherly. We need someone to put a tab on his ex-wife. I know a good San Francisco detective agency with associates in all the major cities. I'm going to talk to the head of the agency as soon as I leave here—man named Willie Mackey—but I can't bring him into the case without Wycherly's go-ahead. You can get it for me."

"Can I?"

"It shouldn't be hard. Wycherly already knows Mackey. Will you put in a call to him? I left him at the Boulder Beach Hotel. If he's checked out, they'll know where he is."

"Why don't you call him yourself?"

"He's a hard man to talk to. You've had more practice at it."

"Have I not." He pressed the button of his intercom and asked his secretary to get him Homer Wycherly on long distance. He said to me: "I'll talk to him in private if you don't mind."

I waited in the anteroom until Trevor called me back.

"Homer wants to talk to you." He handed me the telephone with a helpless shrug of his shoulders.

"Archer here," I said into it.

Wycherly's voice came over the line, strained thin by distance and tension: "I hear you've gone against my express orders. I expressly told you I didn't want my ex-wife brought into this. I'm telling you again, keep away from her."

I didn't like his tone. "Why? Does she know where the body is buried?"

"The body?" His voice became thick. "Is Phoebe dead? Is that the fact you're trying to conceal from me?"

"I'm not trying to hide anything from you, Mr. Wycherly. I have no evidence that your daughter is dead, but she's still very much missing. So is your ex-wife. And I think Mrs. Wycherly may know more than she told me. You're defeating your own ends if you don't let me have her looked for."

"By William Mackey? Is that what you're trying to sell me?"

"He's competent, and he has the connections. This case is

getting bigger than we expected. I can use some help, both private and public. I want your authorization to work with Mackey and the local police."

"You can't have it! I don't trust Mackey, and I don't want the police butting into my private affairs. Do I make myself clear?"

"You do. I don't know whether I have. A disappearance, a possible murder, isn't a private affair. The police are already involved, anyway. Didn't Mr. Trevor tell you about the killing of Ben Merriman?"

Trevor half-rose out of his chair, shaking his head at me.

"Ben who?" Wycherly said.

"Merriman. He's a realtor on the Peninsula who had some business dealings with your wife. He was found murdered last night in her house in Atherton."

"That has nothing to do with me. And nothing to do with Phoebe."

"We can't be certain of that."

"I'm certain." Uncertainty whispered and slithered through his voice.

I said: "It would be a good idea for you to come up here. You'd get a better feeling of what's been going on."

"I can't. I'm to see the college chancellor this afternoon. Tonight I have a meeting scheduled with the entire board of trustees."

"What can they do for you?"

"They're going to admit that they're at fault," Wycherly said grimly. "I'm going to force them to admit official negligence. They claim they cabled me some time after Phoebe left, and notified Missing Persons as well. But I never received any cable. Such a thing could never have happened at Stanford!"

"That's sort of a side issue, isn't it?"

"You may think so. I don't. They're going to know who they're dealing with before I'm through with them."

I suspected they knew already: a foolish man full of passions he couldn't handle.

"If you won't come up here," I said, "please give me the authority to co-opt Mackey. It won't cost more than you can afford."

"It isn't a matter of money. It's a matter of principle. I won't touch Mackey, do you understand. If you can't find my daughter without chasing red herrings up blind alleys—by God, I'll get someone who can."

His receiver crashed down, and there was nothing on the line but angry silence. I gave Trevor the dead telephone:

"He hung up on me. Is the whole family nuts?"

"Homer's naturally upset. He's very fond of Phoebe, and he never could handle situations well. You can be just as glad he isn't here."

"Maybe. But what in hell does he think he's doing, calling meetings with the college trustees?"

"I suppose he's doing the best he can with his problems. He's always been a great one for official meetings." Trevor's tone was mildly satirical. "Incidentally, you were a bit rough on him. I didn't like that remark about where the body was buried."

"I'm a detective," I said, "not a wet nurse. Anyway, I was doing him a favor. He doesn't know what's hitting him. I think it would be better if he knew."

"Do you know, Archer?" A trace of satire lingered in his voice.

"I have a feeling. It isn't a nice feeling."

He sat down heavily. "I think you're dead wrong, about Catherine and Phoebe. For that matter, Catherine and Merriman. It doesn't fit in with what I know of Catherine. She isn't a bad woman, really, underneath her rugged exterior."

"People change, under pressure. She's been under some kind of intense pressure."

"No doubt. I'm beginning to feel the pressure myself." He produced a small brown bottle from a desk drawer and took a capsule from it.

"Digitalis," he said. "Excuse me."

His mouth had turned grey. He leaned forward in his chair and rested his head on the desk-top. It lay there like a big pinkish brown egg half fledged with hair. He groaned, and said to the polished wood:

"Poor Phoebe."

"You love her, don't you?"

He lifted his heavy head, and gave me an upward slanting look, like a man spying up out of a hole. There were bitter lines of grief around his mouth:

"That's a God damn silly question. I don't mess with young girls."

"You can love them without messing with them."

"Yes. I know." His mouth softened, and the color was returning to his lips. "I do love her."

"It would be possible for you to authorize Mackey, you know. It doesn't have to be Wycherly."

"You want me to lose my job?"

"I don't think you're in any danger of losing your job."

"You don't, eh?" He looked around his handsome office.

"Homer's in a chancy mood, and he's never liked me, not really. In-laws never really like each other. If you want the truth, he's been looking for an excuse to push me out of the business. Not that he's capable of running it himself."

"You could get another job. There's only the one girl."

Trevor showed his teeth, not at me. He was bitting into the decision he had to make. He made it:

"Go ahead and use Mackey. I'll pay for him, if Homer won't. And if there's any beef, I'll take the responsibility."

chapter 14

HE WAS WAITING FOR ME in the English room on the ground floor of the St. Francis. A busty brunette hostess pointed him out, sitting at a table in a panelled niche. She had the air of a cathedral guide pointing out the statue of some well-known local saint.

Willie was a flat-faced man in his late forties with black eyes that had never been surprised. He wore a narrow black moustache, a white carnation in the buttonhole of his Brooks Brothers suit; and managed to look a little like a headwaiter. Women adored him, if you could believe his personal decameron.

I liked him pretty well myself. Willie was no saint, but he was an honest man according to his lights, even if the lights were neon. He gave me a grip-testing handshake:

"Nice to see you, Lew. I thought the Los Angeles jungle had swallowed you up for good."

"I like to visit the provinces from time to time."

He leered at me smugly with his moustache. Willie believed that there was an earthly paradise, and that San Francisco was it. We ordered Gibsons and steaks from a hovering waitress. She called Willie by name and looked at him as if she wanted to smell his carnation. He looked at her as if his carnation had a squirt gun concealed in it. When she was out of hearing, I said:

"I'm here on a case, as you know."

"Yeah." He rested his sharp dark elbows on the white tablecloth and pushed his flat face towards me. "You mentioned the magic name Wycherly on the phone. What goes on in the Wycherly family now?"

I told him.

"Daughter's run out, eh?"

"Run out or been run out with."

"Snatch, you think?"

"Not likely. They don't wait two months to make a contact."

"Two months, she's been gone?"

I nodded. "Wycherly's been out of the country, on a cruise. The girl had been going to school in Boulder Beach, living more or less on her own. She came up here to see her father off, was last seen herself leaving the docks in a taxi with her mother, Wycherly's ex-wife."

"Yeah, I saw in the papers she got her divorce. What's she doing?"

"Right now she's wandering around with a bad case of postmarital neurosis, babbling about death and murder. Wycherly's going to pieces, too—I just talked to him on the phone. And I'm supposed to put it together and make it all come right in the end."

"I could see a lot of this coming last year. The family was all ready to fly apart. You know those chocolate apples from Switzerland that fall into pieces when you tap them?"

"The question is who tapped Phoebe."

"Yeah. Last seen with her mother, you say? What does the mother say?"

"Nothing useful. She's practically certifiable, in my opinion."

"I thought they took away your medical license. Have you made any attempt to trace the taxi?"

"I'm working on it now. You could help."

He gave me a bland impermeable look. Our Gibsons came and we sipped at them, watching each other to see how quickly we were drinking this year. Willie put his glass down half-empty:

"You think the girl's dead?"

"I hate to admit it to myself, but I have that feeling in my bones."

"Homicide or suicide?"

"I haven't given suicide any thought."

"Maybe you ought to," Willie said reflectively. "She's a flighty kid. Is or was. I only saw her once, for about five minutes, but she made me nervous. I didn't know if she was going to make a pass at me or run screaming from the room. She didn't relate, if you know what I mean."

"Spell it out."

"She was carrying around a lot of sex that she didn't know what to do with. A lot of sex and a lot of trouble. From what I saw of the family, she didn't have much help growing up. Her mother couldn't give it to her. She's the same type herself, sexy-hysterical. You never can tell what females like that are going to do to themselves."

"Or what other people are going to do to them."

"You think it's murder," Willie said.

"I didn't at first. I do now."

"What changed your mind?"

"Another murder. It happened yesterday, down the Peninsula."

"Man named Merriman, real-estate broker?"

"You make quick connections."

"That was the only murder on the Peninsula yesterday. They had a good day." He grinned. "Incidentally, I heard from a friend in the San Mateo Hall of Justice that they're interested in Catherine Wycherly's whereabouts. If you know where she is—"

"I don't. That's one of my problems. I talked to her in Sacramento last night. A friend of hers hit me with a tire-iron, then they took off for parts unknown."

"I was wondering about the bandage."

"It's nothing serious. But we've got to get our hands on Catherine Wycherly."

"We?"

"I need your help on this case. You're equipped to handle a dragnet operation. I'm not."

He made a sad face. "Sorry, Lew, I have other irons in the fire."

"What happened between you and Wycherly last year?"

He shrugged, and finished his drink.

"You don't like Wycherly, is that it?"

"I love him. I love his type. He's got money in his head instead of brains. And he's tricky, the way those spoiled slobs get. He pulled the rug out from under me." Willie was showing signs of passion: his eyes were blacker and his nose was white. "The slob sent one of his troopers around to take my evidence away from me. Hick sheriff by the name of Hooper."

"What evidence?"

"The letters he hired us to investigate. I handled the case personally, spent three or four solid days on it, between here and Meadow Farms. Just when I was hitting pay dirt, the slob yanked me."

"Why?"

"Ask him. He's your baby."

"You must have some idea."

"Sure. I was getting too close to home. There were indications that those letters were an inside job. Indications, hell. I had the proof. I made the mistake of taking Wycherly seriously and going to him with it. I should have gone to the Post Office Inspectors. Maybe I could have headed this whole thing off."

"I don't follow."

"You weren't intended to. The point is I want no part of Homer Wycherly or his affairs."

Our steaks arrived. I postponed further argument until we had eaten. But even with T-bone in his belly, Willie was adamant:

"No sir. I'm loaded with work as it is. If I was unemployed, I wouldn't go back to work for Wycherly. Tell you what I'll do, though, simply as a favor to a friend. I'll put out the word to my informers to be on the lookout for the girl. Dead or alive."

"That's something."

"You want something else?"

"Copies of those letters, if you have them."

"It wouldn't be ethical." He was baiting me. "But then, neither is Wycherly. Come over to the office, I'll see what I have in the files."

We walked to his office, a four-or-five room suite on the second floor of an old building on Geary Street. His inner sanctum was a large front room furnished with a Persian carpet, old mahogany furniture, a couch. Wanted circulars and mug shots were Scotch-taped to the walls. A glass showcase containing hand-guns, knives, saps and brass knuckles stood in a corner between a water cooler and a set of steel filing cabinets which took up one whole wall.

He unlocked a W drawer, rummaged in it and came up with a folder whose paper contents he spread out on his desk:

"Here's the letter Wycherly sent me in the first place."

I picked it up and read it. It was cleanly typewritten under the letterhead of the Wycherly Land and Development Company, Meadow Farms; and it was brief and to the point:

Dear Mr. Mackey:

A San Francisco representative of my company tells me that you have a good local reputation for skill and discretion as an investigator. I seem to be in need of one. During the past week, my family has received two alarming letters from an unknown person, who is obviously a crackpot and quite likely dangerous. I want him identified.

If you are free to undertake this case, please contact me by telephone and I will make arrangements to fly you here. Nothing of this, of course, is to be divulged to the authorities, the press, or, indeed, anyone.

> Yours truly,
> Homer Wycherly
> President

It was one of those Laocoön signatures, half-choked in its own serpentines and curlicues.

"He gave me the letters when I got there," Willie said. "I Thermofaxed 'em. I'd just as soon you don't tell Wycherly I kept copies. I always keep copies."

He handed me two limp heavy yellowish sheets on which the anonymous letters had been reproduced. They had no dates, no headings. I sat at his desk and read one:

Beware. Your sins will be punished. Remember Sodom. Do you think you can copulate like dogs in the public streets? Do marriage vows mean nothing to you? Remember, sin is punished to the third and fourth generation. Remember you have a child.

If you don't remember, I will remember for you. Rather than see you sink down in your slime, I will strike at a time and place of my own choosing. There will be weeping and gnashing of teeth. Beware.

> ?A Friend of the Family.

Then the other:

You have had one warning. Here is your last warning. Your house is soaked with evil. The wife and mother is a whore. The husband and father is a complaisant cuckold. Unless you expunge the evil, it will be expunged. I speak for a jealous and an angry God. He and I are watching.

> ?A Friend of the Family.

"Lovely stuff," I said. "What did Wycherly have to say about the cuckold angle?"

"I didn't ask him. He didn't encourage me to ask personal questions. He simply wanted me to track down the poison-penner and stop him. So he said. But when I started to get warm, he stopped me."

"Warm in what way?"

"That seems to have slipped my mind."

"You're a liar, nothing ever does. You said something about an inside job."

"Did I?" He half-sat on the edge of his desk and kicked a pointed toe at me sadistically. "I wouldn't want to throw you into conflict."

"Give." I said.

"You asked for it. Take a second look at those letters, the one from Wycherly and the others. You read 'em for content. Now read 'em for physical characteristics, comparatively."

I compared the three documents. Wycherly's letter to Mackey was evenly and neatly typed, with business-school spacing and paragraphing. The letters from "A Friend of the Family" were sloppily done, by amateurish fingers. But all three looked as if they had been typed on the same typewriter.

"Similar typewriter characteristics," I said. "Same type, same degree of wear, same idiosyncrasies. The 'e' is out of alignment, for example. I'd like to see what a typewriter expert has to say about them."

"I did, Lew. Wycherly's original letter to me and the poison-pen letters were done on the same machine—a prewar Royal."

"Whose?"

"That's what I was trying to find out when the slob yanked me. Clearly it's a machine he has access to. I asked his permission to inspect all his typewriters, in his home and in his office. He wouldn't let me. No doubt he had his reasons."

"You think he wrote those letters himself?"

"I wouldn't rule it out. His letter to me could have been typed by a secretary—it's a professional piece of work—and the letters to the family by Wycherly himself. Note that they were addressed to 'The Wycherly Family,' instead of any particular member of it. He could have been trying to stir up trouble in his own family, force his wife into an open confession. I've seen crazier things done, for crazier reasons."

"You take those accusations seriously?"

"I don't know. Catherine Wycherly is a fairly hot dish for a woman her age. And whoever was trying to stir up the animals succeeded. She did divorce him."

I looked the letters over again. "You don't seem to take them seriously as threatening letters. I do. That combination of paranoia and righteousness bothers me. I've seen it in homicidal maniacs."

"So have I. Also in ministers of the gospel," Willie added sardonically.

"In either case, it doesn't go with what I know about Wycherly."

"I agree. But he could have been pretending to be a crackpot. I think whoever wrote them was putting it on. They're pretty exaggerated."

"Wycherly isn't that smart."

"Maybe not." Willie looked at his watch. "I don't want to rush you, Lew."

I got up to go. "Let me take this letter and these copies?"

"You're welcome to them. I have no use for them. You're welcome to the whole damn Wycherly caboodle."

I walked uphill back to Union Square, kicking at pigeons. And got my break, if you could call it that.

chapter 15

A SHORT WIDE MAN in a horsehide windbreaker and a peaked cap was standing with the dispatcher on the sidewalk outside the hotel. He came toward me smiling. His scar made an extra fold along his jaw.

"You the man that wantsa talk to me?"

"If you're Garibaldi."

"That's what they call me since grade school. Giuseppe Garibaldi, he's my personal hero." He laughed, and made an exultant gesture which wrote his personality large on the air. "My real name is Gallorini. Nick Gallorini."

"Mine's Lew Archer."

"Glad to meet you, Lew," he said expansively, and took off his driving glove to shake my hand. He was big-nosed, flap-eared, hammered-down; his dark eyes were wild and gentle like the eyes of certain animals and birds. "You got a problem?"

"Missing girl."

"Too bad. You want to sit in the cab and tell me about it?"

His cab was the last in line. We sat in the back of it and lit cigarettes.

"Your daughter, maybe?" he said. "Or a friend?"

"Daughter of a friend. You drove her and her father to the docks about two months ago. He was sailing on the *President Jackson*. She went aboard the *Jackson* with him, asked you to wait." I got out Phoebe's picture and showed it to him.

"I remember her." There was gloom in his voice.

"Good for you. What happened after that?"

"Nothing *happened*, not that day. I wait like she said, must have been nearly an hour. She finally comes off the ship with one of the officers and this lady with her. Turns out to be her mother, she called her mother."

"How were the two of them getting along?"

"All right." He nodded judicially. "They had a little argument on the way back, but it didn't amount to nothing. The girl had a car stashed someplace, and the mother wanted her to drive her down the Penisula to her home. I caught that, because I live down that way myself—got a nice three-bedroom in Sharpe Park—bought it when North Beach went to the dogs, the wife says move, we moved." He smiled triumphantly, and pointed a downward thumb at a passing cable car.

"What did the girl say?"

"She said she couldn't drive her mother home, she had a date with a man. The mother wanted to know what man. The girl wouldn't tell her. That was what the fuss was about."

"The mother made a fuss?"

"Yeah, she was under the weather, like. She said her loved ones were cutting her out. The girl said that wasn't true. She said *she* loved her. She was a nice girl to hear her talk—lotta good feeling in her." The gloom in his voice was deepening, and staining his susceptible eyes. "I got a daughter of my own almost as old as her, thatsa why we had to move out of North Beach."

I prompted him: "Where did you drive them?"

"Dropped the girl right here at the St. Francis. The mother I took down to the SP station."

"Did the girl go into the hotel?"

"I guess so. I didn't notice."

"Did she say anything at all about the man she had the date with?"

He considered the question. "No. She clammed up about him. That was what the mother didn't like. She didn't calm down until the girl promised to drive down and see her later."

Introducing the first and only complete hardcover collection of Agatha Christie's mysteries

Now you can enjoy the
greatest mysteries ever written
in a magnificent
Home Library Edition.

Discover Agatha Christie's world of mystery, adventure and intrigue

Agatha Christie's timeless tales of mystery and suspense offer something for every reader—mystery fan or not—young and old alike. And now, you can build a complete hardcover library of her world-famous mysteries by subscribing to <u>The Agatha Christie Mystery Collection.</u>

This exciting Collection is your passport to a world where mystery reigns supreme. Volume after volume, you and your family will enjoy mystery reading at its very best.

You'll meet Agatha Christie's world-famous detectives like Hercule Poirot, Jane Marple, and the likeable Tommy and Tuppence Beresford.

In your readings, you'll visit Egypt, Paris, England and other exciting destinations where murder is always on the itinerary. And wherever you travel, you'll become deeply involved in some of the most ingenious and diabolical plots ever invented ... "cliff-hangers" that only Dame Agatha could create!

It all adds up to mystery reading that's so good ... it's almost criminal. And it's yours every month with <u>The Agatha Christie Mystery Collection.</u>

Solve the greatest mysteries of all time. The Collection contains all of Agatha Christie's classic works including *Murder on the Orient Express, Death on the Nile, And Then There Were None, The ABC Murders* and her ever-popular whodunit, *The Murder of Roger Ackroyd.*

Each handsome hardcover volume is Smythe sewn and printed on high quality acid-free paper so it can withstand even the most murderous treatment. Bound in Sussex-blue simulated leather with gold titling, <u>The Agatha Christie Mystery Collection</u> will make a tasteful addition to your living room, or den.

Ride the Orient Express for 10 days without obligation.
To introduce you to the Collection, we're inviting you to examine the classic mystery, *Murder on the Orient Express*, without risk or obligation. If you're not completely satisfied, just return it within 10 days and owe nothing.

However, if you're like the millions of other readers who love Agatha Christie's thrilling tales of mystery and suspense, keep *Murder on the Orient Express* and pay just $9.95 plus postage and handling.

You will then automatically receive future volumes once a month as they are published on a fully returnable, 10-day free-examination basis. No minimum purchase is required, and you may cancel your subscription at any time.

This unique collection is not sold in stores. It's available only through this special offer. So don't miss out, begin your subscription now. Just mail this card today.

☐ **Yes!** Please send me *Murder on the Orient Express* for a 10-day free-examination and enter my subscription to <u>The Agatha Christie Mystery Collection</u>. If I keep *Murder on the Orient Express*, I will pay just $9.95 plus postage and handling and receive one additional volume each month on a fully returnable 10-day free-examination basis. There is no minimum number of volumes to buy, and I may cancel my subscription at any time.   07013

☐ I prefer the deluxe edition bound in genuine leather for $24.95 per volume plus shipping and handling, with the same 10-day free-examination.   07054

Name_____

Address_____

City_____ State_____ Zip_____

AR123

Send No Money...
But Act Today!

BUSINESS REPLY CARD

FIRST CLASS   PERMIT NO. 2274   HICKSVILLE, N.Y.

Postage will be paid by addressee:

The Agatha Christie
Mystery Collection
Bantam Books
P.O. Box 957
Hicksville, N.Y. 11802

"Did she say when?"

"I *think* she said that same evening," Gallorini looked at me sideways through smoke. "Listen, I got a good memory but I'm no electronic brain. Why don't you take it up with her old lady?"

"She isn't talking."

"She won't help find her own daughter? Holy Mother. I knew there was trouble there, that more was going on than they were saying. That's one reason I remember the conversation."

"What are the other reasons you remember?"

Gallorini was silent for a time. He butted his cigarette and dropped the butt into the breast pocket of his windbreaker. Suddenly he gripped my knee:

"Listen, are you a cop?"

"I have been. I'm in private work now."

"You picking her up as a runaway or what?"

"I hope that's all that's happened to her. Her father hired me to find her dead or alive. She hasn't been seen since the day he sailed."

"Thatsa where you're wrong about that." An emotion I didn't understand added faint feminine endings to some of his words. "I saw the little girl myself, week or ten days later. More like ten days, it was."

I sat up straight. "Where?"

"On the road at night—I was filling in nights that week. I had this fare to the airport, eleven o'clock plane, and I was deadheading back. I saw her standing there on the Broadway overpass. It was raining, cŏming down cats and dogs, and she was standing there in the rain beside the parapet. My headlights caught her face, and I sort of reckanized her, or I probably would of gone right on. Also I got a funny idea that maybe she was getting ready to jump down onto Bayshore."

The St. Francis doorman signalled for a cab. The line moved forward ahead of us. Gallorini made a move to get out and climb into the front seat.

"Hold it," I said. "You're on my time. This is important, if you're sure it was the same girl." I showed him Phoebe's picture again. "This girl."

He barely glanced at the picture. "I'm sure. I talked to her, see. I picked her up." Pushing suspicion away with his hands, he added: "I don't mean that the way it sounds. I thought she was somebody I knew, see, maybe a friend of my daughter from the high school. So I U-turned and went back. She was still standing there, no raincoat, with her dress all wet and her hair striped down her face. I didn't know who she was until she said something. I got a good ear for people's voices." He pointed to his ear with a dirty fingernail.

"What did she say?"

"She said she wanted no cab, she had no money. So I said I'd give her a free ride if it wasn't too far. It ain't legal but what the hell, I couldn't just leave her standing there in the rain, in her condition."

"What was her condition?"

"It wasn't so hot," he said compunctiously. "She didn't make too good sense, and I thought what will happen to her if a gang of wolves come along and grab her up. Even if she didn't jump."

"How do you mean, she wasn't making sense?"

"The way she talked, the way she acted. I finally got her into the cab, I pradically had to lift her in." He enacted the scene as he sat, one arm curled around imaginary shoulders. "I asked her where she wanted to go, and she said out of this world. Those were her words. Out of this world."

Gallorini shook his head angrily.

"I said I didn't have rocket propulsion. She didn't think that was funny. I told her she should be home in bed, not running around in the wet. She thought *that* was funny. 'Where's home?' she said, and she let out a laugh. I didn't like the sound of it. I finally got it out of her that she had relatives in Woodside. A long haul, but I said I'd take her there. She offered me her wrist watch—she had on this little gold wrist watch, and she offered to give it to me for the fare. I said to hell with that, I didn't want no wrist watch.

"Then she said she didn't want to go to Woodside anyway. She couldn't face her aunt, something like that, she hated her already."

"Her aunt hated her?"

"Thatsa what she said. I tried to find out her aunt's name, but she wasn't saying. She wouldn't even tell me her own name. I tried to ask her, what about her mother. That was when she broke down, sort of. She said she might as well go back to the apartment. So I took her where she said. It was only a short haul, a couple of miles." He grinned wryly. "It didn't buy the kids no shoes, but I was glad I did it."

I gave him five of Wycherly's dollars. "That's for the short haul."

Pleasure and embarrassment struggled for his face. Embarrassment won. "Hell, I wasn't pressing for pay. I only did what any man would do."

"Keep it. I'm not finished with you."

The words were wrong: fear danced up in his eyes:

"You think I *did* something to her."

"No, I mean I want the rest of your story, all of it."

He said with the fear still bright and hard in his pupils: "That's all there is. I drove her up to her door and she went in. She offered me the wrist watch again, but I couldn't take her wrist watch away from her." He added with a kind of compulsive candor: "Besides, it was one of those deals that maybe next day the cops would be around asking me for it. She was trouble, see. I hate to say it about a young girl, but she was a lot different from the first time I saw her. She'd went downhill in a handcar."

"In a week or ten days?"

"It can happen overnight."

"What sort of a place was she staying at?"

"Nothing special one way or the other. One of those old apartment houses on Camino, down San Mateo way."

"Show it to me."

It was a two-story stucco building with decorative tiling along the roof-edge like red icing on a slightly decaying cake. The once-white façade was dingy, streaked with rust from the iron balconies on the second floor. They gave the place a barred-up, uninviting look.

Gallorini had pulled into the curb across from the building. I parked behind him and leaned in his window:

"You're sure this is the place?"

"Uh-huh. I took a special note of it." He was looking at it as if its shabby attractions fascinated him.

"Why? Were you planning to come back?"

"Maybe. Just to collect for the haul, you know."

"In cash or kind?"

"I don't get you." His whole personality backed away from me. It left his face where it was, close up to mine, but empty. "You trying to get me in trouble? I didn't do nothing to her. Would I lead you all the way down here just to put my own neck in a noose?"

It was an interesting question. Some murderers and sexual psychopaths did precisely that. Their necks kept hankering for the rope: they broke their arms trying to lasso themselves. I offered Gallorini a little piece of string:

"Which apartment is she in?"

"Upstairs corn—" He closed his teeth on the middle of the word.

"Did you go in with her?"

He shook his head so hard that his cheeks wobbled.

"How do you know she has an upstairs corner apartment?"

His eyes were small and troubled, squinched close in to the base of his big nose as if for protection:

"Okay, so I went in with her. She *asked* me to. She said she was scared to go in by herself."

"What was she scared of?"

"She didn't say. She was soaking wet and shivering with the cold. I couldn't just *leave* her that way. I helped her out of her wet clothes, and then she kind of passed out on me."

"Was she drinking?"

"Not with me, she wasn't. Maybe she took a pill. Anyway, she got woozy. I helped her into her bedroom and put her to bed."

"You do this for all your customers?"

"It's happened before. I dunno why you're giving me a bad time. I didn't do anything out of line." He bit on his thumbnail and regarded me over his fist. "I gotta daughter of my own, see. Anyway, I had no chance to do anything even if I wanted to which I didn't. This character barged in, see."

"Who was he?"

"Some blondie guy. I thought at the time he was prob'ly living with her. He acted like he owned her."

"What did he do?"

"Gave me hell and told me to get out."

"Can you describe him?"

"Yeah, he's a blondie guy, about my size. He had a little chin beard, and kind of bulgy blue eyes. He was a nasty-talking son but what could I do? I got."

chapter 16

I LEFT GALLORINI sulking at the wheel and crossed the street. A verdigrised metal sign beside the entrance bore the title, "The Conquistador." Depending from it on a piece of wire was a small sign made of weather-beaten cardboard: "Apartment for Rent."

The wall inside the entrance was banked with brass mailboxes. Most of them showed the owners' names on cards: nobody I knew. The card on number one was printed in green ink. Alec Girston, Manager. I pressed the bell push above it.

The front door buzzed ajar. The door of Apartment One was the first to my left. A stairway rose beyond it to the second floor. The air in the hallway was chilly and oppressive.

A woman's voice said through the door: "What do you want?"

"You have an apartment for rent."

That opened the door. A wispy-haired large-eyed woman looked out at me from the internal dimness:

"Mr. Girston isn't here. Can you come back?"

"Not easily. I'm driving through. I noticed your sign and thought I'd see what you have."

"But I'm not dressed." She glanced down at the pink robe gathered carelessly at her bosom. She spread her hand on the dead white flesh above the robe. "I haven't been too well this winter."

She looked as though she'd been through a long illness. Her eyes were fogged by the basic doubts you get when your body lets go under you. The hollows of her temples and eyes were blue and sharply cut like shadows in snow. Though she wasn't old, her mouth was beginning to seam.

"I'm sorry to hear it."

The cheap words seemed to revive her spirits. "That's all right. I'll put something on and show you the flat myself. I think I can make the stairs all right."

"The vacant one is upstairs?"

"Yessir. Were you wanting something down? Upstairs has many advantages. You get more light and air, especially when you're on the corner."

"This is an upstairs corner flat?"

"Yessir. It's the most desirable one we have, when you consider the furnishings. They're included in the rent."

"How much is the rent?"

"We're asking one-seventy-five on a year's lease. The previous tenant had a year's lease, it just ran out the end of the year. She left all her good furniture, which is what makes it such a steal."

"Why did she leave it? Couldn't she pay her rent?"

"Of course she could pay her rent."

"I was only kidding. I believe I know her family, as a matter of fact." We grew up together in the last twenty-four hours.

"You know Mrs. Smith's family?"

"I think we're talking about the same girl."

"I wouldn't call her a *girl*. She must be as old as I am."
The woman touched her faded hair and looked expectantly
into the mirror of my eyes. What she saw there made her
insistent: "I swear she's as old as I am, though she does
her best to cover it up with her paints and her bleached
hair."

Illness had made her reactions self-centered and dull. I
took the mild risk of showing her Phoebe's picture. She
stabbed at it with her forefinger:

"*This* isn't Mrs. Smith. It's Mrs. Smith's young daughter.
She used the apartment for a while last fall."

"I thought that's what I said."

Confusion puckered her eyes. It changed to concern,
which wasn't for herself.

"I hope she's all right. I was worried about the girl."

"What made you worried?"

"I don't know. I never saw a young girl so sad and
mournful. I would of tried to do something for her, but
I was getting sick myself around about that time."

"Around about what time?"

"The early part of November. She's all right now, though,
eh?"

"I haven't seen her lately. When did she leave here?"

"She was only with us for a week or two—I don't know
how long exactly."

"Did she leave a forwarding address?"

"Not that I know of. Maybe my husband would know.
I was in the hospital when she moved out. The flat's been
standing vacant ever since."

"May I see it?"

"Yessir, I'll put something on." She plucked absently at
her frilly breast. "You don't have any dogs or children,
do you? We don't take dogs or children."

"I live by myself," I said. "Look, why don't you give
me the key and let me go up by myself?"

"I guess that would be all right."

Her mules thumped softly away. I looked in through the
open door. Her living room, if living was the word, smelled
of perfumes and medicine and chocolates. The outside light
sliced fiercely at the cracks between the slots of the Venetian
blinds. Thin slanting rays flaked with dust leaned across
the tangled sheets of a studio bed in one corner. A table
crowded with medicine bottles stood beside the bed.

The woman trudged back into the room with a key in
her hand: "Number Fourteen, it's the last one on the right."

I went up the stairs and along the hallway to the end. While I was fumbling at the lock, a typewriter behind the door of the next apartment drummed a brief inscrutable message and fell silent. The door opened directly into a dark room. The switch in the wall beside it turned on no light. I crossed to the windows and pulled back the heavy drapes.

Through the ornamental iron balcony, I could see Gallorini at the wheel of his cab. His head was cocked up sideways towards me as if he suspected snipers. He saw me, and withdrew his head into the cab's yellow shell. Behind me, behind walls, the typewriter rattled again.

The room was expensively and badly furnished in a stuffy "modern" style that had been fashionable two or three years ago and was already old-fashioned. Bulky square-cut armchairs and a divan covered with *bouclé* were grouped around a heavy free-form coffee-table. It reminded me of the three-walled rooms you sometimes see through the windows of furniture stores.

The bedroom contained a king-sized bed with a bare mattress which remembered the press of bodies. It was decorated in pink, with flouncy curtains and lampshades and wall-to-wall carpeting like pink quicksand. This room was so overpoweringly feminine that it made me feel enwombed.

I raised a blind and let in more light. A picture on the wall above the bed jumped out at me like a bright square chunk of chaos. It was very much like the Rorschach picture over Wycherly's mantel in Meadow Farms. I took it off the wall to examine it: blobs and swirls and jagged lightning strokes of oil paint, in a bleached wood frame, signed with the initials C.W.

I reached up to hang it back on its hook. Two or three inches below the hook, a hole in the pink plaster had been roughly plugged with white plaster. The hole had been about as big as the tip of my little finger, or a .45-caliber bullet. I took out my penknife to dig out the plater plug, and then thought better of it as the typewriter behind the wall started up again like a lackadaisical woodpecker.

I formed a powerful desire to know if the hole had been made by a bullet and went clear through the wall. I made a rough estimate of its height from the floor, about six feet, rehung Catherine Wycherly's painting on it, and went and knocked on the door of Number Twelve.

A startling young woman answered. She had on a fuzzy orange sweater over a black leotard, no shoes. Her brilliant red hair was pulled up tight in a topknot and held in place by an elastic band. The topknot had a pencil skewered through it. Her eyes were the color of slightly adulterated sagebrush honey.

"I thought you were Stanley," she whispered, but she didn't sound particularly disappointed. Her honey-colored gaze poured down my frame. She adjusted hers to take advantage of the light behind her.

"I'm Lew. I'm thinking of moving in next door."

"Oh. Good."

"I heard you typing. It was you, wasn't it?"

"Yes," she whispered. "I'm working at the story of my life. I call it 'Deep in the Heart of Darkness.' You like that title?"

"I do like it."

"I'm glad. Outside of Stanley, you're the first person I tried it on. I thought *you* were Stanley. But Stanley doesn't usually leave the shop until six."

"Stanley's your husband?"

"Not exactly," she said, adjusting her posture a few inches here and there. "He's letting me live with him while I finish my whatchamacallit—autobiography." She was one of those whispering girls who said loud things.

"You're young to be writing an autobiography."

"I'm older than I look," she said. "Twenty-four. I've had a very full life, and people kept telling me I should write it up. I mean, look how Jack Kerouac and Allen Ginsberg cleaned up, writing up their youthful experiences. I've had many varied experiences."

"I bet you have."

"You may have heard of me. Jezebel Drake?"

"The name sounds familiar."

"It's just my professional name, my real name's Jessie. Who wants to be a Jessie? So I called myself Jezebel after the song, and Drake after the hotel. I stayed there once, when I was in the chips. Which I am going to be again. I've got the looks. I've got the talent."

She was talking more to herself than she was to me. I'd run into other young women like her: they believed the dream they lived in was their own dream because they had featured roles in it. She remembered me:

"Can I do anything *for* you?"

"I can think of several things. At the moment I'm trying to find out about the construction of this building."

"The *building?*"

"The building. I work nights and sleep days. I want to be sure the walls are fairly soundproof."

"What kind of work do you do?"

"Confidential work."

She gave me another long slow look, estimating my value as material for autobiography. "Secret scientific stuff, like?"

"If I told you it wouldn't be secret, would it? Do you mind if I check the walls on your side? I've already checked on my side."

"Do you have to use equipment?"

"I tap them, manually. May I come in?"

"I guess it's all right, since we're going to be neighbors. At least I hope we are."

The room was sparsely furnished with cheap black-iron pieces. Uncabineted stereo components and other sound equipment, including a tape recorder, were scattered around it. Against the wall I was interested in, a card table with a portable typewriter and a lighted desk-lamp on it stood in a drift of yellow paper.

I made a show of tapping the wall. There was no sign of the hole on this side. That didn't mean much. A bullet could have expended itself between the layers of plaster, or caught in the lathing.

"How does it sound?" she said.

"All right, I guess."

"You shouldn't have any trouble sleeping in the daytime. I sleep a lot in the daytime myself. This place is real dead in the daytime. Everybody in it works but me." One of her hips swung out as if in comment. She pressed it back into place with her hand. "Stanley keeps me up late at night."

I didn't dare ask her how. She answered the unasked question: "With his equipment. You'd think he'd get enough of it in the daytime, but he blasts my ears off half the night sometimes. He used to be a D-J."

"Delinquent juvenile?"

"Disc jockey. Now he sells the stuff."

Something in the baseboard had caught my eye. I got down on my knees. It was a hole in the wood the size and shape of a bullet-hole, but no bullet had made it. It had obviously been drilled, then refilled with wood paste which had dried a different color from the wood.

"What is it?" she said. "Termites?"

Call them termites. The hole behind the picture, the hole in the baseboard, the tape recorder, which belonged to a sound expert, combined to suggest one thing. The bedroom next door had been wired for sound from this room.

"Could be. How long have you been living here, Miss Drake?"

"Just since the beginning of the year. I was working up until Christmas, but they raided the place. What do termites do?"

"They infest the foundations and penetrate the walls."

"You mean the whole place might fall down?" With a downward shrug of her shoulders, flutter of hands, bending at the knee, she enacted the whole place falling down.

"It could happen. It isn't likely, but I'd better talk it over with your friend." Your friend the termite. "Where does he work?"

"He doesn't work, exactly. I mean, Stanley has his own record shop. It's in the new shopping center this side of San Carlos."

"I think maybe I know Stanley. What's his last name?"

"Quillan."

"Heavy-set blond boy?"

"That's my boy," she said, without pride of ownership. "If you talk to him, do me a favor, will you? Don't tell him I let you into the flat. He's awfully jealous." Her hip popped out, repeating its silent comment.

"Known him long?"

"Just since the first of the year. That's why he's so jealous. I picked—I mean I met him at a New Year's party at his sister's house. It was a kind of a rough party, and I lost my date in the crush. Bad scene. But Stanley took over." She smiled in bright dismay. "That's the kind of thing that's always happening to me. But I always land on my feet like a cat." She jumped a few inches in the air and landed on her feet like a cat. "Speaking of cats, his sister didn't like it me taking up with Stanley. She thinks she's very hot stuff since she got married. But I've known Sally Quillan when she was prowling the Tenderloin for free drinks. And I happen to know that Stanley got canned last year for taking payola. Oops, I'm talking too much. I always talk too much when I meet somebody I like."

She covered her mouth with both hands and looked at me between her heavy eye-shadow. "If you see Stanley, you won't tell him what I said, will you?"

"I wouldn't dream of it."

"He might hit me where it shows," she said smiling. "Don't even *mention* this conversation. We'll keep it between ourselves, huh?"

That suited me. Before I left, I showed her Phoebe's

picture. She had never seen the girl, or heard of a Miss Smith or a Mrs. Smith in the next apartment.

"See you later, neighbor," she said at the door.

I went downstairs and paused outside the door of the manager's apartment to adjust my face. It felt from the inside as if I had it on a little crooked. The manager's wife called out when I knocked:

"The door's unlatched."

She was lying among the pillows on her studio bed:

"Forgive me if I don't get up. All that talking before there tired me out. You took long enough." She peered up through the dimness into my face. "Is there something the matter with the apartment?"

I gave my face another internal yank. When you sense your face as a talking mask stuck to the front of your skull, it's time to go for a long walk on the beach. I didn't have time. I produced a grin:

"I like the apartment very much."

She stirred and brightened. "You won't do better than one-seven-five for a separate-bedroom flat in a good neighborhood like this one. With furnishings like that. How did you like the furnishings?"

"Fine. But I don't quite understand about them. You say they belonged to the previous tenant, Mrs. Smith?"

She nodded. "That's why it's such good stuff. Mrs. Smith has money, I imagine you know that. When she moved in, she threw out everything that belonged to the building and put in all new stuff. It's still in practically new condition, as you can see. She hardly ever used the place. I don't think she was in it one night a week."

"What did she use it for?"

"She said she did some painting as a hobby, and she wanted a place where she could get away and paint." She squinted at me. "Seems to me you're very much interested in Mrs. Smith. Just how well do you know her?"

"She's only a passing acquaintance. But I don't want to get in dutch with her. Won't she be wanting her furniture back?"

"No, she just left it sitting. I think she told Alec she couldn't be bothered moving it. Take it up with Alec, he'll explain."

"Do you and your husband own the Conquistador?"

"Not us. I wish we did. The owner lives in Sausalito. We hardly ever see him."

"How long ago did Mrs. Smith move out?"

"Months ago. I haven't seen her for months. Then that girl of hers used the flat a little while. It's been empty since November. If Mrs. Smith wanted her furniture, she had plenty of chance to claim it. But take it up with Alec, he's the one that had the dealings with her."

"When will your husband be back?"

"He always gets home by suppertime. If you want to set a time for this evening, I'll tell him that you're coming." She hunched herself up to a sitting position. "I don't believe you mentioned your name?"

I mentioned my name, and said that I would be back around suppertime.

chapter 17

GALLORINI CLIMBED OUT OF his cab when he saw me. "Is she there?"

"She hasn't been since early in November—around the time you saw her."

"You still think I pulled something on her?"

"No. I found out who the blond boy is. Will you help me pin it down?"

He lifted his hands as if to feel for rain. "I dunno. How?"

"Drive down to San Carlos and let me show you a subject."

"I can't do it, mister. I lost an hour already—hour-and-a-half."

"I'm paying for your time."

"That's different."

I went ahead and Gallorini followed me down the highway. Vitamins, the signs said, Foreign Cars, Pediatrics and Psychiatry, Fuchsias, Storage and Moving, Remedial Reading Clinic. Bury Your Loved Ones at Woodland, Rejuvenation, Real Estate. Stanley's Stereo Shop was a plastic-fronted hole-in-the-wall with records and record-players in the window. It was one of twenty stores in a cheap new commercial development.

We parked in the off-street area. At my suggestion, Gallorini changed jackets with me and took off his peaked cap. I gave him money to buy a record.

He came out in five or six minutes, carrying a thin square parcel in his hand. He had a hot-eyed look, like a musician:

"The sonabitch reckanized me."

"What did he say?"

"Nothing. But he reckanized me. I could tell, the way he looked me over."

"And you recognized him?"

"He reckanized me, I had to reckanize him, didn't I? He's the one all right. I bet he's got her stashed someplace."

"I hope so, Nick." It wasn't too likely, though. Jezebel Drake would be all most men could handle at any one time.

I paid him off and waited for a while. I put in the time making notes on my expenses: Transportation and witnesses, $45.00; Music, $5.00. Nick had bought *Cavalleria Rusticana,* and I let him keep it.

When I went into the shop, a traffic-noises record was thundering and grinding through the glass wall of a listening-room at the back. Stanley turned the noises off and came out looking excited. He was the blond, goateed young man I had seen the night before in Merriman's office. He didn't seem to remember me.

"Yessir, can I help you?" It was a different voice from the snarl he had used on Mrs. Merriman.

"I'm looking for a girl."

"Afraid I can't help you with that. We don't keep girls in stock, ha ha."

"Ha ha. She called herself Smith, spent some time last fall in the Conquistador. Apartment Fourteen, next door to where you live."

"How do you know where I live?"

"I've been asking around."

"I don't get it." He was trying to be casual, but his voice had changed from baritone to tenor. His vocabulary changed with it. "Why don't you bug off, I got work to do."

"So have I."

"Are you fuzz—from the police?"

"I'm a private detective."

His protuberant blue eyes squeezed further out. He moved behind the counter. I leaned across it and flashed Phoebe's picture under his nose:

"You must have seen this girl. She lived beside you for at least a week in November."

"What if I saw her? What does that prove? I see a lot of people every day."

"Who do you see at night?"

He glanced at me like a tomcat trying to feel like a lion. Muscle or fat bulged under his hidden-button Italian jacket.

"Were you ever in her apartment, Stanley?"

"What if I was?" His hairy long chin waggled at me: "You sent that dago in to spy on me."

"I sent him in to see if he could identify you. He could."

"Did he tell you what *he* was doing in her bedroom? He had her down on the bed and he was stripping her. I heard these suspicious noises through the wall."

"You have very acute hearing."

"Yeah. I heard these suspicious noises, so I rushed in and threw him out on his ear. I was only doing what any fellow would do."

"How well did you know her?"

"I didn't know her. I don't know any of the other tenants in the building. I saw her in the hall a few times, maybe. That's all."

"Why were you so interested in what went on in her bedroom?"

"I wasn't."

"You planted a mike in it."

His face tried various colors and compromised on mottled lavender. I took hold of his hide-the-button lapels and dragged him across the counter towards me:

"Why did you bug her room?"

"I didn't." His voice had risen another octave.

"What happened to her, Quillan?"

"I don't know nothing about her. I'm clean. You turn me loose."

He was dirty. I shook him. His eyes bulged like a bottom fish's jerked up from the sea. He had a fishy odor. I flung him away from me. His thick body slammed back against the record shelves. He leaned there blotched and quivering:

"You can't manhandle me. I'll call the cops."

"Do that. We'll go over to the Hall of Justice and compare backgrounds. Then we'll all go and take a look at that bedroom wall."

His face became drained of blood. His eyes were electric blue bubbles in its pallor. Like a sick man reaching for medicine, he groped under the counter. His hand came up with an automatic in it:

"Bug out now. I'll gun you down like a dog."

"Can you stand that rap on top of the other?"

"The rap is all yours. You come in my place of business and try to put pressure." He punched his cash-register open with his left hand and threw some money at me:

Dollar bills fell like leaves at my feet. "Out of here now or I shoot. You want to make me a hero?"

I didn't think he would shoot, but I couldn't be sure. His personality altered from minute to minute. He was one of the unpredictables who got hot sudden flashes from outer space. A little green man might tell him to squeeze the trigger, and he might squeeze it. I went.

Not very far. I drove around the shopping center and parked in a place at the south end from which I could watch his back door as well as his front. I didn't have long to wait. It was the back door he left by.

He had on a red beret. He climbed into an Alfa-Romeo the same shade of red and turned south on Camino trailing dark oil smoke. I let him get far ahead of me, till his sports car was only a red corpuscle in the traffic stream. I followed him through Redwood City and Atherton, varying the distance between us and gradually decreasing it. His car had no real speed, and he drove it foolishly, changing lanes, spurting and braking.

He made a left turn on a green light in Menlo Park. I sneaked past the oncoming traffic on the tail end of the yellow. For a mile or more we jogged east, past the Stanford Research Center, then into an area so thickly grown with oaks that it was like thin forest. The red car disappeared around a curve.

When I caught it again it had stopped on the gravel roadside and Quillan was stepping out over the door. It was too late for me to stop or retreat, but he didn't seem to notice me as I passed. He was trotting up a flagstone walk to a brown frame cottage half-hidden by trees and shrubs. Below its rustic mailbox, a reflector sign spelled out in three-inch letters: MERRIMAN.

I parked around the next curve and transferred my contact mike from the dash compartment to my jacket pocket. I walked back towards the brown cottage. The late afternoon light fell green and tempered through the overarching branches of the oaks. It was one of those untouched stretches of land which you find here and there on the Peninsula, enclaves of a centuries-old past, when everything was oak forest.

The trees stood thick around Merriman's yard, and I made it unobserved to the side of his cottage. Keeping close to the wall and ducking my head below window-level, I worked my way around to the back and across an imitation flagstone patio shadowed by a jungle of unclipped laurels.

The sliding glass door which let into the house was closed and partly obscured by matchstick bamboo drapes. I could hear voices through it, a man's and a woman's. I lay down full length on the flagstones with my head resting on the doorsill, and pressed my mike to the corner of the glass.

Quillan's voice was rapid and raw: "I need some bread, but fast."

"You want it buttered, maybe with jam on it?" Sally Merriman said.

"It's no joke."

"It's a joke when you come to me for money. I haven't got a red cent. He borrowed on the furniture, even, right up to the hilt. I'll have to bury him on the installment plan. I was counting on you to help me with the down-payment."

"That's a laugh. What did Ben ever do for me?"

"He did plenty, and you know it. He let you in on a big deal, set you up in business. I happen to know he was paying your rent last year, I saw the check-stubs. But you never had any gratitude. What do you want now, with him laying dead at the morgue? The gold out of his teeth?"

"Gratitude!" His angry snicker exploded like static in the mike. "Big-hearted brother-in-law Ben never gave me a damn thing in his life. You think he put me in that apartment because he couldn't resist my baby-blue eyes? Or let me in on the Mandeville deal? I *made* that deal for Ben."

"Yes, God. I happen to know you were just a front, a dummy."

"You're the dummy," he yelled, and went on ranting at her in a high and ugly yammer: "I read you like a book, doll. You want what money will buy, but you don't want to know where it comes from. You let me and Ben sweat out your dirty money for you. But when you get your hooks on it, suddenly it's clean like fallen snow. And all yours. But you're not going to cut me out. I need travel money, and I'm getting it from you. You're sitting here on a bundle of loot, and don't think I don't know it."

"If I had a bundle, you think I'd stay in a dump like this?"

"You've stayed in worse. Let's see your bag, bag."

"Don't you call me that, Stanley Quillan."

"Let's see your purse, sweet little lovie-doll sister of mine."

She must have thrown it at him. I heard the slap of leather in his hands, then the click as he opened the catch.

"It's empty." His voice was empty. "Where's the loot?"

"I never had any of it. You got your share and you know

where the rest of it went. Reno and Vegas and the goddam stock market. He went in at the top of the market and came out at the bottom, through the drain."

"Don't give me that pitch, that was way last summer. I'm talking about here and now."

"What do you think I'm talking about? There hasn't been anything since the Mandeville deal and that went with the wind. We've been on our uppers ever since, paying back what he borrowed to swing it in the first place. Big deal Ben." Her voice was harsh and sardonic, with woodwinds of hysteria shrilling through it. "We were going to be rich, move up to Atherton, join the Circus Club. Some circus. We were always going to be rich. And now he's dead."

"It's a deeply touching story. It'd touch me deeply, only I don't believe it."

"Believe what you like, it's the truth. I haven't suffered enough, with Ben laying dead, cops hammering questions at me." She began to sob, gasping out words between her sobs: "My own brother has to turn against me."

"Buck up, sis, I'm *for* you. Ben was no great loss, and he left you well-fixed."

"He left me stony broke."

"Change the disc, kiddo, and kid me not." Quillan's footsteps vibrated through the floor.

"Keep away from me," she said.

"When I get my share. I need it. You're not the only one they've been questioning. I need it worse than you, and I'm going to have it."

"There isn't any money in the house. You can look if you want."

"Where is it then?"

"Where's what?" she said in bitter mocking idiocy.

"The loot. The wad. When Ben came back from Sac he was loaded for bear."

"You mean the Wycherly commission? That's gone. Most of it went to the agent who sold the place, it was on multiple listing. The rest went to the finance company. They were going to take the car. Anyway, you had no claim on that commission."

"I'm not talking about the commission. I'm talking about all of it—the whole cash value of the house. Ben went to Sac to get it, and he got it. Naturally he didn't tell *me* that, but I have a little bird that keeps me informed."

"It must be a coocoo-bird, then. It doesn't make sense. Why would Mrs. Wycherly give him all that money?"

"You can't be as dumb as you let on. Nobody could."

"Lay *off* me," she said on a rising note. "And don't stand over me. You remind me of the old man."

"*You* remind *me* of the old lady. But we won't argue, sis. I'm in a jam. I swear I have a right to part of that loot. You wouldn't turn your little brother down."

"If it's so important, you can sell the store, or your car."

"The car's shot, I couldn't get my equity. The store hasn't even been paying the lease. Anyhow, I can't wait around to sell it. I need out. Today."

"Did you do something wrong again?" There was family history in the question. "What did you do, Stanley?"

"Ben really kept you in the dark, eh? Maybe he was smart. We'll leave it like that, so if somebody asks you you won't know."

"Are the cops after you?"

"They will be. A private dick jumped me in the store this aft. He won't be the last of them."

"Is it about Ben?" she said in a thin voice.

"Partly. What happened to Ben is one reason I need out." He made a snicking sound between his teeth. "It could happen to me. Song title."

A chair scraped the floor. Her breath came out as she rose. "Did you kill him, Stanley?"

"That's kookie talk." But he sounded almost flattered.

"I mean it, Stanley. *Did* you kill him?"

"If I killed him I wouldn't be here. I'd be on my way to Australia. Travelling first-class."

"On what? I thought you were stony."

"On the wad he was carrying. Somebody got it."

"You don't have to look at me like that. I didn't know about it."

"Cross your heart and hope to die?"

She repeated the childish phrases: "Cross my heart, and hope to die. The cops said he had four bucks in his wallet."

"Christ, he was carrying fifty thousand skins."

"How do you know, Stanley?"

"Jessie told me. I wasn't planning to pass that on to you. But maybe I'll be doing you a favor."

"What happened with him and Jessie?"

"I said last night he made a pass at her. He dropped in the apartment while I was still at the store. Old lady Girston saw him and mentioned it to me. I had to pry the rest of it out of Jessie. Ben wanted her to go away with him. He showed her the loot, he even let her handle it. He said he had fifty grand, in cash, and more coming."

"The dirty dog! I knew he was double-timing me with that floozie."

"He made the pitch. But he didn't make any time—"

"Don't let her fool you."

"Jessie doesn't fool me. She was scared to put in with him, though. I got the whole thing out of her last night. I had to beat it out of her, but I got it. She was afraid it was funny money, that they'd be picked up if they tried to spend it."

"Counterfeit?"

"No, it's the real McCoy, but hot."

"But you said Mrs. Wycherly gave it to him."

"He didn't get it for the Nobel Peace Prize."

"Was she stuck on him? Or what?"

"More like what."

"Did Ben have something on her?"

"You're getting warm."

"He had all that money, and he didn't tell me. He never even told me." Her real sorrow was striking dully home. She burst out: "Who got it?"

"I sort of thought maybe you did."

"You thought I killed him for it?"

"You've threatened to often enough."

"Well, I didn't. I'm *sorry* I didn't." She let out a laugh which went through my head like a knife. "We make a nice pair, Stanley, a lovely family groupee. The heavenly twins."

"Listen, sis—"

Her voice overrode his: "Who do you think got it?"

"Whoever it was killed him."

"Do you have any idea who did it?"

"Not if it wasn't you."

"That's crazy. I thought at first it was old man Mandeville. He's been making a nuisance of himself. But I guess that's crazy, too. The cops say it was a gang of kids."

"Lucky kids," he said with throbbing sincerity. "Listen, sis, we can maybe pull it out—some of it, anyway. There's this tape Ben kept in the safe in the office. If you'll go down and get that for me—"

"I don't know what you're talking about."

"You don't have to know. Just get it. I think I can find a customer for it."

"What kind of a customer?"

"A paying customer. The tape's worth money, see."

"Blackmail money?"

"Call it that."

"I don't want any part of it," she said.

"She doesn't want any part of it. She's too clean, too sweet, too pure." His voice was savage: "Come off it, doll. What do you think you've been living on the last six months? Manna from heaven?"

"Lay *off* me. Maybe you can bully Jessie, but you can't bully me."

He brought his voice under control: "Listen to me. I'm trying to do what's best for you—best for both of us. You don't have to know a thing, I don't *want* you to. All you have to do is go down to the office and get me the tape in Ben's safe. It's in a round paper package—you know what *tapes* feel like. Just make that little trip for me, and I'll give you half of what I get for it."

"And half the rap? I get that, too?"

"There won't be any rap, sis. Leave it to me."

"I am," she said. "I'm leaving it to you. All of it."

"You won't co-operate?"

"I'm not going in on any crooked deal."

"Then give me the office keys and the combination."

"The cops have the keys to the office. I don't know the combination."

"Didn't Ben have it written down someplace?"

"If he did, he didn't tell *me*."

"So what good are you?"

"More good than you are, nothing man."

"Don't call me that!"

"Nothing man. You were going to be a big shot, you and Ben both. The real-estate king and the big movie producer. What did it all add up to? I spent my life trying to make sense out of a couple of cheap hustlers."

"Hustler is a word you shouldn't use."

He slammed out. He was very good at slamming out. The Alfa-Romeo roared away, and I had no chance to follow it.

I went back to Camino Real and stopped at the drive-in across from Merriman's office. The little building had a lockedup, empty look.

It was dinnertime, and I hadn't eaten all day. The chill of the winter earth had crept up through the flagstones into my marrow. I ordered hamburger and coffee and sat listening to the younger generation trying to talk like underworld characters and succeeding. Nobody said anything revealing, except that the carhop who brought me my hamburger called me dad.

Stanley didn't show.

chapter 18

HE WASN'T IN his store, either. I went on to the Conquistador Apartments and buzzed Apartment One. A gaunt man in shirtsleeves came to the door. He had a long unhappy face on which a sense of frustration had settled and caked like dust.

"Mr. Girston?"

"Yeah." His tone was grudging, as if he hated to give anything away, even his identity. "Would you be the gentleman the wife was telling about? Interested in the apartment upstairs?"

"I'm more interested in the occupants of the apartment."

"There's nobody in it. It's been empty for two months."

"That's one of the things that interests me." I told him who I was. "Is there some place we can talk without being disturbed?"

He looked me over suspiciously and said in his grudging whine: "Depends on what you want to talk about."

"This girl." I brought out Phoebe's picture. "She's missing."

He peered at the photograph. It was changing under all the eyes I showed it to. Phoebe looked strange and remote and a little worn like a statue that had been standing in the weather.

Girston's mouth worked softly. "I don't believe I know her."

"That's funny, your wife does. Mrs. Girston said she occupied Apartment Fourteen for some days last November."

"The old woman runs too free at the mouth."

"She's an honest woman. And you're an honest man, aren't you?"

"I try to be, when it don't put my neck in a sling."

"You recognize the girl, don't you?"

"I guess so."

"When did you last see her?"

"Back in November, like you said. She was moving out, and I helped her down with her bags."

"Where was she going?"

"To Sacramento, to see her mother. I asked, because I happened to notice that they were her mother's bags. The little girl wasn't feeling so good, so I helped her down with them." He looked as if he expected me to thank him.

"What was the matter with her?"

"I dunno, stomach trouble maybe. She was kind of bloated-looking in the face."

"Can you pinpoint the date?"

"Let's see, it was the day after the old woman went into the hospital. That was November eleven she went in. She was in for two weeks and three days, came out November twenty-eight. I still haven't got it all paid for." His slow mind made a connection: "The girl's family has money, isn't that right?"

"Some. How do you know that?"

"The clothes she wore—they were Magnin's and stuff like that, the old woman said. And look at the way her mother refurnished the flat. You working for the mother, did you say?"

"For the family."

"Is there reward money?"

"There should be, when the girl is found. I think I can guarantee it."

Girston's manner changed. With protestations of good will, he ushered me down the hallway to his office under the stairs. It contained an old safe, a roll-top desk, a broken-backed swivel chair. He switched on a green-shaded desk lamp, and urged me to sit down in the chair. I preferred to lean in the doorway where I could watch the entrance to the building.

"Getting back to the day she left here," I said, "how did she leave? By taxi?"

"Car."

"Green Volkswagen?"

"Naw, an old Buick, I think it was. She drove away with—with a guy."

"Guy you know?"

He didn't answer immediately. He pawed among some papers on his desk, found a paperclip, straightened it out carefully. His face was green in the lamplight, like ancient bronze. I felt like an archaeologist digging among the ruins of the recent past.

"How much reward money, would you say?"

"I can't say, Mr. Girston. It ought to be substantial, if you give substantial help."

"Okay," he said. "I know him. We do—we did a little business from time to time. He was in the real-estate business—guy by the name of Merriman. I saw on TV where he got himself killed."

"The girl drove away with Ben Merriman in November?"

"That's correct."

"Were they friends?"

"I guess you'd say so. He was the one that brought her here in the first place."

"When was that?"

"Some time around the early part of November. He said she was Mrs. Smith's daughter, said it was okay with her mother to let her use the apartment. It sounded all right to me." Which meant that it hadn't. "He was the one rented it to Mrs. Smith in the first place, and her lease wasn't due to run out till the end of the year."

"How long did the girl stay in the apartment?"

"A week, maybe a little longer. She was as still as a mouse up there. I don't think she ever went out."

"Did Merriman see her in the course of the week?"

"Just about every day he was in and out."

"Were they having an affair?"

"I couldn't answer that, mister." His mouth moved like a chewing camel's. He said out of the side of it, with sour primness: "We're not responsible for what the tenants do in the privacy of their own dwellings."

"Do you think they were having an affair? That information may be valuable."

"Maybe they were. He spent some awful late nights up there with her. He used to bring in groceries, too. And then they went off together, that signifies."

"Went off to see her mother in Sacramento, you said."

"What's what *they* said."

"Which of them said it—the girl or Merriman?"

"Merriman, I think it was. Yeah, it was him said it."

"Did either of them say what she was going to do after that?"

"Not to me, they didn't."

"Did she seem to be looking forward to seeing her mother?"

"I doubt she was looking forward to anything much. She acted like a pretty sad little girl."

"What about her mother? You knew her mother, of course?"

"Sure. She was a tenant here for six or eight months, off and on. Mrs. Smith is a different kettle of fish from her daughter."

"In what way?"

"She's a lively customer. These artists and people like that can be pretty wild sometimes."

"She's an artist?"

"So she said. She rented the apartment to have a quiet

place where she could paint. I never saw her doing any
painting, though. In fact I never saw much of her at all.
Ben Merriman handled the whole deal. Sometimes a month
would go by and I wouldn't see her. She only stayed here
off and on, and she came and went very quietly."

"All by herself?"

"She came and went by herself."

"No visitors?"

"I guess she had visitors. I don't keep watch on their
goings and comings, but I know what you're getting at. You
want to know if she was using the apartment to be with a
man." His prim mouth dirtied the phrase.

"Was she?"

"I wouldn't say yes. I wouldn't say no."

"Did you ever see a man with her?"

"Not so's I could swear to it. There's people in and out
of here at all hours of the day and night. It isn't part of
my job to spy on the tenants."

"Could the man have been Ben Merriman?"

"Could have been at that." He looked into a shadowed
corner. His gaze swung around to me. "What happened to
Ben, mister? It said on TV that he was clubbed to death."

Before I could answer him, the front door opened. It
wasn't Stanley. It was a young woman in a dark hat and
business suit. She closed the door, leaning wearily on the
doorknob for a moment, then saw me and went upstairs.
Her quick steps climbed the slanting ceiling of Girston's
office.

"Who did it to Ben Merriman?" he said.

"I was going to ask you the same question. You knew
him better than I did."

"You couldn't say we were friends. We never visited in
each other's homes. I never thought much of his habits."

"Such as?"

"Gambling and drinking and running around with women.
I don't throw my money away on things like that, and I
try and keep away from people who do. I knew Ben in
line of business, is all."

"What kind of a businessman was he?"

"Ben was a sharpie—a little too sharp for his own good.
He had his little tricks, a lot of them do. Couple-three
years ago, when there was an apartment shortage, he had
a little habit of squeezing cash bonuses out of prospective
tenants. Then he had another little habit of using apartments as a roosting place for house prospects. He'd lease

an apartment to them, then undertake to break the lease if they'd buy a house from him."

"Did he do that with Mrs. Smith?"

"No. She didn't break her lease. She just let it run out at the end of the year."

"I understand she left her furniture."

"Yep, just left it sitting there. Merriman said she didn't want it back. It didn't fit in with his plans for her new house."

"When did he tell you this?"

"Round about the beginning of December. He called up and told me Mrs. Smith couldn't be bothered moving her furniture, I could rent the apartment furnished if I wanted. I didn't know until then that she wasn't planning to renew her lease."

"Did you see Mrs. Smith after her daughter left here?"

"I don't think so. But she might of used the apartment without me knowing. It was here for her to use, all paid up until the end of the year."

I was puzzled. Apparently Mrs. Wycherly had moved into the Champion Hotel at a time when she had a perfectly good apartment in the San Mateo area, as well as the house being sold in Atherton.

"Why did she leave here? Do you know, Mr. Girston?"

"You mean Mrs. Smith? The mother?"

"Yes. Was there any trouble before she left?"

"Now that you mention it, she did have a little trouble with the fellow next door. But that was way last spring."

"What month?"

He wrinkled his forehead and smoothed it with his fingers. "March, I think. March or April. It's one of the few times I ever talked to her, to do more than pass the time of day. She came storming down here, claiming that Mr. Quillan was spying on her. Older women get that idea sometimes, 'specially when they're man-crazy. She wanted me to evict him. I told her I couldn't do that. Told her Mr. Quillan had no more interest in her than the flies on the wall. Luckily she got over the idea."

"How do you know?"

"She said so. She said in a day or so that she was mistaken about it. I should forget it. I said I already did. Mr. Quillan wouldn't be interested in her. He has plenty of girls of his own."

"What kind of a tenant is he?"

"He doesn't cause any trouble. He used to play his records

loud at night but I gave him a quiet talking-to and he got over that. He's a fine young man, has a business of his own."

So had Capone.

"Is Quillan home now?"

"I didn't see him come in yet."

I went upstairs to Quillan's apartment. Jessie Drake answered the door, and smiled when she saw me:

"Did you make up your mind to take it?"

"I haven't decided. I want to talk to Stanley first."

"Isn't he at the shop?"

"No, I just drove past there. May I come in and wait for him?"

"I wouldn't want him to find you here." She rubbed her shoulder through her sweater. "He didn't like it the last time I let a man in."

"You mean Ben Merriman."

"Yeah." She went through an exaggerated double-take, widening her eyes and mouth, then narrowing them suspiciously. "How do you know about it? Did Stanley tell you?"

"Stanley wouldn't tell me the time of day."

"Are you a cop?"

"A private one. Don't get excited, Jessie. I'm not after you. Ben Merriman showed you some money yesterday."

"I *knew* it was hot," she whispered. "I didn't touch it. I didn't touch him *or* the money."

"I wouldn't care if you rolled in it like catnip. I'm interested in where it came from." And where it went.

"Me, too. Naturally. He came busting in here with a jag on and wanted to take me to Mexico. Just like that. We could live like kings in Mexico, he said. I asked him what on, just to keep the conversation going, you might say. And he unfurled his roll. It was big enough to choke a rhinoceros, so big he had to carry it in a satchel. Hundreds and hundreds of hundred-dollar bills." Her eyes were like glass.

"What kind of a satchel?"

"Little black leather case with his initials. He said he just got back from Sacramento. He made a deal with some woman—nobody I knew. He sold a house for her, he said, and he said she liked him so well she gave him most of the cash. Gave *him* the cash, he said, and kept the commission for herself. Which didn't make sense to me. People don't *give* money away, not in my experience which has been varied. They grind it out of you, like coffee. So I knew the money was hot. Anyway, you don't want to go and live in Mexico the rest of your life unless you're hot."

"He intended to stay there for the rest of his life?"

"So he said. He was high, though. I didn't put too much stock in what he said. I never have."

"Did he ever ask you to elope before?"

"Not elope, I mean technically not elope. Sure, he's been after me. He made a heavy pass at the New Year's party, right in his own house. He suggested we ought to take off our clothes and dance around in our bones. I wasn't interested, but he's a hard man to discourage. Was."

"How long have you know the Merrimans?"

"Sally I've known for years. I hardly knew Ben at all, I only met him three or four times in my life. But he was a fast worker, or so he liked to think. I have that effect on certain types. That's probably why I didn't see much of Sally after she married him."

"What did she do before she married him?"

"She was an actress, like me. I met her when we were both trying out for the chorus line at the old Xanadu. I got the job, she didn't. They told her she was too old. She had it rough for a while, and I helped her out. She paid me back when she got a job with Ben Merriman. Then he married her."

"How long ago was that?"

"I don't know exactly. Four-five years. For a long time I was out of touch with Sally. I was over in Nevada for a year. Or was it two years?"

The telephone rang in the room behind her. She jumped as if it had sounded an alarm, and left me standing in the doorway.

"Hello, Stanley," she said into the receiver.

There was a lengthy silence while she listened and I listened to her listening. Her head turned gradually towards me. Her heavily shadowed eyes reminded me of a grease-monkey.

"Will do," she whispered into the phone. "I get the message, darling."

She hung up, carefully, as if the instrument was fragile and she was very clumsy.

"You've got to excuse me," she said. "I have to do some things for Stanley."

"What things?"

"I don't have to tell you, and I'm not going to."

"Where is Stanley?"

"He didn't say. Honest," she added in a dishonest voice.

I didn't try to argue with the girl. I went downstairs. Girston was standing in his doorway. He looked at me like

a lost soul whom I was cheating out of his hope of heaven.
He lunged for me as I went by, digging his fingers into
my arm and breathing into my face:

"What about the reward money?"

"If your information leads to the girl's recovery, I'll recommend you for a reward."

"How much?"

"That will be up to my principal."

"Couldn't I get a percentage of it now? Just a small percentage?"

I gave him twenty dollars as you throw a dog a bone,
and went outside. The sky above the rooftops was streaked
green and yellow like an old bruise. Night was gathering
in the corners of the buildings. Most of the cars in the
road had their lights on.

I joined the traffic stream. From her second-floor window,
Jessie watched me drive away. I turned off Camino at the
first corner, U-turned and parked a hundred feet up the
side street, ready to go north or south. The street was
shadowed by broad-leaved trees whose name I didn't know,
and there were children playing in the twilight.

I walked back to the corner, where I could watch the
entrance to the Conquistador. Two cigarettes later, a green
cab with a pulsating light on the roof honked at the curb
in front of it. Jessie came out wearing a coat. She had a
suitcase in either hand, a brown one and a white one. The
driver scrambled out to take them from her. He slammed
the door on her and drove on north.

His pulsating light was easy to follow, even in the evening
rush. He went through Burlingame and turned right on
Broadway. When he crossed the overpass at Bayshore, where
Phoebe had stood in the rain above the river of traffic,
I was close behind him. The lights of International Airport
silhouetted Jessie's head through his rear window.

Circling the parking lot, the taxi deposited her and her
suitcases on the sidewalk in front of the main terminal.
I found a green curb, and followed her into the building.

She took an elevator up to the main floor and lost me
for a while. I picked her up about ten long minutes later,
coming out of the ladies' room. She passed within five feet
of me in the crowd. She had fresh lipstick on, a bemused
glitter in her eyes. She didn't see me. She didn't seem to
see anyone.

She moved through the people like a bright-headed shadow passing among shadows. Men's eyes trailed her. Keeping
my distance, I followed her to the newsstand and saw her

buy a magazine with an anguished female face on the cover.
She settled down on a bench with it, crossing her legs.
She was wearing high-heeled shoes and stockings, and under
her coat a low-cut black dress that looked like a party dress.

I bought a *Chronicle* and sat down on the far side of the
newsstand. Ben Merriman's picture, the same one he used
on his blotters, was on the third page. The accompanying
story told me nothing I didn't already know. It concluded
with a statement from Captain Lamar Royal of the San
Mateo County Sheriff's office, to the effect that his depart-
ment was co-operating closely with local law-enforcement
agencies in tracking down the hoodlums responsible for the
brutal killing, and arrests were expected momentarily.

I glanced over the edge of the paper at Jessie. She was
reading her confession mag with avid intensity, as if it
was telling her the story of her next ten years. The roar of
planes taking off below the windows, the hubbub of passengers coming and going around her, made no impression
on her. From time to time she looked up at the clock.

The minutes went by so slowly that time itself seemed
to be running down. Jessie began to get restless. She looked
up at the clock again, stood up and scanned the whole
enormous room, sat down again tapping her toe on the floor.
She fumbled a cigarette out of her coat pocket and inserted
it between her lips.

A dark man in a form-fitting overcoat froze like a bird
dog near her, looked at her feet and body, swarmed in on
her with clicking lighter. She twitched her cigarette away
from the flame. I didn't catch the look she gave him, but
it sent him scurrying. She lit her cigarette and went back
to her magazine.

This time it failed to hold her. She consulted the clock
four or five times before she finished her cigarette. She
threw down the butt and ground it under her shoe, standing
up as she did so. She began to circle the newsstand, peering
at all the waiting faces on the benches. I hid my face
with the newspaper until she went by.

She returned to her place on the bench and put in some
time crossing and recrossing her legs. The place was warm
enough, but she looked cold. She wrapped her coat around
her, plunging her hands in the pockets. She lay back stiffly
with her head against the back of the bench and watched
the clock like somebody on salary. The minutes were drib-
bling out as slowly as molasses in January.

It was an hour and a half since Stanley had telephoned
her. We had been sitting in the terminal for over an hour.

I'd read my way through the paper to the classified ads. An anonymous benefactor at a Grant Street address was offering the only authenticated photograph of Jesus Christ for sale or rent. I was so bored I felt like getting in touch with him.

I was on the point of approaching Jessie when she gave up. She threw a final furious glance at the clock, as if it had betrayed her, and took an elevator down to the ground floor. I caught up with her at the cab-rank outside:

"Don't waste money on taxis, Jessie. I'll drive you where you want to go."

She backed away from me with her fist at her chin. "What are *you* doing here?"

"Waiting for Godot."

"Is that supposed to be funny?"

"Tragicomic. Where do you want to go?"

She concentrated on this problem, slipping one knuckle in between her teeth. With a slight wrench, she removed it. "Back to the apartment, I guess. I was supposed to meet somebody. Their plane was delayed, I guess."

"Is Godot travelling by plane these days?"

"Har dee har," she said.

"My car's parked on the other side. Do you want me to get the bags?"

"What bags?" She overacted, exaggerating her natural stupidity.

"The brown bag and the white bag you checked an hour ago. It looks as though you won't be needing them."

Her pentup anger burst out on me. She came up close to me shaking and whispering, calling me various names. "You've been spying on me."

"A little. Give me the checks and I'll go and collect the bags. You can wait in the car."

"The hell I will."

But when I gave her my arm she came along quietly. She was a girl who needed an arm, any arm. I made sure the key wasn't in the ignition and left her sitting in the front seat while I reclaimed her baggage.

The bags were surprisingly light. Neither of them was locked. I opened them on a bench inside the entrance. The brown one held several men's sports shirts, a dark blue suit on the verge of shabbiness, a set of the "trail clothes" affected by sports-car drivers: white ducks and black wool sweater; an electric razor, and a pair of military brushes in a pigskin case which had Stanley's initials engraved on it in gold.

The other bag smelled of Jessie. Her meager wardrobe

was wadded into it: sweaters and slacks and underwear with her initials on it, a couple of gaudy dresses, a little collection of toilet articles, a carton of cigarettes, and her typescript. It began: "I was always wild from the time my mother's currant love siezed me in a passionate embrace on my twelfth birthday." With my hands in the flotsam of her life, I was oddly relieved that the trip with Stanley hadn't taken place. It would have been a trip to nowhere anyway.

I closed the bags and carried them out to my car. Jessie said when I got in:

"Stanley stood me up. I guess you figured that out for yourself."

"Where were you supposed to be going?"

"Away, he said. That suited me. I've had enough of this place." She looked around at the great lighted buildings.

"You were going to take a plane?"

"No, we were going to travel by oxcart. That's why he told me to meet him at the airport."

"Where was he calling from?"

"His store, maybe. I heard music behind him."

"He could still be there."

"Yeah." Her voice brightened. "Maybe he got held up by something."

I put the car in gear. Bayshore took us up in its rush and disgorged us in San Carlos a few minutes later. I drove across the town to the shopping center on Camino Real. The parking space around it was almost deserted. Not quite. Stanley's red sports car was parked in front of his shop. There was a light inside, and the sound of music.

Jessie took hold of my shoulder with both hands. "You stay out of it. Please? Just set the suitcases out and blow. He'll hit me again if he sees me with you."

"I won't let him."

It sounded like a commitment, the way it came out. Her hands became more conscious of my shoulder; they lingered there with something like possessiveness. Her breast came up against me:

"You're sort of sweet."

"I always thought so."

"Conceited, too," she said indulgently.

She kissed me lightly. I think she was trying to nail me down just long enough to see if she still had Stanley. She climbed out of the car, and I handed her the suitcases. With one in each hand, like a German wife, she marched up to the front door of Stanley's shop.

I heard the surge of music when she opened it. It was

musical-comedy music, loud and insistently happy. I followed her in under cover of the music. It burbled out of
the glass-walled listening room at the rear of the store.

Stanley was sitting in the glass room with his back to
me. He was listening very intently to the music. I couldn't
see Jessie, but the two suitcases were standing outside the
door of the cubicle. I took out my gun and approached
the open door.

Jessie was down on her knees behind the door. She was
picking up money like a red-headed chick in a corn bin.
Hundred-dollar bills spilled from a black leather satchel
onto the floor. Jessie was stuffing them into the pockets
of her coat.

Stanley was paying no attention to her. He was sprawled
in his chair with a bullet hole in his forehead, listening
to the happy music with dead and dreamy eyes.

It was the perfect time for the law to arrive. It arrived.

chapter 19

A BAD HOUR LATER the case was all
wrapped up and I was discussing it with Captain Royal on
the second floor of the Hall of Justice and Records in Redwood City. The case was all wrapped up in wet tissue
paper. I suggested this fact to Royal, more than once, but
he was not impressed by my criticisms. My status in his
clean, well-lighted office was somewhere between witness and
suspect, veering towards the latter.

It was Captain Royal's theory, to put it in the nutshell
where it belonged, that Stanley Quillan had murdered Ben
Merriman for the fifty thousand dollars, that Jessie Drake
had murdered Stanley Quillan for the fifty thousand dollars,
and that I had knowledge, probably guilty knowledge, of
both crimes.

"This isn't an open-and-shut case," I told him for the
second or third time. "Even if Quillan killed Merriman,
which I very strongly doubt—"

"He very strongly doubts it," Royal said to an invisible
poltergeist beside his desk. To me he said: "Do you have
evidence that you're suppressing?"

"No," I lied. "But I do know Quillan and Merriman
were partners."

"Thieves fall out. They both wanted the fifty grand. They

both wanted the Drake woman. She admitted that herself."

"But she also said she wanted no part of Merriman. She had her chance at Merriman and the money."

"You believe that?" Royal gave me a pitying look and a smile which resembled a crack in granite.

"I believe it. In any case, she couldn't have shot Quillan. I was at their apartment with her when he phoned from his store. Since then I've had her under constant surveillance."

"So you tell me," Royal said blandly.

"You can check it out. I'll give you a complete account of her movements and you can match it with her story. That is, if you want to go to the trouble. I realize it's a lot less trouble sitting here on your can think-talking."

Royal's granite smile didn't change, but his eyes glinted like mica. "I'm a patient man. Don't take advantage of it."

"Or you'll throw me in a cell along with Jessie Drake, no doubt."

"A different cell," he said equably, "on a different floor. How do you know it was Quillan who phoned the apartment?"

"I have no reason to doubt it."

"He has no reason to doubt it," Royal said to his poltergeist. "It could have been somebody else. Quillan was dead already, maybe, and maybe the redhead was using you for a patsy."

"It's possible," I admitted against my will.

"There are other possibilities. I'm not throwing any of them out. Just how well do you know this Drake woman?"

"I met her today."

"Pickup?"

"You can call it that if you want to."

"I want to call it what it was. What was your business with her?"

"I had some questions to ask her about a case I'm on." He leaned across his desk in a confidential way. "Tell me about the case you're on."

"I prefer not to."

"You have no preference in the matter, mister. You're a private detective, not a lawyer, and you have no right of privilege. You're obliged to co-operate with the properly constituted authorities. Me."

"I'm obliged to answer questions in court. Your case against Jessie Drake will never get that far."

"We'll see." The Captain's face was very close to mine. I examined it with all the interest of a rock-hound who had just discovered a mineral specimen resembling human flesh. "Did you know she has a record?"

"I'll lay odds it isn't a violent one."

"Narcotics and prostitution. They often lead to violence. In the long run they nearly always do."

"Come off it, Captain. Jessie Drake didn't shoot Quillan. He phoned the apartment while I was there. After that she was hardly out of my sight."

"She was out of your sight long enough to shoot him, according to both your accounts."

"When?"

"When she walked into his store."

"I would have heard the shot."

"Maybe." Royal leaned back in his chair. "Deputy Snider said the music was turned up loud—it's what attracted him to the scene. You have to admit Drake had an opportunity to shoot him. She certainly had a motive. All that money."

"But no gun."

"You were carrying a gun," Royal said mildly.

"It hasn't been fired since I had it out on the range three weeks ago Sunday. Incidentally, I want it back. I have a permit to carry it, and I need it in my business."

"Sure you do. You'll get it back when our ballistics men are through with it—provided that the tests turn out in your favor."

"You know that gun wasn't fired tonight."

"Do I? You could have cleaned it and loaded it right there in the store."

"I had no time."

"So you tell me. I don't know how long you were in there. I don't know *you*. Tell me about yourself. Tell me about this case you say you're on. Where did all those hundred-dollar bills come from?"

"I've been trying to find that out." I was on shaky ground, and I decided to bolster it up with a little truth: "Merriman evidently made some kind of a deal."

"With anyone you know?"

I avoided a direct answer. "I believe it was some kind of a real-estate deal involving several people. Have you been through his office records, the contents of his safe?"

"No. Have you?"

"I'm not in a position to get a search warrant."

Royal got up cumbrously out of his chair. I stood up, too. He was taller than I was, broader, a little older, perhaps a little stupider. "What would you look for if you had a warrant to search Merriman's office premises?"

"Whatever I found."

"Is that supposed to be funny?"

"Not so very. You made an accusation which amounts to murder. You don't believe in your lousy accusation. You're simply trying to use it for leverage. I'm not playing."

Royal shook his head at me in a disappointed way. "I don't know how the people down South deal with people like you. Maybe you got a pull in Southland enforcement circles. Up here you don't have the pull of a broken elastic. Think about it."

"I've thought about it. And I'm not playing. You can book me, or let me go."

"Or I can hold you for twenty-four hours on an open charge. Which is precisely what I'm going to do." He switched on the box on his desk and spoke into it briskly: "Thorne? I have another roomer for you. Come and get him, will you?"

I was bothered. A night in a nice modern jail was one thing. Sitting still for twenty-four hours while the Wycherly case went on without me was another thing. I said to Royal:

"Do you know Colton of the Los Angeles D.A.'s staff?"

"Heard of him."

"Call him, will you? His home number is Granite 3-7481. Ask him about my record."

"I'm not interested. Also, the County doesn't have funds for long-distance calls on behalf of private parties. Call him yourself if you like—you're entitled to a call."

A stout man in deputy's uniform came in without knocking. He gave me a practised look. "This the man, Captain?"

"This is the man. I want him in a cell by himself, and be sure to take his belt. Mr. Archer is very emotional."

"Are you kidding?" I said.

Royal turned and looked at me the way men look at dogs. "This is no practical joke, if that's what you're thinking. You're in, brother."

"You said I could make a call."

"To Colton in L.A.? You'll be wasting your time. Colton or nobody else cuts any ice with us. This is a clean county, even if you and your buddies have been littering it up with corpses."

I almost swung on Royal. I think he wanted me to, if only to take the dubiety out of the situation. Thorne inserted his shoulder between us and nudged me with it. "Do I take him away, Captain?"

"First I'll make my call."

"That's your right and privilege," Royal said with some

unction. "My best advice to you is call your principal, if you have one, get his release on the information you're sitting on. Maybe then—I say maybe—you and me can have a meeting of minds."

"Intellectual slumming bores me."

He missed it, or let it pass. "I'll get your principal for you. Say the word." He picked up one of the telephones on his desk.

"I'll talk to Carl Trevor in Woodside."

Thorne and Royal looked at each other. Then they both looked at me, with dawning approval. The atmosphere in the room began to warm up, as if Trevor's name had jiggled a thermostat.

"Mr. Trevor was in this office just last night," Royal said. "You're working for Mr. Trevor?"

"I'm working for his boss."

"You're on the Wycherly disappearance?"

I nodded.

"Why didn't you say so?"

"I don't like being squeezed."

"You got to admit you were asking for it," Royal said. "Here. Sit at my desk."

The atmosphere was getting so warm it made me a little sick. Royal dismissed Deputy Thorne, placed me in his own chair, gave Carl Trevor's home number to the switchboard. He didn't have to look it up.

He exchanged a few cordial words with Trevor and handed me the receiver. Trevor sounded old and spent:

"I've been trying to get in touch with you, Archer. Why didn't you tell me you were going to be in Redwood City?"

"I didn't know it. I walked in on a killing."

"Another killing?" he said wearily.

"Man named Quillan, ran a hole-in-the-wall record shop in San Carlos."

"Who killed him?"

"Captain Royal thinks I did."

Royal began to smile and wag his head.

"Is everybody going crazy?"

"Yes," I said with my eye on Royal. "Everybody is going crazy. Do you feel like coming over here and straightening the Captain out?"

Royal made a pooh-pooh mouth and pantomimed with his hands a smooth unbroken flow of good fellowship and tolerant understanding.

"I'll talk to him on the phone, that will be quicker." Trevor's voice faltered as though it had come up against an obstruction. "Archer. I want you to make a journey with me. Tonight."

"Where to?"

"Medicine Stone. I have a summer place there, as I think I told you. The local sheriff knows I'm Phoebe's uncle, and he called me a little while ago. He thinks they may have found her car."

"At your place?"

"A few miles from there. Underwater, in the sea. A fisherman spotted it the other day, but Sheriff Herman isn't on the ball and he didn't think anything of it until he got the teletype on Phoebe's disappearance. I urged him to try and dredge it up tonight."

"Is it a Volkswagen?"

"Apparently it is."

He took a shuddering breath, as if he was coming up from underwater. I said I would pick him up in a few minutes. Royal followed me downstairs to give me back my gun.

chapter 20

THE FLOODLIGHTS were on at Leafy Acres. Helen Trevor came out when I mounted the front steps. She shut the door softly behind her:

"May I speak to you for a moment, Mr. Archer?"

"Go ahead."

"Please don't tell my husband I intervened. I'm worried about Carl, deeply concerned for his health. I'm convinced he shouldn't make this—this nocturnal excursion with you."

"It's his idea."

"I realize that." She sighed, and rubbed her gray throat. The glare of the floodlights made her eyes seem huge and frantic. "Carl has always taken on more than his strength can bear. I know he appears to be a powerful man. He isn't, really. He had a coronary less than two years ago."

"How bad a coronary?"

"He barely survived it. Only my prayers brought him through, I do believe. The doctor told me another attack would—might possibly kill him. And I can't live without him, Mr. Archer. Please don't let him go with you."

"I can hardly stop him. Don't worry, I'll do the driving."

"It's not just the driving I'm worried about. It's the emo-

tional shock he may meet at the other end. He's had a night
and a day of terrible strain already. The only thing that's
kept him going is the hope that she is alive. If he should
discover that Phoebe is dead—"

Her voice lost itself in dry shallows. She turned her face
away from the light, perhaps for fear of what I'd see
in it. Her hatchet profile was caricatured by her shadow
on the door. She was an unattractive woman who knew she
was unattractive, had probably known it the day she lifted
her bridal veil for her husband's kiss. Such knowledge could
make a wife possessive as hell.

"You'd better take it up with your husband directly, Mrs.
Trevor."

"I tried to. He wouldn't listen. He treats me as an enemy,
when all I'm trying to do is save his life. He insists on
rushing around like a madman—it's part of his illness."

"I doubt that. Phoebe is important to him."

"Too important," she said bitterly. "He puts her ahead of
me—ahead of his own welfare. I wasn't able to give him a
child, you see. He's been fixated on my brother's child ever
since she was born." She added on a deep breaking wave
of feeling: "God chose to make me barren."

Her fingers crept down from her throat to her meager
breast. Her face was fierce and haggard. I was beginning
to feel some of the angry strain that knotted Trevor's arteries.

"Will you please tell your husband I'm here? I promise
to look after him as well as I can. If his heart kicks up
I'll take him to a doctor. But I think you're borrowing
trouble, Mrs. Trevor."

"I assure you I'm not. He looked like death itself when
he came down from the city. He didn't even take his nap,
and he was up all last night."

"He can sleep in the car."

"You don't *care* about him."

"I care in a different way. A man has to do what he has
to do."

"You men!"

It was a declaration of war. She turned abruptly and
went into the house, not inviting me to go along. I leaned
on the wall and looked across the weirdly shadowed lawn.
A fuller moon than last night's was rising behind the trees.
It gleamed through their branches like a woman's breast
pressing against wrought iron.

Trevor came out quickly, slamming the door. He nodded
to me and glanced up at the moon as if its rising was an

augury. His features had sharpened in the course of the day. His eyes were bright and dry.

"I'm not so sure you should make this trip," I said. "How are you feeling?"

"Fine. I feel fine. Has Helen been putting bees in your bonnet, by any chance?"

"She brought up the fact of your coronary."

"Nonsense. It's completely healed." He doubled his fist and struck out at the air, to demonstrate his fitness. "I ride, I swim. But she goes on trying to make a bloody invalid out of me. Let's go, eh?"

He practically raced me to the car. Inside, I could hear him breathing hard and trying to conceal it. His wife called from the veranda:

"Carl? Have you got your digitalis?"

He growled something inarticulate. Her voice rose to a bird's scream:

"Carl? Your digitalis?"

"I have the damn stuff," he muttered, and I amplified his answer: "He has it, Mrs. Trevor."

She watched us go, rigid and gray-faced. Following Trevor's directions, I turned right out of the driveway onto a black-top road that rose between black trees towards the moon.

"It's good of you to do this for me, Archer. I wouldn't admit it to Helen but frankly I didn't feel like driving to Medicine Stone by myself."

"I'm not doing it for you. I'm just as interested in the outcome as you are."

"How could you be? You don't even know her."

"No. But I haven't entirely given up hope of that."

"Then you don't think it's her car they found?"

"We'd better wait and see. How far is it to Medicine Stone?"

"Just about a hundred miles from my driveway."

The trees increased in size as we climbed into the hills. The road became a tunnel cut by my headlight beams out of branching darkness, which closed behind us. Trevor said after a while:

"This killing you say you walked in on—is it connected with Phoebe in any way?"

"In several ways. Through her mother, for one. I'd give a good deal to talk to Catherine Wycherly again."

"I thought you were going to have her looked for."

"Willie Mackey refused to take the assignment."

"Why?"

"He's too busy," I said diplomatically. "Then other things came up. A lot of other things came up. I'll get back to the problem of having her looked for tomorrow."

He turned towards me heavily. I could feel his straining eyes almost palpable on my face:

"You think Catherine killed Ben Merriman, don't you?"

"And possibly Stanley Quillan, the record-shop proprietor."

"I can't believe it. What motive would she have?"

"They took her for her money. Merriman used his brother-in-law Quillan to buy the Mandeville house for less money than it was worth. They turned around and sold it to Catherine Wycherly for more money than it was worth."

"You don't commit murder because somebody cheats you in a real-estate deal."

"It wasn't just a real-estate deal. Merriman sold the house again the other day and forced Mrs. Wycherly to give him most of the money she got for it."

"How could he force her to do that?"

"The obvious answer is blackmail."

"Blackmail for what?"

"I only know what people tell me. I talked to a man in San Mateo today—manager of an apartment house called the Conquistador. Phoebe stayed there for some days after her disappearance, in an apartment which her mother had leased. Quillan lived in the apartment next door. He had Phoebe's bedroom bugged. I don't pretend to understand the situation, but it wasn't a good one. The manager, Girston, told me further that Phoebe left the Conquistador in Merriman's company."

"Where did they go?"

"Apparently she was on her way to see her mother in Sacramento. She never got there, if Catherine Wycherly can be believed; which I doubt."

"All of this is new to me," Trevor said thoughtfully. "At least it means that Phoebe has been seen alive since November second."

"I have several witnesses to that."

"You think she's been killed since then?"

"We'd better let the evidence tell us, when we get to it."

That held Trevor, as it was intended to. We had begun the long descent from the ridge. The trees fell away; the darkness opened; the sea spread out before us, paved down the middle with broken moonlight. We drove south on the coastal highway for over an hour, between bare fields and deserted beaches, through redwood forest that blotted out the sky, along rising bluffs. On our right the moon slid

up the darkness, trailing its broken silver on the surface
of the ocean.

Trevor glanced at the water every now and then. "I can't
believe she's in there," he said once, but he was shivering.

Medicine Stone was a wide place in the highway among
the redwoods. It seemed to be largely composed of tourist
lodges faced with unpeeled logs. Its main building was a
combination of general store, gas station, motel, post office,
and coffee shop. The coffee shop spilled light through its
front window. Someone had scrawled in soap on the glass:
Breakfast Twenty-four Hours. Above it a red neon sign,
incongruous with the surrounding trees, bore the name Gayley.

Trevor and I went in. The little café was empty, but
I heard the slop and clatter of dishwashing in a back room.
I rapped with a quarter on the formica counter. An old man
came out of the back room wiping his hands on the front
of his long white apron.

"Sorry, gemmen," he said around ill-fitting false teeth,
"I can't serve you. Mrs. Gayley's cook, and she ain't here.
Nobody's here 'ceptin' me, and they don't let me cook. Ac-
count of I ain't been checked by the County Health."
The spiderwebs of senility dimmed his eyes and drew his
mouth into a one-sided grin.

Trevor said: "Where is everybody?"

"Down at the beach. They're trying to bring up a car
that went over the cliff. That's what they get for racing
around in their roadsters. Bang. Kerplash."

"Can you tell us where the place is?" Trevor said impatiently.

"Let's see. You headed south?"

"South."

"Then it's the second turn on your right, about two miles
down the road. Just follow it all the way. Only not too
far all the way." He guffawed. His false teeth slipped down
and lent him a ghastly look, like a laughing skull.

"Did the car go over at Painted Cove?"

"That's right. Take the road to Painted Cove. You know
these parts?"

"I have a summer cottage about halfway between here
and Terranova."

"Thought I reckernized your physog."

I gave the old man the quarter, and we drove down the
highway. The road to Painted Cove was rutted dirt eked out
here and there with gravel. It wound interminably through
redwood forest. The trees hung over us like pyramids held

up by rough brown columns. Then there were lights beyond
them.

The road unwound onto a mesa which broke off suddenly
in a sheer sea cliff. A heavy tow truck had been backed
to its edge. Several cars, official and unofficial, were parked
near it, and twelve or fifteen people were standing rather
aimlessly around. The crane on the back of the big truck
stuck out over the cliff edge like a gallows, with a cable
hanging from it.

We walked towards it across the uneven ground. The
truck had the legend, Gayley's Garage, painted on the door
of the cab. The only active man in sight was a uniformed
deputy handling a searchlight on the rear end of the truck-
bed. Its beam fell down the basalt face of the cliff and
shone on the moving water thirty-five or forty feet below.
A black head like a seal's broke the surface; I caught the
gleam of a diving mask. The diver submerged again.

Trevor reached up and touched the deputy's leg. "Did
you get the car out, officer?"

The man turned on him fiercely. "You don't see it, do
you? Stand back from the edge."

Trevor stepped back, and almost lost his balance. I took
his arm. Muscles were like straining wood; a steady tremor
ran through them under my fingers. I tried to pull him
away. He wouldn't budge. He stood sighting down the cable
at the water, trying to penetrate its black-and-silver surface.

A broad old man came up to us. He had a face like
carved redwood burl under his wide-brimmed hat.

"Mr. Trevor!"

He offered Trevor his hand, and after a moment of complete blankness Trevor took it: "How are you, Sheriff?"

"Tolerably well. I'm sorry to drag you away from home
on an errand like this."

"It can't be helped. You didn't get the car out?"

"Not yet. It's wedged between two boulders and filled
with sand. I'm commencing to think it'll take a sky-hook
to yank her."

"Is there anyone in it?"

"There was."

"What do you mean, there was?"

"We got her out of there and brought her up a couple
hours ago." He glanced down at the sea as if it was his
personal enemy. "What was left of her."

"My niece?"

"It sure looks like it, Mr. Trevor. It's her car, and she
was in it. I never knew the little lady myself."

Trevor thrust his peaked face towards him. "Where is she?"

"Over there."

The sheriff pointed with a solemn arm towards a covered thing on the ground in the furthest zone of light. I saw as we moved towards it that it was a blanket-wrapped body strapped to a stretcher. The Sheriff said to Trevor:

"If you feel up to looking at her, I'd sure appreciate it. We haven't got a positive identification."

"Of course."

"It won't be nice. She's been in the water for a couple of months."

"Don't beat around the bush. Show her to me."

The sheriff uncovered her face and turned his flashlight on it. The sea-change she had undergone had aged her rapidly and horribly. She was beaten and bloated and ravaged. A blur of tears stung my eyes, and a blur of anger. The people stood around in absolute silence.

"It's Phoebe," Trevor said.

His face was bone-white, bone-hard. He looked around helplessly, as if he could feel the early shocks of an earthquake that was going to topple the cliff. The shocks went through him visibly. He fell to his knees beside her. I thought he was trying to pray. But his body continued its loose downward movement until his head struck the earth.

He rolled onto his back, his upturned face turning blue, his white teeth shining in it. I kneeled beside him, slipped his tie, unbuttoned his button-down collar. He forced out words:

"Digitalis. Right coat pocket."

I found the bottle and gave him a capsule from it, returning it to his pocket. He said through grinning teeth:

"Thanks. Bad one. Oxygen."

I touched his left breast. His heart was pounding like the dull random blows of doom. The Sheriff bent over us, his jowls hanging out from the bone structures of his face:

"Cardiac?"

"Yes," I said. "I shouldn't have brought him here."

"I better rush him into Terranova Hospital. We might as well fold up this operation for tonight."

He brought his car to Trevor. We helped him in. The storm of pain had gone through him and left him terribly slack.

"Good luck," I said.

He nodded and tried to smile. The Sheriff drove him away.

chapter 21

I WENT BACK to the cliff. The deputy on the truck-bed was switching his searchlight off and on. Down below, the black seal head broke water, and the diver turned his masked face up into the eye of the light. The deputy made scooping motions at him.

A man wearing overalls over a red shirt climbed into the cab of the truck and started the motor. Slowly, the winch began to wind in the cable. It lifted the black-suited diver from the water. With both hands grasping the loop at the end of the cable, he walked up to the cliff like a space man liberated from gravity. Some of the bystanders clapped as he stepped over the edge.

I saw when he took off his mask that he was a boy of eighteen or nineteen. He reminded me of Bobby Doncaster. He was very big for his age, with swimmer's shoulders exaggerated by his thick rubber suit. An aqualung was strapped to his back. A canvas bag, a long sheath knife, and a miniature crowbar swung from a web belt around his waist.

The man in overalls got out of the truck and helped him remove his aqualung and other gear. He growled at the boy in pride:

"Have you had your fill of the water for once?"

"Can't say I did, Dad."

The boy wasn't breathing hard. He didn't even look cold. He took off his flippers and swaggered around a little in his bare feet. The deputy interrupted his promenade:

"Did you get the trunk open, Sam?"

"Yep. There was nothing in it but some tools. I didn't bother to bring 'em up."

"What about the registration slip?"

"I couldn't find any sign of it. That doesn't mean a thing, though. The wave-action down there is pretty terrific."

I said: "It's a green Volkswagen, isn't it?"

"Used to be. Like I said, there's a lot of wave action under the cliff. It sand-blasted most of the paint off of her already."

"Are you the one who brought the body out?"

His face went sober. "Yessir."

"Was she in the front seat or the back?"

150

"The back. She was wedged down on the floor between the front and back seats. I had to dig her out of the sand in there. The car's chuck full of sand."

"Did you notice her clothes?"

"She wasn't wearing any," the deputy said. "She was wrapped in a blanket. You got a special interest in her, mister?"

"I'm a private detective, and I've been looking for the girl for some time. I came here with her uncle, Carl Trevor." I turned to the boy: "Do you mind if I ask you some more questions, Sam?"

Sam was willing, but his father intervened. "Let him get some dry clothes on first."

He helped his son to pull off his rubber suit, revealing long woollen underwear; and brought him jeans and a sweater from the truck. Sam's big moment was fading. The onlookers were straggling back to their cars. I followed the deputy to his:

"Do you have any witnesses to the accident?"

"No direct witnesses." He added grimly: "It was no accident, mister."

"I know that. Were there indirect witnesses?"

"Jack Gayley and his son think they saw the Volksie the same night it went over. Of course there's lots of green Volksies on the roads."

"Where did they see it?"

"Going past their place in Medicine Stone, headed this way. This was a couple of months ago, along about midnight. They were just closing up their station for the night, and this guy went by in the Volksie. The thing is both of them knew him, or so they claim. Young Sam says he even yelled hullo at him, but the guy didn't stop. I guess he had his reasons, if he had the body in the back seat."

"Who was he?"

"They don't know his name, or where he's from. He camped near Medicine Stone for a while last summer. Sam saw him at the beach a couple of times, and Jack says he was in their coffee shop more than once."

"Could they give you a description?"

"Yeah. Sheriff Herman's sending out an all-points on it. Young fellow with reddish hair, over six foot tall, good-looking, well-built." He clucked. "The damnedest types are taking up murder these days. He probably got the girl in a jam and figured that this was a way out."

"Yeah," I said absently. The description fitted Bobby Doncaster, who had been at Medicine Stone the previous August.

He had met her here, I thought, and parted with her here.

"The deputy looked into my face: "This ring any bells for you?"

It rang a dull dead tolling bell, but I denied it.

I caught the Gayleys before they took off in their tow-truck. They confirmed the deputy's story of the red-headed boy in the green Volkswagen driving through their little town at midnight. The boy said:

"He was going like a bat out of hell."

"Watch your language, Sam," his father put in.

"Hell isn't swearing."

"It is in my book. You don't want to get too big for your britches just because you can swim good under water."

The boy grinned sheepishly. I said to both of them: "Are you certain of your identification?"

"Pretty certain," the boy said. His father nodded, and he went on: "We still had our bright lights going, they shone on his face. I shouted something at him, but he didn't stop. He didn't even look sideways."

"But it was definitely someone you knew?"

"I wouldn't say I *knew* him. I saw him on the beach a couple of times last summer. We said hello."

"When last summer?"

"I think it was in August."

"Yeah," Jack Gayley said. "It was in August, couple of weeks before Labor Day. I remember he came into the coffee shop."

"You have a good memory."

"A thing like this sharpens up the memory."

"Did you ever see him with the girl?" I asked them.

The boy answered: "I did, once, at the beach. He was trying to teach her to use his surfboard. She wasn't doing too good at it."

"Where is the beach?"

"About a mile up that way." He pointed north. "There's a reef that makes pretty good breakers for surfing. He was camped near there."

"But you don't know who he was, or where he came from?"

They both shook their heads.

"Can either of you pin down the date you saw him drive through?"

Jack Gayley leaned on the side of his truck and looked out across the moony sea. "Deputy Carstairs asked us that. It isn't possible to palce it for sure. I think it was about two months ago, give or take a week. What do you say, Sam?"

"Couple of months ago."

"What were you doing when you saw him?"

"Getting ready to close up. We were late that night because of an emergency call we had. A guy from Candad had a blowout on the Terranova road and we had to go out about eleven o'clock and change his tire for him. He didn't even have a jack in his car."

"Anyway," Sam said, "you sold him a new tire."

"Do you keep a record of your tire sales, Mr. Gayley?"

"Sure, I keep duplicate sales slips on everything like that."

"Dated?"

"Yessirree."

"Let's go back to your place and see if we can find that particular sales slip."

He nodded briskly. "I get your point. Maybe we can put a date on it, after all. Let's see, it was a General tube-type black-wall."

I followed the tow-truck back to Medicine Stone and had two cups of coffee while the Gayleys went through their garage records. They found the sales slip; it was dated November 2.

"Does that mean anything to you?" Jack Gayley said.

"Yes. I don't know what."

Except that someone was lying. According to my witnesses, the cab-driver Nick Gallorini, the apartment manager Alex Girston, and the late Stanley Quillan, Phoebe had been alive in San Mateo for at least another week. I was sure it wasn't the Gayleys who were lying.

On my way through Terranova I stopped at the hospital, a flat-roofed one-storied building on the southern outskirts of town. The front door was unlocked, but there was nobody in the dim little lobby or behind the information desk. I started down a softly lighted corridor, and a nurse materialized in front of me.

She was a big woman who used her bigness to block my way. "Where do you think you're going?"

"I'm a friend of Mr. Carl Trevor's. He was brought in tonight with a heart attack."

"You can't see him. Nobody can see him."

"I know that. How is he doing?"

"As well as can be expected. He's resting comfortably."

"May I talk to his doctor?"

"Dr. Grundle has gone home. He'll be called if there's any change, I can assure you."

"Is Dr. Grundle a heart specialist?"

She answered tartly: "I'm not authorized to discuss doctors' qualifications."

"You can give me a yes or no."

"No then." She made an impatient movement. "I can't stand here talking. I'm the only R.N. on duty."

She sailed away under full spinnaker. I found a phone booth in the lobby and a dime in my pocket, which I used to place a collect call to Trevor's house in Woodside. His wife answered on the first ring:

"Of course I'll take the call." Her voice was a controlled screech. "What is it, Mr. Archer? What has happened?"

"The thing you were afraid of. Phoebe is dead. Your husband had to identify her, and it was a bad exp—"

Her voice cut in on mine: "He's had another coronary. Is he dead?"

"Nothing like that. He's in the Terranova hospital, doing all right. But you may want to get his own doctor to him."

"Yes. I'll call Dr. Wallace right away."

There was silence on the line, which seemed to need filling. I said:

"I'm sorry about this, Mrs. Trevor."

"You have reason to be, Mr. Archer."

She hung up on me.

chapter 22

IT WAS A ROUGH NIGHT, and it got no smoother. About three o'clock I pulled into the north side of Boulder Beach, where motel neons hung their cold lures on the darkness. I turned off the highway towards the college area. The campus lay like a city of the dead under ectoplasmic fog rolling up from the sea. The moon had a halo.

On the second floor of the Oceano Palms, light filtered through the drapes of the apartment which Phoebe Wycherly had shared with Dolly Lang. I didn't want to see Dolly just yet. I knocked on Mrs. Doncaster's door.

She answered with surprising speed, almost as though she'd been waiting for my knock. Her voice came thinly through the panels:

"Bobby? Is it you, Bobby?"

I knocked again, more softly. The door opened a few inches on a chain. Mrs. Doncaster peeped out over the brass links.

"May I come in?" I said. "I have news for you."

"Is it about Bobby?"

"Yes. It concerns your son."

She unhooked the chain and stepped back, swallowed up by the darkness. "I'll turn on a light. I've been sitting here in the dark."

She switched on a standing lamp. In a worn flannelette robe, her hair down in braids which hung limp on her limp breast, she looked old and defenseless. She said in a hushed voice which tried magically to deny what it believed:

"Bobby has been in an accident?"

"You could call it an accident. Please sit down, Mrs. Doncaster. We have things to talk about."

She backed into a chair under the pressure of my eyes. Her breath came out as she sat down:

"He's been killed."

"Bobby isn't the one who's been killed."

"Tell me what happened. I have a right to know."

I sat down near her on the piano bench. "You may know more than I do about what happened. Phoebe Wycherly's body was found in the sea near Medicine Stone, north of here. We made the identification tonight. Her car had been pushed or driven over a forty-foot cliff with her body in it."

Mrs. Doncaster looked up at her husband's photograph. The moustached man in the black frame smiled at the edge of the lamplight. In the full glare of the light, she blinked as if I'd slapped her across the eyes.

"What has this to do with my son?"

"He was seen driving her car through Medicine Stone the night of November the second. You told me he spent that entire weekend at home in bed."

"He did."

"We both know he didn't."

She swallowed. "I may have been mistaken. It's possible it was the weekend after that he had the flu."

"Are you ready to change your story?"

She nodded dully. Her braids twitched like dying grey snakes on her breast. She fingered one of them as she spoke:

"He went off by himself that weekend. He never told me where. He phoned me in the morning from the bus station—asked me to go down there and pick him up. Which I did. The poor boy looked like the wrath of—" She glanced up at her black-framed icon: "The wrath of gosh."

"How long had he been gone?"

"Just the one night."

"Did you ask him where he spent it?"

"Of course I asked him. I asked him over and over again,

if he was with that girl—with Phoebe. Over and over again
he denied it." The enormity of the situation silenced her.
She wrung her hands, and said in a breaking voice: "I did
my best for him. I did my best to bring him up without a
father's guidance. What can you do when they lie to you?"

"You can give up lying yourself."

"He's my only son, I was only trying to protect him. Anyway, you've got no proof that Bobby had anything to do with
her death. You can't have. He wouldn't hurt her. He was
fond of her, over-fond."

Her voice ran down. She sat hunched in her robe with the
pinched face of a little old woman. Her gaze flickered here
and there about the room.

"Where is Bobby tonight, Mrs. Doncaster?"

"I don't know. If I did know I wouldn't tell you."

"That's a queer line for you to take. You're supposed to
be a respectable woman."

She looked down at her shapeless body. "He's all I've got."
Perhaps that was the trouble.

She lifted her head slowly. "It's been such an effort, I've
racked my brain, trying to serve as mother *and* father to
him. I know he resents me, he always has. A woman can't
bring up a man. But I thought our life together was working
out." Tears glittered in the corners of her eyes. She drew
her fingers across them. "What am I to do?"

"Tell me the truth. Where is your son now?"

"I don't know. I swear." She shook her head, and the
tears ran down like mercury into the folds of her cheeks.

"If I can get to him and talk to him, we may be able to
make some sense out of this business."

She snatched at the forlorn hope: "You don't believe he
did it either, do you?"

"I don't want to believe it. His going on the run doesn't
help me much."

"Bobby isn't on the run. He's only been gone since suppertime. He said he had important business to attend to."

"Where?"

"He refused to tell me. It isn't like Bobby. He's never had
secrets from his mother. But when I tried to question him
this evening he walked out of the flat and drove away without a backward look."

"What kind of a car is he driving?"

"His same old jalopy. I believe it's an A-model Ford."

"Did he seem frightened?"

"He was more excited than frightened. It worried me."

"Why, Mrs. Doncaster?"

"I suppose I've got into the habit of worrying—the way he's been moping around these last months. Then all of a sudden he received this telephone call, and he started acting like a cat on a hot stove. He could hardly contain himself, it didn't seem *healthy*. He wouldn't even stay to eat his supper."

"You didn't mention a telephone call."

"Didn't I? I meant to. That was what set him off."

"Who called him?"

"He wouldn't say. He wouldn't tell me anything about it."

"Was it a local call, or long distance?"

"I have no way of knowing. Whoever it was made a mistake, you see. Or more likely they were trying to get to him behind my back. They called him on Dolly Lang's telephone."

"Dolly Lang took the call?"

"That's right. Afterwards I tried to get it out of her who it was on the phone. The little minx claims she doesn't know." Her eyes were bright and hostile. The tears in them had evaporated. After her moment of vulnerability, her nature was closing and hardening up like scar-tissue over wounds. "Maybe she'll be willing to talk to you. You're a man."

I climbed the outside stairs, feeling as grey and vague as my late moon-shadow climbing the wall beside me. Dolly's light was still on. She must have heard me coming. Before I could knock, she opened the door and looked out eagerly, her head thrust forward birdlike on her neck.

The eagerness wilted when she recognized me. "Oh. It's you."

"Who were you expecting?"

She answered with forced airiness. "Nobody. I don't make a habit of entertaining at this hour of the night."

She was still wearing the sweater and jeans in which I had last seen her. Her face had a grey and greasy pallor. She looked as though she hadn't washed in the interval, or combed her hair.

"I didn't pick the hour," I said. "It picked me. You're up late, Dolly."

"I gave up sleeping for Lent. I know it isn't Lent yet, but I'm anticipating."

"It was nervous chatter. Her eyes were flat as dimes. In the room behind her a sleepy girl's voice said something loud and inarticulate, like "Grahh!"

Dolly stepped outside and closed the door quietly. "My roommate's sleeping. She hasn't broken the habit. What's on your mind?" Her tone was brittle. She seemed older and more aggressive, at the same time less assured, than she had the day before.

"What's on your mind, Dolly?"

"Nothing much. We could talk about the weather."

She glanced around her pertly, like a slightly mechanical bird. The fog streamed up the slanting street from the ocean. The substance of the night itself seemed to be moving and dissolving below and above and around us.

"Foggy, isn't it?" she said.

"Let's dispel a little fog."

"That would be nice. I hate fog. It always reminds me of clammy shrouds and things." A spasm of shivering took hold of her, and let go. "Don't pay any attention to me. I'm on a coffee jag. For Lent."

"Could we go somewhere and talk?"

"I don't want to go somewhere and talk," she said with a little-girl's whine in her voice. "We can talk right here if we have to."

"We have to, all right. You took a telephone call for Bobby this evening."

"Did I?"

"We won't play word games. That telephone call may be a matter of life or death. For him."

Her grey little anxious face tilted up beside my shoulder. "That's what *he* said. I promised him not to tell anyone about it."

"I'm going to ask you to tell me."

"Why is it so important? Is it about Phoebe?"

"What gave you that idea?"

"The way he reacted. I mean, his face lit up when he—" She drew in her breath sharply. "I promised not to *tell* anyone. I wouldn't even tell his mother, and she got really nasty."

"I'm not his mother."

"I didn't think you were. But you are a detective, and all. I wouldn't want to get Bobby into trouble."

"You can't get him in any deeper than he is. I simply want to reach him before the police do."

"The police? Are they after him?"

"They will be by tomorrow."

"What did he do?"

"I'm afraid I can't answer that. You wouldn't like the answer, anyway. If you really want to help him, and help me, you can do it by giving me all the details of that call."

"I don't *know* any details. He asked me to leave the room when he was talking."

"Who was he talking to?"

"I tell you I don't *know*."

"I thought you answered the phone."

"I did, but it was just the operator. She said she had a person-to-person call for Mr. Robert Doncaster, so I went down and got him."

"What time was this?"

She hesitated. "About a quarter to six."

"Did the operator say where the call was from?"

"Palo Alto. That's where Stanford is, where Phoebe used to go, and I got the wild idea that it was Phoebe calling. I guess I'm not over it yet—I couldn't sleep tonight for thinking about her. You know, like maybe she lost her memory and all she remembered was Bobby's name and her own telephone number—"

I cut in harshly, speaking to myself as well as her: "Lay it to rest, Dolly. It wasn't Phoebe."

"I know that, really. Bobby said it wasn't, and he wouldn't lie to me, not about that."

"Did he give you any hint as to who it was?"

"No. He said it was his private business."

"What else did he say?"

"He thanked me, quite effusively. That's all. About five minutes after that I saw him drive away in the direction of the highway. He took off like jets."

"And you say he seemed pleased or excited?"

"Very excited."

"In a good sense? Or was he high?"

She pondered. "I don't really know. Bobby's been so low all winter, it's hard to say what's natural for him. He was pretty tense tonight. But happy, too—out of this world, sort of. As if he was off to seek the Holy Grail." She looked up at the moon, which had become hardly more than a dimness in the darkness. She shivered, and hugged herself. "I'm cold, Mr. Archer. And I don't even know what this is all about."

"Neither do I, Dolly. Give me another minute or two, though, will you?"

"Certainly, if it's any help."

"You're being a great help. Tell me—you're a sociologist—has Bobby ever shown signs of neurotic or emotional trouble?"

"Of course, he's very neurotic. Who isn't? Phoebe and I used to talk about his mother-fixation. He's got a bad one, but he's been fighting it."

"How?"

"By growing up. You know, untentacling the tentacles, living his own life. He's had some terrific fights with his mother this year. They come up through the floor."

"Physical fights?"

"I don't mean that. Just words."

"Does he threaten her?"

"Not that I know of. It's mostly about quitting school and going off on his own."

"Is that what he's done, do you think?"

"I wouldn't be surprised."

"Did he ever threaten anyone with physical harm? You or Phoebe, for instance?"

Dolly giggled cheerlessly. "Of course not. Bobby's always been fantastically meek and mild. That was one of Phoebe's objections to him. She used to call him Christian Slave, from 'When I was a king in Babylon you were a Christian slave.'"

"Would you consider him capable of violence?"

"Violence to Phoebe?" she said with her hands at her breast. "Is that what you're getting at?"

"Yes."

She shook her head in a narrow jerky movement. "He would never hurt Phoebe, you can be sure of that. I never saw a fellow so gone on a girl. Honestly." But she touched my arm for reassurance. "Has something happened to Phoebe?"

"I'm afraid so, Dolly."

"Is she dead?"

"I'm afraid so."

She pulled back her hand as if she had burned it on me. At the same time she fell towards me, literally fell. I found myself holding her up, stroking her tousled head. It was not a sexual occasion.

"God damn it," she said in a very young voice. "I gave up praying when I was a kid. For Lent. I took it up again last November. I prayed every night for two months. And Phoebe is dead anyway. There is no God."

I said she could be right, she could be wrong. If there was a God, He worked in mysterious ways. Like people. She turned away from me and my platitudes and leaned on the door, her forehead against the wood. Her hand was on the doorknob. She seemed to lack the will or strength to turn it.

"I'm sorry I had to be the one to tell you," I said. "Still it's better than reading it in the newspapers."

"Yes. Thank you. How did she die?"

"We don't know yet. But she's been dead for two months." I touched her shoulder. "Will you do one other thing for me?"

"If I can. I don't feel well."

"Just let me use your phone."

"But my roommate's sleeping. She hates when I wake her up."

"I'll keep my voice down."

"All right."

She let me in. A girl with pull-taffy hair lay huddled under a blanket on the studio bed. The telephone stood on the desk beside the big old typewriter. The same half-filled sheet of typescript was in the machine. I sat in front of it and reread Dolly's unfinished sentence:

"Many authorities say that socio-economic factors are predominate in the origins of antisocial behaviour, but others are of the opinion that lack of love" . . .

The e's were out of allignment. The e's were out of alignment, and it was an old Royal typewriter. I took out the letters that Willie Mackey had given me and made a quick comparison. They checked. Homer Wycherly's original letter to Mackey, the threatening letters, and Dolly's essay, had all been written on the same typewriter. This one.

"What are you doing?" she whispered at my ear.

"I just discovered something. Where did you get this typewriter?"

"Phoebe lent it to me. When she didn't come back, I went on using it. Is that all right?"

"It was until now. I'm going to have to take it with me now."

"What for?"

"It's a clue," I said. "Do you know where Phoebe got hold of it?"

"No. It's an old one, though, it must be twenty years old. She must have bought it secondhand. But that isn't like Phoebe. She bought things new."

The girl on the studio bed turned over and called in a sleep-filled voice: "What are you doing, Dolly? Go to bed."

"You go back to sleep."

The girl turned her face to the wall and complied.

"What does the clue mean?" Dolly said.

"I couldn't begin to guess." I glanced up at her tense small face: she looked like a bunny after a hard Easter. "Why don't you settle down now and take your friend's advice.

Warm yourself some milk and drink it down like a good girl and by that time I'll be out of here. You can get some sleep."

"I guess it's worth trying," she said in a doubtful voice. She went into the kitchen and rattled pans.

I dialled the long-distance operator and told her: "This is Robert Doncaster. I had a person call from Palo Alto last evening shortly before six. Can you tell me what number in Palo Alto the call was placed from?"

"I'm sorry, sir, we don't have a record of that. On incoming calls, we only keep a record of the numbers called at this end."

"Is there any way I can find out who called me?"

"I don't know, sir. I'll put you in touch with my supervisor."

There was a click and a wait. An older, brisker, female voice said: "This is the long-distance supervisor. Can I help you?"

"I hope so. This is Robert Doncaster speaking. I received a person call from Palo Alto at this number around six o'clock last evening. I'm trying to find out what number called me."

"Was it a direct-dial call? If so, we have no way of knowing."

"It was handled by an operator," I said.

"In that case, Palo Alto will have a record of it."

"Can you get the number from them?"

"We don't do that except in case of emergency."

"This is a very serious emergency."

She took my word for it. "Very well, I can try. What was your name again, sir?"

"Robert Doncaster."

"And the number?"

I read it to her off the dial.

"Do you wish me to call you back, or will you hold?"

"I'll hold on, thanks."

I sat and listened to faint fragments of conversation dangling at the verge of intelligibility; names of places, Portland, Salt Lake City; wisps of thought in the great empty mind of the night. The brisk voice drowned them out:

"I have your number, Mr. Doncaster. It's Davenport 93489 in Palo Alto."

"Whose number is it?"

"We don't give out that information even in an emergency. The Palo Alto office might tell you if you contacted them in person. That would be up to them." She added: "Or you could call the number."

"Of course. Do that, will you?"

The early-morning circuits were open, and the call went through right away. The telephone at the other end of the line rang in its unknown place. It rang sixteen times.

"I'm sorry, sir, your party does not answer. Do you wish me to call again later?"

"I'll call again later. Thank you."

I made a note of the number and got up to go. Dolly appeared in the kitchen doorway. She had a steaming cup in her hand, and a white milk moustache on her upper lip.

"Good night," I said. "No dreams. But don't stop praying."

She slumped into beat position, and made herself look like a maltreated idiot child. "What's the use of praying?"

"It keeps the circuits open. Just in case there's ever anybody on the other end of the line."

chapter 23

      I LUGGED THE OLD ROYAL out to my car and drove across town to the Boulder Beach Inn. At ten minutes to five in the morning the place was like a catacomb. The night clerk looked at me the way night clerks were always looking at me, with dubiety tinged by the suspicion that the customer might be right and I might be a customer:

"What can I do for you. Sir."

"Is Homer Wycherly still here?"

He didn't answer me directly. "Mr. Wycherly wouldn't wish to be disturbed at this hour. If you'd like to leave a message—"

"I work for Wycherly. What time did he ask to be called?"

He consulted his schedule. "Eight o'clock."

"Call me at the same time, please. I'm checking in. How much for a room?"

He told me.

"I'm renting, not buying."

He simpered delicately and handed me a pen. I registered. A Negro bell hop emerged from the shadows and led me to a room at the rear of the building where I stripped to my underwear, crawled dirty between clean sheets, and went out like a light.

I caught three hours of sleep at five dollars an hour. But the old movie projector I was using for a brain wouldn't

shut down. It kept on grinding out aquatic scenes in which
I became immersed, sinking like a spent swimmer in coiling
cold water, through deeping zones of chill where the dead
thronged like memories, their lank hair drifting in the underwater currents. I saw her plainly, frayed flesh worn dowdily
on her skeleton, little fish swimming in and out of the sockets
of her eyes.

I woke up with Phoebe's name in my dry mouth and a bell
ringing inside my head or just outside my head. I opened
my eyes to the full white horror of morning. The bedside
telephone rang at me again. I picked up the heavy iron dumbbell which the management had substituted for the receiver.

"You asked to be called at eight, sir," a girl's voice said.

"I must have been insane."

"Yessir."

"Wait a minute. Have you called Mr. Homer Wycherly
yet?"

"Yessir, just this minute."

"Get him on the line for me, will you please?"

"Yessir."

I propped myself up on the pillow. Something peculiar happened: I lost my sense of orientation in space. The facing
wall slanted over me, the bed leaned backwards under me. I
was stuck with my legs up in a corner of space, and space
tipped over like a chair.

"Who is it?" the iron dumbbell said in a voice like Wycherly's.

I answered doubtfully, upside down in the angular white
horror: "This is Archer."

Space jiggled a little. It started to right itself. I tried to
lean forward and help it but I was stuck in its corner, immo-
bilized by a stronger pull than gravity. I didn't want Phoebe
to be dead. I didn't want to have to tell her father that she
was.

"Archer? Where are you calling from?"

"I'm here in the hotel. I have news for you."

"What news? Have you found her?"

"No. You haven't heard then."

"Heard what?"

"I'd rather tell you in person. May I come around to your
bungalow in fifteen minutes?"

"Please do."

I hung up. The walls of the room were vertical. Space was
back where it belonged, up and down and across and from
side to side. I took advantage of this circumstance by getting

out of bed and having a quick shower and a shave. My eyes in the bathroom mirror looked scared as hell, or of it.

On the way to Wycherly's bungalow I got the typewriter out of the trunk of my car.

"What on earth is that?" he said when he opened the door.

"A Royal typewriter, vintage about 1937. Do you recognize it?"

"Bring it in and let me see it properly."

I followed him into the living room and set down the heavy machine on a coffee table near the windows. He looked it over with eyes like boiled blue onions.

"It could be Catherine's old typewriter. At least she had one very like it. Where did you dredge it up?"

"Your daughter's roommate had it. Phoebe lent it to her before she left."

Wycherly nodded. "I remember now. Catherine left it behind in the house, and Phoebe took it off to college last fall."

"Where was it last Easter?"

"In my house in Meadow Farms. Catherine used to keep it in her sitting room. She liked to have an office model handy."

"Is she an expert typist?"

"She was at one time. She used to be a secretary before I married her. This machine dates from that period."

"Did she ever do any typing for you in more recent times? Last spring, for instance?"

"She helped me out occasionally, yes." An edge of old malice entered his voice: "When she was in a conciliatory mood, and available."

"You wrote a letter to Willie Mackey last spring, about the threatening letters you received. Did Mrs. Wycherly type it for you?"

"I believe she did. On second thought, I remember that she did. I preferred to keep it in the family—the fact that I was hiring a detective."

"Can't you type yourself?"

"I never learned, no."

"Not even with one finger?"

"No. I've never manipulated one of these things in my life." He stroked his hair with a nervous hand. "What is the relevance of all this, if any?"

"I had a talk with Mackey yesterday. At my request, since I'm employed by you, he filled me in on those 'Friend of the Family' letters. It's my opinion they were typed on this typewriter."

"For God's sake!" He slumped on the mohair sofa and

pressed his hand to the side of his face as if it needed holding together. "You're not suggesting that Catherine wrote them herself."

"The facts suggest it."

"But you don't know what was said in them. It's impossible."

"Nothing is impossible in this case. Who else had access to the typewriter?"

"Anyone in the house, anyone who came to the house. Servants, guests, anyone. Catherine's rooms were in a wing by themselves, and she was seldom in them. There's no lock on the sitting room, either. Understand me, I hold no brief for my ex-wife, but she simply couldn't have written those letters. They slandered her."

"People have been known to slander themselves."

"But what purpose could she have had?"

"To make trouble, break up the marriage. She wouldn't have needed to have a rational motive."

"Are you implying that Catherine was irrational?"

"Is. I saw her the night before last, Mr. Wycherly. I don't know what her emotional state was nine months ago. She's in a bad way now."

He lifted his hands and thrust them out away from him, fingers stiff. He might have been trying to fend off furies.

"Is this your great news? I thought you were going to tell me something—something hopeful about Phoebe." His arms dropped to his sides, and his fingers plucked at the buttons on the sofa. "What good are these excursions into the wretched past? I know that Catherine is capable of anything. I even suspected that she wrote those letters."

"Is that why you took Mackey off the case?"

He nodded. His head stayed low, as if it was too heavy for his neck.

"Were the allegations in the letters true? Specifically, was she having an affair with another man last spring?"

"I suspected that she was. I had no proof. I had no real desire to look for proof. I loved my wife, you see."

I didn't see, but I heard him saying it.

"From the first of last year," he went on, "she spent a great deal of time away from home. She never would tell me where she went, where she stayed. She claimed to have a studio somewhere, that she went away to paint."

"She had an apartment in San Mateo," I said. "The chances are she was sharing it with a man or men. Assuming that, do you have any idea who he or they might have been?"

"No."

"Did you ever question her on the point?"

"Not directly. Frankly, I hesitated to. She sometimes had such violent reactions."

"Did she ever offer to kill anyone?"

"Many times."

"Who did she threaten?"

"Me," he said dismally.

"I'm going to ask you a question you won't like. Did you prepare those 'Friend of the Family' letters yourself, to satisfy your doubts about your wife?"

Mrs. Wycherly wasn't the only one who had violent reactions. He got up blotched and roaring, shaking both fists at me like a child in a tantrum: "How dare you, you garbage-raker!" He called me other names. I waited for him to subside. It didn't take long. He fizzled out like a damp firecracker, sputtering: "That's insane. You must be crazy."

"Then humor me. Answer the question."

"I had nothing to do with those ugly letters. They came as a fearful blow to me."

"How did they affect Phoebe?"

"She was upset, in her quiet way. She takes things quietly, but deep and hard."

"And your wife?"

"Catherine was very cool about the whole thing. It's one reason I asked her to type the letter to Mackey. I wanted to see how she'd react."

"How did she?"

"She was perfectly cool and calm—which wasn't usual for her. She stayed that way throughout the entire business. Then the week after Easter she went to Reno, and her lawyers wrote me asking for a settlement."

"Were you surprised by that development?"

"I'd reached the point," he said, "Where nothing had the power to surprise me. Nothing in this world."

"How did Phoebe feel about the divorce?"

"She was deeply hurt and shocked."

"Children take sides when their parents divorce. Which side did your daughter take?"

"Mine, naturally. I thought I'd made that clear the other day. We seem to be going back and forth over the same old ground."

I was putting off breaking new ground, for fear the shock of Phoebe's death would make him unavailable for questioning. I still had questions to ask him:

"You recall the day you sailed, and Mrs. Wycherly came aboard?"

"To wish me bon voyage," he said wryly. "I'm not likely to forget it."

"Were you aware that Phoebe left the ship with her mother?"

"They left my stateroom together, at least Phoebe followed her out. I had no idea that they left the ship in each other's company."

"They rode away together in a taxi. They seemed to be good friends for the moment. At least Phoebe agreed to visit her mother in Atherton that evening."

"How do you know all this?"

"It's my business to find out such things. It's also my business to ask you if you left the ship that evening."

"For heaven's sake, are you suspicious of me?"

"Suspicion is my occupational hazard, Mr. Wycherly. You didn't tell me the sailing was delayed till the morning of the third. You let me assume it went off on schedule."

"I'd forgotten about the delay. It slipped my mind."

"That could happen, I suppose. Surely you remember, though, if you left the ship that evening."

"I did not. I resent the question. I resent your whole line of questioning. It's insulting and contemptible and I won't put up with it." He glared at me with warmed-over rage in his eyes. He couldn't hold it. In a voice that was almost querulous, he said: "What are you getting at?"

"I'm trying to get at a situation that led to a death. Three deaths, as a matter of fact, and one near miss. How's your cardiovascular system, Mr. Wycherly?"

"All right. At least it was all right when I had my last checkup, shortly before I sailed. Why?"

"Carl Trevor had a heart attack last night."

"Carl did? I'm sorry to hear it," he said in a light queer voice. A strange expression entered his eyes, a foxy curiosity. "How is he?"

"I don't know. It's his second attack, and it hit him hard. I left him in the hospital in Terranova."

"What on earth is he doing in that primitive hole?"

"Recovering, I hope. He and I went to Medicine Stone to look into a report that a car had been found in the sea. It turned out to be your daughter's car, and it had a body in it, a woman's body. Trevor identified her. Then he keeled over."

"Was it Phoebe?"

"I'm afraid so, Mr. Wycherly."

He went to the window and stood there for quite a long time looking out at the empty morning. Something indescribable happened to his body. It seemed to me as I watched him that the knowledge of his grief entered his body. When he turned back into the room the foxy look had been wiped from his eyes and mouth. He said in a deeper voice than I'd heard from him:

"So that's your news. My daughter is dead."

"I'm afraid so. There is one element of doubt—a discrepancy among the facts I've collected. According to one set of facts, Phoebe went into the sea the night of November second: her car was seen around midnight going through Medicine Stone."

"Was she driving it?"

"I'm not prepared to report on who was driving it. As I said, there's a discrepancy. According to another set of facts, Phoebe was living in her mother's apartment in San Mateo for a week after November second. I should say that a girl who called herself Smith and who fits Phoebe's description was living there."

Hope flared up in his eyes. "Smith was my wife's maiden name. Phoebe would naturally use it. It means she's still alive."

"I'm afraid it doesn't, Mr. Wycherly. Your brother-in-law Trevor made a positive identification of her body. You might say it was confirmed by his heart attack."

"I see what you mean. Carl was very fond of her." He paced up and down the room, a fat bear of a man caged by reality. "No fonder than I was," he said, as if that helped. He turned to face me, his face slack and naked in the light. "Where is Phoebe now?"

"In the morgue in Terranova. It might be a good idea for you to go up there, today. Please don't get your hopes up. She isn't pretty or easy to look at, and I'm very much afraid that you'll recognize your daughter."

"But you said she was alive in San Mateo, long after she was supposed to be dead. It must be another girl you found in the water."

"No. It's more likely that it was another girl who was seen in San Mateo."

chapter 24

I DROVE BACK UP to the Peninsula. I was bone tired, in spite of my fifteen-dollar sleep. Still I was tugged along by a sense of people and places and meanings coming together, filled with that abstract kind of glee which a mathematician has when he's just about to square the circle. He thinks.

The assistant manager of the telephone company in Palo Alto admitted after some palaver that the number from which Bobby Doncaster had been called belonged to a public telephone in a booth on the grounds of a gas station at Bayshore and Cedar Lane.

There were no cedars on Cedar Lane, no trees of any kind. Its asphalt roadway, pocked by traffic, ran through a housing tract that was already decaying into slum, and ended abruptly at the roaring highway. Harry's Service Station (We Give Blue Chip Stamps) was on the corner. I noticed the metal and glass telephone booth standing by itself like a sentry box at the edge of Harry's lot.

I pulled in beside the pumps, and a quick gray man came running out of the office. He looked very eager and a little punchy, like a retired welterweight or a superannuated Navy mechanic. The name Harry was embroidered on the chest of his white coveralls.

"Yessir," he announced.

"Fill her up. She ought to take about ten."

While the gas was running, I got out and looked at the number of the telephone in the booth. Davenport 93489. I returned to my car and Harry. He was wiping away at the windshield as if he had a cleanliness compulsion.

"Need change to phone?"

"No thanks. I'm a detective working on a murder case."

"What do you know." I couldn't tell if he was being sardonic or naïve.

"One of our suspects had a telephone call last night from that booth over there. That was shortly before six. Were you on duty?"

"Yeah, and I think I know the one you mean. You ain't the first one that's been asking for her."

"A woman?"

"You're not kidding." He made the hourglass gesture with his hands. His wiping-rag flapped in the air. "Big blondie in a purple dress. I made change for her."

"Change for what?"

"So she could phone long-distance. She gimme a fifty-dollar bill out of her shoe."

"Where did she come from?"

"Up the hike." Harry pointed up Cedar Lane towards the

central section of Palo Alto. "She ankled in here like her feet were hurting."

"Walking?"

"Yeah. That struck me funny, too. She looked like class."

"Describe her."

He described her. It was the Wycherly woman.

"You're sure she was the one who made the phone call?"

"I couldn't be wrong about that. Right in the middle of it, while she was still talking, she hailed me over to the booth. She wanted to know the name of the nearest motel. That happens to be the Siesta. I told her she wouldn't want to stay there. She said she would."

"And did she?"

"I couldn't say. She ankled off in that direction after she finished her phone call."

"Which direction?"

"San Jose direction. The Siesta's about a quarter mile that way, you can see the sign. It's a crummy joint, like I tried to tell her. But she shut me up and went on talking into the phone."

"Did you hear what she said?"

"Not a thing. I didn't listen."

"How was she acting?"

"Acting?"

"I mean, was she drunk or sober—did she seem to know what she was doing?"

"That's what the other fellow wanted to know." Harry scratched his head with black fingernails. "She walked straight, she talked straight. I guess you could say she was plenty nervous, though. Like I told the other fellow."

"Big boy with red hair?"

"Naw, he wasn't red-haired, and he was no boy. I think he was some kind of a doctor. He had the emblem on his car."

"What kind of a car?"

"1959 light blue Impala two-door."

"Did he give you his name?"

"Maybe he did. I don't remember. I was pretty busy at the time."

"What time?"

"Couple hours ago. I told him everything I told you. He went off in the direction of the Siesta."

"Can you describe him?"

"I dunno. He looked like a doctor. You know how they give you the once-over like you was a patient. He had

thick glasses, I noticed that, and he was well-dressed. He
had on a brown tweed topcoat that must of set him back
plenty."

"How old?"

"Forty-five—fifty maybe. He had grey in his moustache.
Older than me. And heavier."

A road-grimed station wagon with an Oregon license came
off the highway and stopped on the other side of the pumps.
Three children in the back seat peered around with travel-
drugged eyes, wondering if this was Disneyland. Jets went
over. The driver of the station wagon gave Harry a Barney-
Oldfield look across his wife. This was a pit-stop.

Harry said to me: "That will be five-oh-nine. You want the
stamps?"

I paid him. "Skip the stamps. Keep the change. Thanks
for the information."

"Thank you."

He ran around the pumps flapping his rag.

The Siesta Motor Court stood on scorched earth near a
truck-stop diner. Its sign advertised Modern Housekeeping
Facilities. Its cabins had cracks in the stucco as if they'd
been leaned on by a giant hand, not lovingly. The place
was a couple of levels below the Champion Hotel, which
was not the Ritz.

I stopped beside the hutch marked Office, and climbed out
onto crunching cinders. A cutdown A-model Ford was
parked in front of a cabin at the rear. I went and looked at
the steering-post. Bobby Doncaster's name and his address
in Boulder Beach were on the registration slip. I wrenched
at the door of his present address. It was locked. The window beside it was covered with a cracked green blind.

A door opened somewhere behind me. A fat woman wearing a man's sweater-coat over a flowered print dress came
out of the office and undulated ponderously towards me.
Earrings the size and color of brass curtain rings swung
from her ears. She had soot-black hair with a single slash of
white running back from her widow's-peak like a lightning
scar.

"Roust out of it, you," she said in a deep raw voice. "I
know how to use this."

She showed me a little nickel-plated revolver. It looked
tiny as a toy in her large dimpled hand. She was breathing
hard.

"I'm not a burglar, ma'am."

"I don't care who you are. Roust out of it."

"I'm a detective. Put the gun up."

I displayed an old special-deputy badge that the L.A. sheriff had given me for not particularly good conduct. She was impressed. She pushed the gun down her dress, where the bivalve of her bosom swallowed it.

"So what you want with us? We run a clean place. All that trouble last year was under a different management."

I was keeping one eye on the door of the cabin. "Is the red-headed boy in there?"

"You want him?"

"I'm not the only one."

She made a mournful face. "We're not responsible for the people—"

"That's not the point. Is he in there?"

"I don't think so. I didn't see him come back."

I said to the cabin door: "Come out, Bobby, or I'm coming in."

There was no response from inside. I leaned my shoulder against the flimsy door.

"What you think you're doing?" the woman cried. "You don't want to bust the door. Wait a minute now."

She went away and came back jingling a key-ring. While she unlocked the door I took my gun out. It was gun day. I stepped into the dim blinded interior. It smelled of breaths and bodies. The furniture in the greenish gloom resembled underwater wreckage at a depth where nothing stirred.

The fat woman pulled a chain that turned on the ceiling light. It shone through a white glass globe like a fly-specked moon on a peeling veneer chest of drawers, a rug the color of packed earth, a double bed that had been slept in. Its sheets looked as if a pair of cell-mates had passed the night twisting them into ineffectual ropes for some frustrated escape. On the floor beside the bed a canvas overnight bag lay unzipped. It was stencilled with the initials R.D. and contained a change of underwear, some shirts and handkerchiefs, toothbrush and toothpaste and razor, and a checkbook whose last stub showed a balance of two-hundred-odd dollars in a Boulder Beach bank.

I glanced into the kitchenette. On the sinkboard a half-eaten hamburger with pink insides reposed on a paper plate. The dusty bland eyes of a cockroach regarded me from behind the remains of the hamburger. He was almost big enough to have eaten the other half. I didn't shoot him.

Back in the main room, the fat woman was lowering herself onto the bed. The springs groaned under her. Her voice was like a continuation of their sound:

"I didn't know if he came back or not, or if he was coming back. He must be, though. He left his bag and his car, and they didn't check out."

"Who's with him?"

"His wife." She couldn't say it without a peculiar look. "Anyway, they registered as man and wife. I wondered if there was something funny at the time. But what can you do when you're in the cabin business? Ask to see their marriage license and the results of their Wassermann test?" Her smile was rough and wry, like her wit. "What is he wanted for?"

"Suspicion of murder."

"Too bad," she said without turning a hair. "He *looks* like a decent boy. Maybe with her he was stepping out of his weight class. What did he do, kill her husband or something like that?"

"Something like that. When did they check in?"

"She came in last night around six, said her husband was joining her later. He got in around eleven or so."

"What name did she give you?"

"Smith. Mr. and Mrs. Smith."

"Did they walk away from here?"

"No, this older man came asking for them—for her. He had a car—new blue Chevvie."

"What did he look like?"

"Older man with a moustache." She fingered her upper lip. "More of an Adolphe Menjou type moustache than a Charlie Chaplin. A nice-looking man, even *with* those great big glasses. He treated her nice enough, too, considering the provocation."

"Provocation?"

She looked down at the twisted sheets, the mashed pillows. She took one of the pillows into her lap and began to plump it up. "He's her husband, isn't he?"

"No. I'm trying to find out who he is."

"So who got themselves killed?"

"Her daughter."

The woman's mouth drooped in sympathy. "No wonder she looks so sad. I know what sadness is. I lost a husband in the World War Two. That's when I started eating. I went right on even after I married Spurling."

She placed one hand on her breast. Her fingers were pale and speckled like breakfast sausages. All of her flesh was lardlike: if you poked it the hole would stay. Some of it had run like candle wax down her ankles and over her shoes.

"Getting back to the man with the moustache, Mrs. Spurling, what did he say when he came here asking for her?"

"Just was she here, and he described her—big blonde, platinum blonde, in a purple dress. I told him she was here. He knocked on this here door and they let him in and then they had a pow-wow. It went on for fifteen or twenty minutes."

"What was said?"

"I couldn't hear—just their voices. But it was quite a pow-wow. I guess she didn't want to go with him, she wanted to stay here with her little red-headed friend. I saw her hanging back when he marched her out to his car."

"Did she resist him?"

"She didn't *fight* him, if that's what you mean. But she was putting up an argument. The three of them were still arguing when they drove away. Funny thing is, the red-head appeared to be arguing *against* her."

"Was the man taking them into custody, do you think?"

"It didn't look like that to me. Is that what you're planning to do?"

"Yes. The boy should be coming back for his car. I'll wait here for him, if it's all right with you."

"No fireworks."

"I don't expect any."

She got up, and the bed groaned in relief. In her slow mind, two thoughts came together with an impact which made the flesh of her face quiver: "My God, you mean he killed the blondie's little girl?"

"That's what I want to ask him, Mrs. Spurling."

"And she spent the night with him? What kind of woman is *she?*"

"That's what I want to ask her."

I closed the door behind her and turned off the light. After a while my eyes got used to the green twilight, and I could see the cockroaches coming out like a small guerrilla army.

They retreated, as if they had outlying scouts, when Bobby came back to the cabin. I heard his footsteps on the path, and was waiting at the door when he came in. He saw the gun in my hand and went still. He had blue rings under his eyes, as if the night and the morning had drained his youth.

"Sit down, Bobby. We'll talk."

His feet arranged themselves to run. He couldn't decide where to run to.

"Come in and sit down and hurry up about it."

"Yes sir," he said to the gun.

I turned on the light and frisked him. He shuddered as if my touch was contagious. Almost in reflex, regardless of the gun, he threw a short right uppercut at my chin. I caught it in my left hand and pushed him backwards. He took two tanglefooted steps and fell sideways across the bed. He wasn't hurt, but he made no attempt to get up. I said:

"Your mother has changed her story, Bobby. You have no alibi. We know you went to San Francisco with Phoebe."

He was silent, his face half-hidden in the tangled sheets. From the corner of his head one wide green eye watched me.

"You don't deny it, do you?"

"No. But Mother didn't know I went with Phoebe. I let on I was going to school early, and Phoebe picked me up at the edge of the campus."

"What did you have in mind?"

"It's none of your business."

"It's everybody's business now," I said.

"All right." His voice rose defiantly. "We were going to get married. After she saw her father off, we were going to drive to Reno and get married. We were old enough, it's no crime."

"Getting married is no crime. But you never did get married."

"It wasn't my fault. I wanted to. It was Phoebe who changed her mind. She ran into a family situation. Don't ask me what it was because I don't know. I gave up and took a bus home."

"From San Francisco?"

"Yes."

"You're lying. That same night, or early next morning, you were seen driving Phoebe's car through a place on the coast named Medicine Stone. You know the place. The car was found yesterday, where you pushed it over the cliff. Her body was in it. And your feet are wet, boy, all the way up to your neck."

He didn't move or speak. He lay still as catatonia under the weight of my accusation.

"Why did you have to kill Phoebe? You were supposed to be in love with her."

He raised himself on his arms and turned to face me, not quite squarely:

"You don't understand anything about what happened."

"Enlighten me."

"A man doesn't have to incriminate himself."

"You're a man?"

He stared up at the ceiling light, fingering his sad pink moustache. "I'm doing my best to be one."

"You don't prove manhood by killing girls."

He brought his gaze down to my level. His eyes were bleak and dubious for twenty-one. "I didn't kill her. I didn't kill anyone. But I'm willing to take the consequences for what I did do."

"What did you do?"

"I drove the car down to Medicine Stone, like you said. I shoved it over the bluff and walked out to the highway and caught a bus."

"Why did you do that?"

He peered into various corners of the room. "I don't know."

"Tell me the truth."

"What's the use? Nobody will believe me, anyway."

"You haven't given it much of a try."

"I tell you I didn't kill her."

"Who killed her if you didn't? Catherine Wycherly?"

He let out a kind of snuffling laugh. It was neither loud nor long, but it played hell with my nerves.

"What is it with you and Catherine Wycherly? A mother-image you couldn't resist? Or is it more of a business relationship?"

"You don't understand," he said. "You'll never understand."

"Tell me what happened last November second."

"I'll go to the gas chamber first."

His voice was high and cracking. He looked around the cabin walls as if he was in that final place and could smell cyanide. Outside, heavy feet shuffled on the path. There was a tentative knocking at the door:

"Is it all right?"

"It's all right, Mrs. Spurling." Everything was dandy. "We'll be out of here shortly."

"That's good. The sooner the better."

She went away. I said to the wretched boy:

"You have about one more minute. If you can't come up with something sensible, we'll shift the proceedings over to the Hall of Justice. Once I've delivered you there, with the evidence against you, you're practically certain to be held for trial. This isn't a threat, it's one of the facts of life. You don't seem to know too many of them."

I could see the workings of his mind flickering in his eyes. "You don't know everything you think you know, either. I didn't kill Phoebe. She isn't even dead."

"Don't give me that. We found her body."

"I can prove she's alive, I know where she is." The words came out in a rush, ahead of the hand he raised to cover his mouth.

"If you know where she is, take me to her."

"I will not. You'll give her a going-over, and she can't stand it. She's been through enough. She's not going through any more, not if I can help it."

"You can't help it," I said. "There was a body in that car. You say it wasn't Phoebe. Who was it?"

"Her mother. Phoebe killed her mother in November. I got rid of the body for her. I'm just as guilty as she is."

He straightened, breathing deeply, as if he'd got rid of a weight he couldn't hold any longer. I felt it settling on me.

"Where is she, Bobby?"

"I'm not going to tell you. Do what you want to with me. You're not going to touch her."

He had that knight-errant look in his eyes, that Galahad fluoresence compounded of idealism and hysteria and sublimated sex. Not so very sublimated, perhaps. I put my gun away and sat and tried to think of the right words.

"Listen to me, Bobby. You realize I have to have more than your word for all this. I have to see her in the flesh. I have to talk to her."

"You just want to get your hooks on her."

"What hooks?" I held out my hands. "I'm on her side, no matter what she's done. Her father hired me, remember. I've been breaking my neck trying to find her for him. You can't sit there and prevent it."

"She's in good hands," he said stubbornly. "I don't want her taken out of them."

"What's the doctor's name?"

That startled him. "You'll never get it from me."

"I don't need to get it from you. Knowing as much as I know, the police could locate her before dark. But let's keep them out of it, for now."

He sat with his head down. I couldn't tell what was going on inside his young passionate skull. It came out in fragmentary sentences:

"It wouldn't be fair, you can't punish her, she's not responsible. She didn't plan it or anything."

"Were you there?"

His head came up sharply. His face was the color of cooked veal. "I was there in a sense. I was waiting outside in her car. Phoebe didn't want me to come into the house with her. She said she had to talk to her mother alone."

"You're talking about her mother's house in Atherton?"

"Yes. I drove Phoebe down from San Francisco that evening. She didn't feel like driving herself. She was awfully jittery."

"When was this?"

"About eight o'clock at night. She met her mother on the ship that afternoon and promised to come and see her. They hadn't seen each other for a long time. Phoebe said she wanted to be reconciled with her before we got married. But it didn't work out. Nothing worked out."

His voice broke. I waited.

"She was in the house for about twenty minutes, and I thought everything was fine. Then she came out with—she had the poker in her hand, dripping red. She said I had to get rid of it for her. I asked her what she'd done. She took me into the house and showed me. Her mother was lying in front of the fireplace with her head all bloody. Phoebe said we had to get rid of the body and cover the whole thing up." His eyes were tormented. He closed them and spoke from a blind face: "I wanted to save her from punishment. You mustn't punish her. She didn't know what she was doing."

"I'm not in the punishment business. I'll do everything I can for her. You have my word."

"You won't tell the police where she is, if I tell you?"

"No. I'll have to tell her father, of course. Sooner or later the police will have to be told."

"Why?"

"Because a crime has been committed."

"Will they put her in jail?"

"That depends on her condition, and the nature of the crime. It may have been murder, or manslaughter, or even justifiable homicide. Phoebe may be psychologically unable to stand trial."

"She is," he said. "I realized last night how badly disturbed she is. She talked strangely, and she kept laughing and crying."

"What does the doctor say, Bobby?"

"He didn't say much to me. He thought that I was the one who talked her into walking away from his sanitarium. It was the other way round. She phoned me after she left his place and asked me to meet her here at this motel." He looked around the room as if it was an image of his future, dismal and disreputable and confined. "When I saw this place I wanted to take her out of it right away, but she was afraid to show herself in the open. I spent half the night trying to talk her into going back to the sanitarium. Then today the doctor tracked her down, and between the two of us we got her back there."

"You haven't told me where yet."

"I don't know if I'm going to."

He looked at me with stubborn suspicion. Like so many other young people, including some of the best ones, he acted like a displaced person in the adult world.

"Come on, Bobby. We're wasting valuable time."

"What's so valuable about time? I wish I could take a sleeping pill and wake up ten years from now."

"I wish I could take one in reverse and wake up ten years ago. But maybe it's just as well I can't. With all that practice, I'd probably make the same mistakes all over again, in spades."

That was the right thing to say, for some odd reason. Bobby responded:

"I've made some terrible mistakes."

"Twenty-one is a good age to make them. You don't have to go on compounding them."

"But what is going to happen to us?"

"We'll have to wait and see. A lot depends on you right now. Take me to her, Bobby."

"Yeah," he said with a final look around. "Let's get out of this place."

I locked my car and rode along with Bobby. The sanitarium wasn't far, he told me over the noise of the exhaust. It was run by a Palo Alto psychiatrist named Sherrill, whom Phoebe had consulted in her last semester at Stanford.

"Did she come back to him on her own?"

"She must have. There wasn't anybody with her."

"How did she get here from Sacramento?"

"I didn't know she was in Sacramento. She wouldn't tell me anything about the last two months."

"When did she come back to the Peninsula?"

"Yesterday morning. Dr. Sherrill said she turned up at his place about eight o'clock."

"When did she leave the sanitarium?"

"Some time yesterday afternoon. It doesn't matter now. She's safe now."

He stopped for a red light, and made a right turn off Bayshore. I was thinking of Stanley Quillan listening to happy music in the back room of his shop, not many miles from where we were.

"Did Phoebe have a gun with her last night?"

"Of course not. She doesn't have a gun."

"Can you be sure?"

"She had nothing with her at all. Just the clothes that she was wearing, and they weren't hers.'

"How do you know that?"

"They didn't fit her. She's put on a lot of weight, but even so her dress was too big for her. It didn't suit her, either. It made her look *old*. It made her look like her mother when—"

The car swerved under the pressure of his hands. We were on a quiet, tree-lined street named after the poet Cowper. He pulled the car into the curb and braked abruptly. I left handprints on the windshield.

"I saw her mother when she was dead," he went on in a hushed voice. "She had no clothes on. She was big and white. We wrapped her in a blanket and put her in the back of Phoebe's car. I had to bend up her legs." He bowed until his forehead touched the steering-wheel. Both of his hands were gripping the curved steel. His knuckles gleamed white. "It was a terrible thing to do."

"Why did you do it?"

"They said—Phoebe said that it was the only way. We had to get rid of the body. I couldn't leave her to do it by herself."

"She wasn't by herself."

He turned his head, his cheek pressed hard against his straining knuckles. "I was with her. Is that what you mean?"

"Who else was?"

"Nobody. We were alone in the house."

"You said 'they.' The dead woman didn't tell you to put her in the water."

"It was a slip of the tongue."

"It was a slip, all right. Who else are you trying to cover up for, Bobby?"

"I'm not trying to cover up for him."

"It was a man, then. Name him."

The glaze of stubbornness came down over his face again.

"I think I can name him for you," I said. "Did Ben Merriman walk in on the festivities?"

"He didn't say who he was."

From the magpie nest of my inner pocket, I produced the blotter with Merriman's picture on it. It was getting dog-eared.

"Is this the man?"

"Yes."

"Why didn't you mention him before?"

"Phoebe said last night I wasn't to."

"Did she give you a reason?"

"No."

"But without a reason of any kind, you let a disturbed girl make your decision for you?"

"I had a reason, Mr. Archer. I saw his picture in yesterday's paper. He was beaten to death in that same house. Now Phoebe will be blamed for that, too."

chapter 25

THE SANITARIUM WAS in a neighborhood of large old frame houses and new apartment buildings. A massive one-story structure that looked like an overgrown ranchhouse, it stood far back from the street behind a wire net fence masked with a cypress hedge. The driveway curved around a broad lawn where outdoor furniture was set out, chaises and gaily colored umbrellas. A solitary white-haired woman sat on one of the chaises in the middle of the intensely green grass. She was looking at the sky as if it had just been created.

A concrete ramp for wheel chairs sloped up from the driveway to the door. There was a judas window set into the door, and a bell push in the bare wall beside it. I got out of the car. Bobby stayed where he was.

"Are you all right?"

"I'm all right, but I better stay out here. Dr. Sherrill doesn't like me."

"I want you along."

Reluctantly, he followed me up the ramp. I rang the bell and waited. The little window in the door snapped open. A nurse in a cap peered out at us:

"What is it, sir?"

"I have to see Dr. Sherrill."

"Is it about a patient?"

"Yes. Her name is Phoebe Wycherly. I represent her father. My name is Archer." I added, though the words felt strange on my tongue: "This is Mr. Doncaster, her fiancé."

She left us standing in a drab green corridor which ran the length of the building. Twelve or fifteen doors opened on to it. At the far end a young man in a bathrobe was walking towards us very slowly like a diver with weights on his feet. We were there for several minutes, but he didn't seem to get any nearer.

A man in a white smock opened one of the doors and said, "Come in here, gentlemen."

He stood with careful formality beside the door as we entered. I wasn't impressed by my first look at Sherrill. His thin moustache had a touch of vanity. Magnified by thick glasses, his dark brown eyes seemed womanish.

His office was small and unimposing. A bare oak desk with a swivel chair behind it, a leather armchair, a leather couch, took up most of the floor space. A wall of shelves spilled books onto the floor: everything from Gray's *Anatomy* to *Mad* magazine.

Bobby started to sit on the couch, then flinched away. He balanced himself tentatively on one arm of the armchair. I sat on the couch. I had to resist an impulse to put my feet up. Sherrill watched us over the desk with eyes like mirrors: "Well, gentlemen?"

Bobby leaned forward, hugging one high knee. "How is Phoebe?"

"You left her only two hours ago. I told you she should be sequestered for at least two days, possibly much longer. You certainly can't see her again today, Mr. Doncaster." Sherrill spoke without much emphasis, but there was a steady force behind his words.

"I brought him here," I said. "He told me a story which has legal repercussions, to put it mildly. You may know parts of it."

"Are you a lawyer?"

"I'm a private detective. Homer Wycherly, the girl's father, hired me several days ago to look for her. Until this afternoon, when I talked to Bobby here, I thought she was dead. Murdered. It turns out she was a fugitive from justice."

"Justice," the doctor repeated softly. "Do you represent justice, Mr. Archer?"

"No." I did, in a sense. It would take too long to figure out what sense. "I simply want you to understand the situation."

"It's good of you to share your understanding with me."

"I haven't, doctor. That's going to take some time."

"I'm afraid I haven't much time. As a matter of fact, I have a patient scheduled now. Perhaps we can arrange to discuss this later on tonight, if you feel we have to."

"It won't wait," I said bluntly. "Have you had a chance to talk to Phoebe at all?"

"Not really. I plan to see her after dinner. You must realize I'm a busy man, I had an hour set aside for her last night, but that was washed out when she ran away. Fortunately she came back today, more or less of her own free will."

"Did she come here of her own accord in the first place?"

"Yes. I'd seen her twice last year, and when she felt troubled again she had the good sense to come back. She seems considerably more troubled now than she was last year. But she did come back on her own, and that's an excellent sign. It means she recognizes the need for help."

"How did she get here?"

"She flew over from Sacramento early yesterday morning and took a taxi from the airport."

"Why did she run away again yesterday afternoon?"

"It's hard to answer that. Evidently she's more upset than I thought, and needed more security. She was given ground privileges, and I suppose she panicked. I shouldn't have exposed her to so much freedom."

"What time did she take off?"

"About this time. Speaking of time, the patient I'm supposed to be with sweats blood when I miss an appointment." He rose, and looked at his watch. "It's five-ten. If you'll come back at eight, I'll have had my hour with Phoebe, and we can go further into these matters."

"Where is she now?"

"In her room, with a special nurse. After yesterday's fiasco, I'm taking no further chances with her security." He added, with a withering glance at Bobby: "I spent a good part of the night trying to trace her. She's a valuable girl."

Trevor had used the same words about his niece.

"How ill is she?"

The doctor spread his hands. "You're asking impossible questions, at an impossible time. I'd say offhand she's more upset than ill. She's over four months pregnant, and that's enough by itself to account for—ah—unconsidered behavior on the part of an unmarried young woman. She's been doing a certain amount of acting-out."

"What do you mean by acting-out?"

"Enacting her fantasies and fears instead of suffering them." Sherrill's long patience was fraying. "This is hardly the occasion for me to give you a short course in psychiatry."

My patience had never been long: "When you get around to talking to Phoebe, there are some specific questions you'd better ask—"

"You mistake my function. I don't ask questions. I wait for answers. Now if you'll excuse me."

Sherrill reached for the doorknob. I said to his back:

"Ask her if she shot and killed Stanley Quillan yesterday afternoon. Ask her if she beat Ben Merriman to death the other night."

Sherrill turned. His eyes were black and opaque as charcoal. "Are you serious?"

"I'm serious. She killed her mother with a poker last November. Doncaster was a witness."

His black glance shifted to Bobby, who nodded solemnly.

"Who were these other men?" Sherrill said to me.

"A pair of blackmailers."

"You say she killed them?"

"I want you to ask her whether she did. If you won't ask her, let me. There are some answers we can't just sit around waiting for, and some problems that aren't just in the mind."

"I'm well aware of that," Sherrill said. "I'll talk to her now. Wait here."

He went out with his smock flapping around his legs. Bobby subsided into the armchair. He looked at me as if he was sick of me, sick of the world and everybody in it. In twenty-one years he hadn't had time to get ready for so much trouble. You had to start training for it very young these days.

"You didn't tell me she was pregnant."

"That's why we were going to get married."

"You're the father?"

"Yes. It happened last summer at Medicine Stone."

"Everything happens at Medicine Stone. You've put it on the map, boy."

He hung his head. I went to the window and looked out between the slats of the Venetian blind. The window overlooked a large enclosure paved with flagstones and surrounded by a ten-foot wire fence. A brightly frocked woman holding a raised parasol stood like a mannequin in one corner of the fence. Her face was so heavily powdered that she looked as though she'd stuck it into a flour barrel. A middle-aged man with his chin on his chest was shuffling back and forth across the flagstones, taking one step on each.

"You really think she killed Merriman?" Bobby said in a weak voice.

"It was your idea."

"I was afraid—" He tried to complete the thought but didn't know how to.

"For a boy who's afraid you've got yourself into deep trouble."

"I'm not a boy." He clutched the arms of the big chair and tried to fill it, to become old and large.

"Boy or man, you're up against it."

"I don't care. I don't care what happens to me if Phoebe—if she's really finished. I never expected much out of life anyway."

I sat on the couch near him. "Still, life has to go on."

"My life doesn't."

"It will. Why fight it? You don't want to be a dead loss to the world. You have certain qualities it can use. Courage is one of them. Loyalty is another."

"Those are just abstract words. They don't mean anything. I've studied semantics."

"They do, though. I learned that studying life. It's a course that goes on and on. You never graduate or get a diploma. The best you can do is put off the time when you flunk out."

"I've already flunked," he said. "They'll never let me finish college or anything. They'll lock me up, probably for the rest of my life."

"That I doubt. What sort of a record do you have?"

"With the police? I have no record. None at all."

"How did you get involved with Phoebe Wycherly?"

"I didn't get involved with her. I fell in love with her."

"Just like that, eh?"

"Yes. From the first time I met her on the beach, I knew that she was for me."

"Have you ever been in love before?"

"No, and there won't be anybody else, ever. This is it. I don't care what she's done."

He had courage, as I'd said. Or stubbornness raised to the nth power, which is almost as good as courage.

"We still don't know for certain," I said. "Tell me about Merriman. How did he get into the picture?"

Bobby ran his tongue along the lower edge of his moustache. "He just walked in. He had an appointment with Mrs. Wycherly, and the front door was standing open. He must have heard us in the living room. Phoebe was crying and I was doing my best to comfort her. Merriman walked in and caught us red-handed. He was going to call the police. Phoebe begged him not to, and he relented. He said he would co-operate with her—with us—if we would co-operate with him."

"What did he mean by that?"

"It was something to do with selling the house. Mrs. Wycherly was going to sell the house through him, that's what their appointment was about. He was angry because the—because her death interfered with the sale."

"Did Merriman suggest hiding the body?"

"Yes. We were going to bury her at first, in the garden behind the house. But he said sooner or later it would be found there. I was the one who thought of throwing it in the sea. He helped me carry her out to Phoebe's car."

"You said she had no clothes on, is that right?"

"Yes. We wrapped her in a blanket." A shadow of that image cross his eyes.

"What happened to her clothes?"

"They were lying on the chesterfield."

"Did Phoebe undress her?"

"No. I don't think so. I don't understand what happened, Mr. Archer. I took off right after that."

"And left Phoebe with Merriman?"

"I had to." His forehead was wet. He wiped it with the back of his hand and stayed with his head leaning sideways on his fist. "He told me to get out and not come back. I had to co-operate with him. The one thing I had on my mind was keeping her out of jail. I know now there are worse things than jail."

He sighed. He was coming out of two months in the moral deep freeze, beginning to feel himself alive in the world once more. His face was painful to look at. I stood up at the window. The woman with the parasol hadn't moved. She looked as though she hadn't moved or changed her style since 1928. A flight of blackbirds blew across the green and yellow sky. The man with the hanging head lifted his head and shook his fist at the disappearing birds.

The light was beginning to fade. Somebody called the bird-hater into the building. Dutifully, he plodded in out of sight. A nurse wearing a cardigan over her white uniform approached the woman with the parasol. The two of them walked towards the building in slow time. A door closed.

Twilight sifted into the room and gradually filled it. Neither of us bothered to turn on a light. I felt as cold and still as a fish in a dark bowl.

The chair-leather creaked under Bobby's hand. All I could see of him was his white face and his hands gripping the chair arms.

"I can't explain why I did what I did. I couldn't see any other way to handle it. Afterwards I just kept waiting and hoping. Waiting to hear from Phoebe, hoping that something possible would come of it. I might have known that nothing possible would." He said in a despairing voice in which a man's deep tones were somehow mingled: "This is going to kill my mother."

"I don't think so. I talked to her last night."

"Last night she didn't know."

"She was suspicious, from the first. She believed that you'd done something seriously wrong."

"Mother thought that?"

"Yes. She believed she was protecting you for a murder you'd committed."

"That's funny," he said. "I felt as if I had committed a murder. I dreamed on the bus going home that I had murdered her."

I didn't know if he meant Phoebe or her mother or his own mother. I didn't ask him. It seemed almost irrelevant in this slow-motion underwater world.

Dr. Sherrill irrupted into the room. He closed the door quickly behind him, as though pursuers were reaching for the tail of his smock. He switched on the desk-lamp.

"Mr. Archer, can you tell me how to get in touch with Phoebe's father? I promised her yesterday not to, but the situation has altered."

So had he. His face was deeply troubled in the upward light.

"Homer Wycherly should be in Terranova. We can probably reach him through the sheriff there. That can wait until you tell me what she said."

"What she said is confidential." The steady force behind his words was running stronger than ever. His voice shook with it.

"It will stay confidential with me."

"I'm sorry. As a doctor, I have the right of silence where my patients are concerned. You have no such privilege under the law."

"You're assuming trial conditions."

"Am I?" Sherrill threw a distrustful look at Bobby. "We'll continue this in private, Mr. Archer."

"You can trust me," Bobby said. "I'd never repeat anything that would hurt Phoebe. Didn't I prove that in the last two months?"

"This isn't a personal matter. Please wait outside, Mr. Doncaster. All the way outside, if you don't mind."

Bobby got up and went out, looking rejected. When Sherrill had closed the office door, I said:

"Did the girl confess those killings? You can at least give me a yes or no."

Sherrill's lips were tight. They expelled the word, "Yes," as if it tasted sour.

"Did she go into her motives?"

"She outlined the circumstances. They provide a motive, certainly. I don't think we'd better discuss them."

"I think we should."

"I can't and won't break a patient's confidence." The doctor sat down behind his desk with a kind of magisterial formality.

"You may not have to. I got it from Bobby Doncaster that Merriman walked into Mrs. Wycherly's house in Atherton and caught the two of them with her body. He used the situation to set up a blackmail scheme—not his first. Merriman and his brother-in-law Quillan had been blackmailing Catherine Wycherly before they got their teeth into Phoebe. They simply transferred the bite from mother to daughter. They kept Phoebe on ice for a while in her mother's San Mateo apartment, then hauled her off to Sacramento and forced her to impersonate her mother—made her put on weight, wear her mother's clothes, and so on, so that she could pass for her. The point of all this was to go on collecting Catherine Wycherly's alimony checks, and eventually the check for the sale of the house which Merriman was negotiating for the dead woman. Phoebe had to keep her alive, you might say, long enough to cash the check and turn the proceeds over to Merriman."

"I see you know all about it," Sherrill said. "It was a horrible scheme, a cruel refinement of punishment. The most horrible aspect of it was that it fitted in with the girl's need to punish herself for what she had done to her mother. She also had a very strong unconscious need—I noticed it last spring—to identify with her mother. Even the forced feeding to put on weight coincided with her unconscious urges, as well as the fact of her pregnancy."

"You're going too fast for me."

"Deliberately putting on weight, as Phoebe has been doing, can be an expression of anxiety and self-hatred. The self feels itself as heavy and gross and tries to invest itself with a gross, heavy body. I'm simplifying, of course, but the general idea is recognized in the literature—in Binswanger's classic case-history of Ellen West, for example. Lindner's more popularized study of bulimia in *The Fifty-Minute Hour* is an even closer parallel, since Ellen West was psychotic, and Phoebe almost certainly is not."

"What is she, doctor? The question is legally important, as you know."

"I can't make a diagnosis. Not yet. I think she hasn't decided herself which way she's going to go—towards reality, or towards illness. She's still the same essentially neurotic girl who came to me last year, but now she's under really terrible pressures. As she keeps saying, she's been living in hell." Sherrill's face drooped with sympathy.

"Why did she come to you last year?"

"I never really got to the bottom of it. I only saw her twice, and then she terminated. Her resistance was very high: I couldn't get her to talk about herself. Ostensibly she came to me because she was concerned about her family. Her mother was suing her father for divorce at the time. Phoebe blamed herself for the family breakup."

"Did she say why?"

"It had to do with some scurrilous letters the family had received. Apparently they were the proximate cause of the blowup between her parents. I don't pretend to understand the situation."

"Did Phoebe write those letters?"

"It's possible that she did. While she didn't come right out with it, she seemed to feel responsible for them. You have to remember, on the other hand, that she's a self-blamer, as many neurotics are. She tends to blame herself for everything that happens. This Merriman was lucky in his choice of a blackmail victim."

"Lucky is hardly the word. He ended up as the victim."

Sherrill looked at me as though he intended to speak. Instead he busied himself packing a pipe from a leather pouch. He lit it with a match whose leaping flame was reflected in his glasses. The circle of light from his desk-lamp filled up with shifting layers of blue-grey smoke. He narrowed his eyes, as if he was trying to descry a permanent shape or meaning in the smoke.

"We're all victims, Archer, until we stop victimizing each other. Not that I'm crying over Merriman. He deserved to die, if any man does."

"We all die, anyway, sooner or later. Too bad a sick girl had to be his executioner."

"She didn't actually carry it out herself," the doctor said. "At least she claims not. I shouldn't be telling you this, but you know so much already it seems pointless to hold back. She employed a professional killer to do the job, on both Merriman and—what was the other blackmailer's name?"

"Quillan, Stanley Quillan. Did she name the killer?"

"She says she never knew his name. According to her account—and frankly I'm dubious about its accuracy—she ran into this thug in the bar of the hotel where she was staying, the Hacienda on the outskirts of Sacramento. She'd been drinking, and she was in a dark and vengeful mood. This fellow picked her up, they got into conversation, she happened to notice that he was carrying a gun. She invited him to her room and after some further conversation she paid him money on the spot to kill the man who had been tormenting her. That's her story."

"But you don't believe it?"

"I have to believe that something of the sort happened. Her story is pretty circumstantial, but it can't have occurred as casually as she says. You don't just walk into a bar and pick up a gunman to do your killing for you."

"It has happened. Did she describe the gunman?"

"Yes, in some detail, and it wasn't the kind of detail you get in hallucination or delusion. There's no doubt in my mind that he exists. He's a man in his early forties, quite good-looking in a raffish way, she says, with dark hair, blue-grey eyes; about six feet one or two, heavily built and muscular, with the air of an athlete. She took him at first for a professional athlete." Sherrill puffed more smoke and peered at me through it. "She might very well have been describing you."

"She was."

He yanked his pipe out of his mouth. "I don't understand. You can't mean she hired you to murder those men?"

"She tried to hire me to liquidate Merriman. That was two nights ago: Merriman was already dead. I went along with the gag, up to a point, because I believed she was Catherine Wycherly and I was trying to find out what she knew about Merriman's death. She didn't know about it at all, unless she's a very good liar. She simply wished him dead, *ex post facto*."

"She's certainly been lying to me." Sherrill's eyes held a hurt expression. It changed to a more hopeful one: "Isn't it possible, in the light of this, that her entire confession is a tissue of lies? She may be trying to attach to herself all the guilt that's floating around loose."

"Or she may have made a false confession to avoid making a true one." I stood up. "Why don't we ask her?"

"Both of us?"

"Why not? I'm walking evidence that she lied. The issue has to be settled one way or the other."

"But she's in a very chancy condition."

"The whole world is," I said. "If she can survive Merriman and Quillan, she can survive me. Anyway, you said yourself she didn't know which way to jump, in the direction of illness or reality. Let's give her another jump at reality."

chapter 26

SHE WAS WITH a white-uniformed nurse in a softly lighted room. It was furnished almost as barely as a nun's cell with a bed, a wardrobe, two chairs, in one of which she was sitting. Her face was turned towards the wall, and she didn't move when we entered, except that the cords in her neck stood out more starkly. Under her plain hospital robe her large body was still as a beast in ambush.

The doctor said: "I have to ask you to leave again, Mrs. Watkins. Stay within call, please."

The nurse got up and went out. The set of her back expressed her disapproval.

"What is it now," the girl said without looking at Sherrill. "Have they come to take me away?"

"You're staying here tonight, I told you that. I hope you can stay indefinitely, until you're perfectly well."

"I'm perfectly well now. I feel perfectly well."

"That's good, because I want you to do something for me. I want you to have a look at this gentleman here and tell me whether or not you recognize him."

He closed the door and turned on the overhead light. I stepped forward under it. Slowly, on a tense reluctant neck, her head turned towards me. Her face was clean and gleaming pale. With the heavy make-up gone from around her eyes and mouth, she had dropped about ten false years. But she still seemed old and harried for twenty-one. Her bruised flesh-padded features were like a thick mask through which her eyes looked out at me fearfully.

We recognized each other, of course. I said with the best smile I could muster:

"Hello, Phoebe."

She didn't respond. She set the knuckles of one fist against her open mouth, as though to cut off any chance of speech.

"Do you know this man?" Sherrill asked her. "His name is Mr. Archer, and he's a private detective employed by your father."

"I never saw him before."

"He says you have—that you met at the Hacienda Inn in Sacramento the night before last."

"Then he's a liar."

"Somebody's lying," I said. "We both know it isn't me. You offered me money to kill a man named Merriman. He was dead at the time. Were you aware of that?"

She stared at me over her fist, stared and flared and glared, in fear, in anger, in doubt, in surmise, in bewilderment. I'd never seen such changeable eyes as she had.

"I killed him." She turned to the doctor. "Tell him about the people I've killed."

He shook his head slowly. I said:

"I'd like to know how you did it. You didn't do it through me."

"No, that was just play-acting. I knew he was dead, naturally. I had already killed him. I did it with my own hands."

Her voice was calm, almost toneless. Sherrill caught my eye. He held out his hands and brought them close together. Cut it short. But I was convinced that the girl was lying, that she was one of that strange and devious tribe who improvised confessions to other people's crimes. I did a little improvising of my own:

"They found poison in Merriman's stomach—enough arsenic to kill a horse. You poisoned him first and then beat him. Where did you get the arsenic?"

Her head rocked back, but she answered smoothly, too smoothly: "I bought it in a drugstore on K Street in Sacramento."

"Where did you get the shotgun you used to blow Stanley Quillan's head off?"

"I bought it in a pawnshop."

"Where?"

"I don't remember."

"Because it never happened. Quillan was shot with a small hand-gun. Merriman had no arsenic in his stomach that I know of. You're confessing to crimes that never even occurred."

She looked at me as if I was trying to rob her of something precious. Her hand fumbled at her face, pushed back her dyed tinsel hair from her forehead. She said in a voice that sounded ventriloquial, piped in from another room where a child was reciting a lesson:

"I did so kill them. I can't remember the details, it all seems so long ago. But you've just got to believe me."

"Why do we have to believe you? Who are you covering for?"

"No one. I did it all by myself. I want to be punished for it. I killed three people, including my own mother."

She was being punished now. Her forehead was a helmet of white pain pressing down on her eyes. She hid them with her hands.

Sherrill took me by the elbow and drew me to the far side of the room. "I can't let this go on," he said in an earnest whisper. "There are limits to what you can get out of people by cross-questioning."

"But she's been lying. I don't believe she killed anyone."

"Neither do I now. I am her doctor, however, and I don't like the quality of her lies. They're very important to her. If we take away the whole structure at once, I can't predict the consequences. She's been living for weeks in a half-world where lies and truth are all mixed up. It's dangerous to try and pull her out of it in one night."

"Why?"

"Her lies are probably being used to mask an actual guilt which she can't face."

"Or an actual person whose skin she wants to save?"

"Perhaps. I don't pretend to have all the answers. I'm groping just as you are."

Phoebe was watching us between her fingers. She closed them like scissors when I looked directly at her. I turned back to Sherrill:

"You think she's really guilty of something?"

"I think she thinks she is." He was pale and sweating in his earnestness. "I'm more concerned with what she thinks than with the objective fact. That has to come to me refracted through her mind, otherwise I can't reach her."

"You can guess at the objective fact."

"Yes. It may have to do with those letters her family received. They've been very much on her mind."

"I hear you talking about me," Phoebe said across the room. "It isn't good manners to whisper about a person in her presence."

"I'm sorry," the doctor said.

"I don't care, not really. If you want to talk about the letters, why don't you say so out loud?"

"All right. Did you write them, Phoebe?"

"No, that's one sin I haven't got on my conscious—on my conscious. But I was the cause of it all."

Sherrill sat on the bed, suddenly and completely absorbed in his patient. "What were you the cause of?"

"The whole awful mess. I told Aunt Helen about them, you see." She added with a kind of hushed melodrama: "I lit the fuse that blew everything to pieces."

"Who is Aunt Helen?"

"Father's sister, Helen Trevor. She drove me home to Meadow Farms last Easter, and on the way I mentioned that I'd seen them. I didn't realize what it meant—" She shook her head violently. "I'm lying again. I did know what it meant. I was jealous of them."

"Who were you jealous of?"

"Mother and Uncle Carl. I saw them together late one night, when I was coming down from the city with a boy. We stopped for a red light in San Mateo, and this taxi stopped beside us. Mother and Uncle Carl were in it, with their arms around each other. They didn't notice me. They were all wrapped up in each other.

"I brooded about it for a week or two, and then when I had the chance I told Aunt Helen. She didn't say a word. She didn't say a word all the way to Meadow Farms. But when the letter came next day I knew who had written it. I could see it on her face at the breakfast table."

"But you didn't tell anyone?"

"I was afraid to. I've always been afraid of Aunt Helen. She's so sure of herself, so pure, so righteous. Besides it was really my fault. I knew what I was doing when I told her about them, and what would happen." She said in a rough, hoarse voice which didn't sound like her own: "Divorce, and destruction, and death."

"Did Aunt Helen kill your mother?" Sherrill said.

"No. It was partly her fault. But mostly mine."

"You didn't do it yourself, did you?"

She shook her bright unkempt head. Her eyes were changing again. She looked like a girl with a secret she wanted to lose:

"Mother was already dying when I got there. The door was open, and I heard her moaning." Phoebe moaned. "I don't want to talk about it." But she went on, as though a barrier had broken in her mind: "I found her in the drawing room lying in her blood. I held her poor head in my arms. She knew me. She couldn't see, but she knew me by my voice. She said my name before she died."

"Did she say anything else?"

"I asked her who hurt her. She said it was my father. And then she died. I sat there on the floor with her head in my lap. I was afraid to move for a long time. I'd never seen a dead person, except for Grandfather a long time ago.

But after a while I wasn't scared any more. All I felt was pity for her. Pity for both of them." She raised her face. It was bright with candor. "They had such a rotten life together. It was such a rotten way for it to end."

I said: "Did your father ever threaten to kill your mother?"

"Lots of times."

"That day on the ship?"

"Yes." She was breathing quickly through widened nostrils. "She said he was going away and leaving her practically penniless. He said she threw her money away and would never get another cent from him. She said if he didn't help her, she'd ruin his name in California. That's when he threatened to kill her. Then he got some ship's officers to take her away.

"I felt sorry for her. I invited her to ride along in my taxi and I tried to cheer her up a little bit. She wanted me to come to Atherton with her. I couldn't, because Bobby was waiting at the hotel. I promised to come and visit her that evening. But Father got there first."

"Did you see him in Atherton?" I asked her.

"No. All I have to go on is what she said. I remember her exact words. I think I do. 'Your father did this to me,' she said, and then she died. I told Bobby I did it so that he would help me. It was a dirty trick to play on Bobby, but Father came first. I had to protect Father. When the Merriman fellow came in, I told him the same thing, and he believed me."

Phoebe had slumped forward with her elbows on her knees. She pressed her head between her hands as if she hoped to squeeze it empty of pain. Sherrill and I exchanged a long look across her. She said:

"I still don't understand how Father got there. He was already supposed to be at sea. Did he use a helicopter or something?"

"He didn't have to. The sailing was delayed by engine trouble."

"What will they do to him? Will he be executed?"

"There's no danger of that," I said. Men with money never saw the inside of the gas chamber.

"They'll put him in jail, though, won't they? Father is so sensitive. He won't be able to stand that."

"He may not be so very sensitive. Remember that three people have died violent deaths."

"Father didn't kill those horrible men. I'll never believe that he did."

"You've been acting on the belief," I said. "Isn't that why you tried to take the blame for all three killings?"

She answered my question with another: "But why would he do such a thing? He didn't even know them. Father had nothing to do with people of that sort."

"He probably made their acquaintance very quickly in the last few days. My guess is they approached him and tried to blackmail him, just as they'd been blackmailing you, and your mother before you."

"I see. So that's my fault, too."

"Do you want to explain that, Phoebe?" Sherrill asked her.

"No. There are things that can't be said."

"There's nothing that can't be said."

She gave him a slanting sidewise look. "You don't know what I did, what I *really* did."

"I'll know if you tell me. It can't be so very terrible."

"You think not?" She was full of guilt again. She seemed to have an inexhaustible reservoir of guilt.

I said: "Did you finally break down and tell Merriman that your father had killed your mother?"

She nodded almost imperceptibly.

"When did you tell him, Phoebe?"

"The last time I saw him. Was it three days ago? Anyway, I betrayed my father. I made the whole thing in vain. The whole horrible two months were all in vain. I told that man my mother's dying words. I should have cut out my tongue first."

"Did he use force to get it out of you?"

"No. I don't even have that excuse. It was afterwards that he hit me, when he wanted to make love to me, and I wouldn't let him. I never let him."

"Why did you tell him that your father was guilty?"

"I'm a moral weakling, I guess. I couldn't take it. I spilled out everything to him that last time. I'm always spilling out everything I know and then there's death and destruction and it's always all my fault.

Her voice had taken on a hysterical rhythm. Sherrill leaned forward and touched her anguished face:

"Don't blame yourself, Phoebe. You can't assume all the sins of the world. You've had a dreadful two months and nobody blames you for anything you did."

"Yes," she said. "It was dreadful. I almost decided to kill myself more than once. But I couldn't do that to my unborn baby. I took up drinking instead, drinking and eating. I had to do something to take my mind from the way I was forced to live. The crumminess of it." She grimaced. "It was the *crumminess* I couldn't stand—that awful apartment where Mother used to stay, and Merriman and his brother-in-law watching me all the time. They kept me there like a prisoner and made me practice Mother's signature.

"Then in Sacramento they told me to get my hair dyed and wear Mother's clothes."

"So that you could cash her checks?" I said.

"The checks were part of it. Merriman also said if I assumed her identity that no one would know she'd been killed. He wanted to keep the whole thing quiet until we got the big check at the end, the one for the house. Until *he* got it," she said bitterly. "He promised me if I co-operated and signed the check over to him, that he would give me money so I could go away somewhere and have my baby in peace. But he didn't do it. He paid my hotel bill and gave me a few dollars for food and that was that, he said. Why should he finance a murderer? he said. And I broke down and told him I wasn't a murderer." She looked at us with the agonized purity of an addled saint. "I wanted to make sense out of all the suffering, but I couldn't."

"You are making sense of it," the doctor said. "You'll be making more sense of it day by day."

"But look what I've done to Father."

"He did it to himself, Phoebe. It's a fact you're going to have to learn to live with. You can't incorporate yourself with your father—with either of your parents. This isn't entirely your tragedy. You tried to make it yours, but your part in it was really peripheral." He sifted his weight forward, ready to get up. "Don't you think we've talked enough for tonight now?"

"Let her finish," I said. "I won't be here tomorrow."

"Yes. Let me finish."

She held out her hand in an imploring way. It was the first outward gesture I'd seen her make. Sherrill stayed where he was on the edge of the bed. He nodded slowly, and her voice rushed on like jangled music trying to follow the metronome of his head:

"After Merriman went away, I sat up most of the night. Father's ship had come in that day—I saw the notice in the Sacramento newspaper—and I told myself that I should go and warn him. But I couldn't go. I couldn't face him. I started to think all the terrible things, from the time I was three or four years old listening in bed at night. Listening to the two of them cutting each other. I was sitting there by the window of my room and it was three o'clock in the morning or so, it doesn't matter, Scott Fitzgerald says in the real dark night of the soul it's *always* three o'clock in the morning. And I could actually hear them quarrelling through the walls and through the window. My poor dead mother and my poor live father.

"They never stopped quarrelling. They were still quarrelling the day she died. I could see them in the dirty window mixed up with my reflection. I could hardly tell if they were in my head or in the night outside, or if *I* was just a reflection in the window, and only those jabbering words were real, whore and crazy and I'll-kill-you. I started to say my name out loud, Phoebe, over and over. It's a name they gave to the goddess Diana in Greek mythology. And the voices went away."

"You wrote your name on the window," I said.

"Yes. To keep them away." She produced a wan half-smile, which faded as she turned to look at Sherrill. "That's magical thinking, isn't it? Does it mean I'm really insane?"

"No. We all do it from time to time."

"I've been so afraid that I was going insane."

Sherrill smiled at her. "You're not."

"But I've done so many terrible things." She said to me: "The worst thing I did was when I tried to get you to shoot that Merriman."

"He was already dead. It did no harm."

"I must have been crazy. There was such a darkness on my mind." She touched her temple with her fingertips. The memory of the darkness moved like clouds behind her eyes.

"It's lifting," Sherrill said. "The proof of it is that you're here, and of your own accord."

She flushed slightly and looked away. "I have a confession to make. Another confession. I didn't really come back here from Sacramento of my own accord. I didn't want to come. I wanted to go far away and never see anyone I know again. But Uncle Carl said that would be really crazy. He made me come back here with him. He drove me right up to the door yesterday morning."

"It's not important how you got here. The point is that you came."

"It may be very important, doctor." I turned to Phoebe: "How did Carl Trevor get in touch with you?"

"He made me promise not to tell anyone. But it doesn't matter now, does it? He came to the Champion Hotel the other night."

"Which night?"

"The night before last, I think it was. I've been losing track of the days and nights, but it must have been the night be-

fore last, because he made me move to the Hacienda. He said
I couldn't go on living in a place like the Champion. Actually, I lived in worse places than that while I was in Sacramento."

"How did he know you were there?"

"He didn't. He thought I was Mother. He threw his arms
around me and kissed me and called me by her name." She
flushed more deeply. "When he saw that I wasn't Mother, he
broke down and cried." She added grudgingly: "He must
have loved her very much."

"Did you tell him she was dead?"

"Yes."

"And that your father had killed her?"

"Yes. He said I mustn't tell anyone else, ever." Clefts of
pain like knife-cuts appeared before her eyes. "But now I
have."

"You've done the right thing."

"No. There was no right thing for me to do. All my choices
were wrong. When all I wanted was a chance to go away
and have my baby in peace."

"You'll have your baby," Sherrill said. "In peace."

She seized on the words with hungry eyes and mouth.
"Will it be all right to have my baby? In spite of the heredity
and everything?"

"It would be all wrong not to."

"And Bobby? Can I see Bobby?"

"Tomorrow if you like. It's getting late, and you need rest."

"Yes. I'm very tired."

chapter **27**

> I PASSED ON SOME OF MY new informa-
tion to Bobby Doncaster. He was hardly able to believe that
Phoebe was innocent of her mother's death. I left him at
the Siesta stunned with joy, I think.

I still wasn't wholly satisfied with Phoebe's story. Unanswered questions nagged at my mind. One of them, the question of Homer Wycherly's availability on the night of the
crime, could possibly be answered by the steward Sammy
Green.

The case was coming to a focus, in space as well as meaning. Green's house in East Palo Alto was only a five-minute

drive from the motor court. He was even at home, according to his wife.

Green came into his living room through the kitchen, a quick-moving young Negro wearing an apron emblazoned with the legend "Master Chef." His smile was slightly defensive, as if I'd caught him performing a doubtful ritual:

"I'm barbecuing some steaks. They always take longer than you think. What can I do for you, Mister——?"

"Archer," I said. "I came at a bad time and I'll try to make it fast. I'm a private detective, and I've been talking to the Master-at-Arms of your ship. McEachern tells me you looked after Homer Wycherly's stateroom this last voyage."

"I did, yessir." His smile faded, and only the defensiveness remained. It was like watching a human face turn to smooth black stone. "Is there some trouble?"

"I only want a little information, Mr. Green. Wycherly came aboard on the afternoon of November the second. The ship was due to sail at four o'clock, but it didn't actually sail until the following morning. Right?"

"Yessir. We went out at dawn."

"Did Wycherly leave the ship on the night of November second?"

"Not to my knowledge. No, sir. 'Course, I wasn't sitting there watching him all evening. I had plenty of things to do."

"Did you see him at all in the course of the evening?"

"Yessir, I did. I was in and out of the stateroom several times. Mr. Wycherly is a man who likes things the way he likes them. I'm not complaining," he added with a professional grin. "He gave me a good tip the other day. A hundred dollars buys a lot of steaks."

"You say you were in and out of the stateroom. How frequently?"

"Every hour, anyway. Oftener than that. He kept asking for things and I kept bringing them."

"What sort of things?"

"Drinks. Food. Speaking of food, my steaks are going to be incinerated."

"I took them off the fire," his wife said from the kitchen doorway. "The children are eating theirs, and I put ours in the oven to keep warm." She retreated out of sight.

"I'm sorry to be a nuisance."

"It's perfectly all right," he said with formal politeness. "Is there anything else you wanted to know?"

"Just this. Could Wycherly possibly have left the ship that evening long enough to get to Atherton and back?"

"I don't see how. He couldn't make the round trip to Atherton in less than an hour-and-a-half. And that would be cutting it real fine."

I thanked him and left, with more unanswered questions in my mind. I took them across the city to Merriman's house. My headlights caught the reflector sign that spelled out the dead man's name in three-inch letters. There was a light in the cottage among the trees. I made my way up the dark walk and knocked on the door. Sally Merriman answered through it:

"Who is it?"

I reached back for the name I had given her. It was a long reach. "Bill Wheeling. We talked about houses the other night."

She said in a tired voice: "I'll put something on."

Her footsteps went away and after a time returned on clicking heels. She switched on the outside light and opened the door. What she'd put on was a scarlet muumuu worn over tight black Capri pants.

"Come in, Mr. Wheeling."

I stepped directly into her living room. It was poorly lit by a fussy silk-shaded lamp which stood on top of the blank-eyed television set. A battered-looking tape recorder stood on a coffee table. Newspapers cascaded from the chesterfield and chairs onto the floor.

The room was mirrored and repeated by the glass doors on the far side. I could see myself and the woman in the glass, like actors playing out a television drama which went on and on without any station breaks.

She gathered a sheaf of newspapers from one of the chairs and stood holding them. "I'm sorry, the place is a mess. My husband died, I guess you know that. I haven't been doing much around the house."

"You've had a rough time."

"Yeah, a rough time."

Its marks were on her face. She still had her beauty, though, in spite of death and gin, and the money problem that nags like a chronic disease under the heart. I was ashamed of using it against her.

She pulled herself together with a visible effort. From some incredible reserve she dredged up a smile and fixed it on her face and talked through it:

"I don't have the listings here at the house, but I can tell you in general about our offerings. We have some very nice offerings."

The words were a little out of synchronization with the

movements of her mouth. She flapped her blue eyelids at me as if it was herself she was trying to sell. Thirtyish blonde, available at a bargain, abandoned by previous owner, needs some work. More work than I felt up to.

I remained standing with my back to the door, watching my mirror-image using my face in the glass. The man who knocked on any door at any time with any kind of a story.

"I have to admit something, Mrs. Merriman."

Her body went rigid.

"I'm not actually here to buy a house. I'd like some help from you."

"Help." Her red lips curled over the word. "I need it. I don't give it."

"We may be able to help each other. I'm a detective looking into your husband's death, and certain other matters."

The rigidity rose to her face. "You can go back and tell your cohorts that I've done all the talking I'm going to. There's no use *me* talking. I've told you people over and over my brother Stanley didn't knock off Ben. It's a dirty libel on a dead man who isn't here—"

"I agree with you."

The blue stuff on her eyelids exaggerated her look of surprise. "You mean you boys at the Hall of Justice have come to your senses?"

"I'm not from the Hall of Justice."

I told her my real name and occupation. The information did nothing for our relationship:

"So you're just a lousy gumshoe!"

"A pretty good one," I said. "I've come to the conclusion that the answer to who killed your husband is in his office safe."

Her lips parted and shaped the word, "How—?" before she clamped them shut. She was a lousy actress.

"I think the answer is on a tape recording which your brother made for your husband some time last spring. Your brother tried to get it from you yesterday."

"Did Jessie Drake hire you and put you onto me?"

"No, but I would like to ease her out of this bum rap."

"You expect me to help you with that? I wouldn't cross the street to save her neck."

"Aren't you interested in who killed your husband?"

"Of course I'm interested."

"Then come down to his office and let me into the safe."

"I don't know the combination."

"That's kind of hard to believe. You were pretty close to your husband's business."

"His *legitimate* business. I wanted no part of the other."
She narrowed her eyes at me and tried to look shrewd. "What
about this tape? Is it really worth money?"

"Yes. I wouldn't try to collect the money it's worth if I
were you. Your husband and your brother tried. Look
what it got them."

She looked, and shuddered. "They were killed on account
of that tape?"

"That, and other things."

"How do you know about it?"

"I told you I was a pretty good gumshoe."

The woman didn't smile. "You're trying to take me for
something."

"What have you got besides trouble?"

"God knows I've got plenty of *that*—more than I can use."
Her expression softened a little. "You think it was one of
the people on that tape who knocked off Ben?"

"You've heard the tape, Mrs. Merriman?"

She froze, still and flat-eyed. Finally she said:

"All right, so I heard it. Don't go jumping to conclusions.
I wasn't in on the deal with Ben and Stanley. I wasn't in on
any of Ben's deals. I watched the money come and I watched
the money go and damn little of it ever rubbed off on me.
He threw away thousands on the tables and he didn't even
leave me a house I can call my own. Then the cops had the
gall to impound the money they found in Stanley's shop. I
say it rightfully belongs to me."

"Forget that money. You don't want the rap that goes
with it."

"More dirty blackmail money?"

"It smells like it to me. What was said on that tape?"

"I don't remember too well. It was a couple of people, a
man and a woman. It sounded like they were arguing in bed."

"How long ago did you hear it?"

"Just last night. I went down and got it out of the office
last night. The way my brother talked, it was worth money,
like you said. So I rented a machine and put it on, but I
couldn't tell who the people talking were. Who is it worth
money to?"

"Me."

"How much money?"

"I'd have to listen to it first. Is it here in the house?"

She did some quiet writhing. "Yeah, I have it here. I hid it
in the kitchen."

"Let's play it over."

She went out to the kitchen; I heard her moving pans. She

came back with the tape, handling it as if it were made of platinum; put it on the recorder and set it for playback. I sat on a hassock beside the coffee table. After a rustling silence, Trevor's voice spoke from the machine:

"That was Phoebe, you know. In that car."

"I didn't see her," a woman's voice said

"I did. And she saw us."

"Does it matter so much? She's old enough to know the facts of life. Christ, I *had* her when I was two years younger than she is now. As you well know."

"I wish you wouldn't swear."

"Listen to the man. Are you getting religion or something? Is Helen making a Christian out of you?"

"We won't get off on Helen. I simply dislike hearing a woman swear. Especially in bed."

"You like women to do other things in bed."

"Not women. Just you. But we're going to have to be much more careful in future. If Phoebe goes to Homer with this—"

"She won't. She's got more brains."

"But what if she does?"

"I wouldn't give a damn."

"I'd give a very big damn, as you choose to put it. I have a lot to lose."

"You'd still have me." There was wistful irony in the woman's voice.

"You, and nothing else. Helen would take everything. Naturally I'd lose my job. At my age, with my health record, I'd never get another one on my own level."

"We could make do. I could get money from Homer."

"For the two of us to live on? Don't fool yourself. Even if he did give you a settlement, I wouldn't live on Homer's money."

"You're living on it now."

"I work for the money I live on," he said sharply.

"Money, money, money. We wouldn't need money if you loved me enough. We could go to Mexico or Tahiti and live very cheaply."

"Sure, and rot away into the landscape. We've been into that romantic fantasy before. I'm not Gauguin and neither are you."

"I suppose *this* is your idea of real romance."

"It's all there is," he said.

"But don't you want to *live* with me?"

"It's too late."

"Yah, it was always too late for you. The trouble is that

you don't love me enough. Sometimes I think you don't love me at all, that you're just using me to scratch an itch."

"People who love each other use each other."

"No."

"Yes," he insisted. "I love you better than anything or anybody."

"Except your goddam job and your goddam income and your goddam house and horses and for all I know that goddam frigid wife of yours. You've stuck with her long enough."

"That's my business."

She let out a laughing cry. "Business is the word for Cully. Poor cautious Cully, he wants to eat his cake and keep it, too."

"Satirize away. I've been poor, remember. I intend to go on keeping what I've got."

"Even if it means losing me?"

"I don't intend to lose you. Let's not quarrel, hon. We have to do some thinking."

"This is a hell of a time and place to do some thinking."

"It's the only time and place we have."

"Or ever will have." She said after a time: "I wish the two of them would go off on a plane together and crash or something."

"Homer and Helen aren't the type. They'll outlive us both."

"I know. I almost wish you'd never come back to me, Cully. When I'm away from you, I want you all the time. And then when we do get together, you want to talk about money and problems and things."

"I didn't *make* this problem."

"Who made it if you didn't?"

"All right, we made it together. The fact that we're both in it doesn't help much. The overriding fact is the fact that Phoebe saw us tonight, in compromising circumstances."

"So I'm compromised. Again."

"You don't seem to get the picture," he said urgently. "Everything is on the point of blowing up in our faces."

"Let it blow."

"No," he said emphatically. "We have to keep the situation as it is."

"Why do we have to keep it as it is?"

"For the sake of everyone concerned. Not just you and me, but Phoebe too."

"Okay. I'll talk to her."

"What can you say?"

"She might as well know the truth. If I tell her you're her father, that ought to head her off."

"Tell her that she's a bastard?"

"Bastard is just a word. I think of her as a love-child. I've wanted to tell her that she was our love-child ever since she got old enough to understand. This seems like a good time to do it."

"I absolutely forbid it," Trevor said. "If Phoebe is told, if anyone is told, the whole thing's bound to come out."

"What if it does?"

"It's not going to. I've lived a split-level life for twenty years, suppressing my real feelings, covering up. I'm not going to let you make nonsense of it now."

"You want her to inherit the money, don't you?" she said softly.

"It's a reasonable wish for my daughter."

"Always money. Haven't you learned it isn't that important?"

"You can say that because you've had it."

"I haven't always had it, any more than you. Anyway, she could inherit the money, whether or not I told her who she is."

"You're wrong. You don't know Phoebe."

"I ought to, she's my daughter."

"She's my daughter, too," he said, "and in some ways I know her better than you. In the long run she's incapable of lying—"

"So we go on doing her lying for her?"

"I'm certainly not going to let you tell her the truth about her parentage. The truth is supposed to make you free, but it doesn't. The less people know of the truth, the better for them." He spoke with a kind of dry and abstract anguish.

"Okay, Cully, don't tie yourself in knots. I won't tell her. We'll let things lie. Let them lie." She seemed to savor the doubleness of the words. "Now let's think happy thoughts for a change. Shall we?" She waited. "Think about me?"

"I think about you every day of my life."

"That's better. And you really love me, don't you?"

"I love you passionately," he said without much passion.

"Show me, Cully."

The bed creaked. Sally Merriman bent forward and switched off the recorder. Her eyes and mouth were bright.

"That's all there is. Who are they, anyway?"

"Paola and Francesca in middle life."

"Paola and Francesca? They don't sound much like foreigners to me. They sound like you and I. Besides, she called him Cully."

I made no comment.

"Did this Cully knock off Ben?"

"I don't know."

"You said the tape would clue you in on who did it."

"Did I?"

"You're trying to con me. You know who they are."

"Maybe. I don't intend to tell you. One of them is dead. The other might as well be."

"Which of them is dead?"

"The woman."

Her eyes went dark. "But she sounded so *alive!*"

"She looks so dead."

She took it as a personal threat. "Is everybody dying?"

I looked past her at our images in the glass. We were huddled together in a small lit space suspended in darkness over the long fall. "Sooner or later," I said.

"How old was she?"

"Thirty-nine or forty."

"What did she die of?"

"Life," I said.

"Is that supposed to be a gag?"

"I'm feeling a little depleted."

She sat in silence for a while, then rose and stretched, letting me see the weight of her breasts lifting under her muumuu. "So am I feeling depleted, if the truth be knownst. How about a little drinkie? I have some gin in the kitchen."

The voices on the tape seemed to have excited her. Whatever her feelings were, they accentuated her beauty. Her eyes were like peepholes into starred purple darkness. I suspected that she could be had for the taking.

"Thanks. I have to be going."

"But we need to talk about the money. I thought it would be nice if we talked about it over a drink like friends."

"What money?"

"The money you're going to pay me for the tape."

"Oh. That."

I stood up and took out my wallet and counted the money in it: two hundred and ninety-eight dollars. I separated out five fifties and handed them to her:

"Here's two-fifty. That leaves me forty-eight bucks to get back to L.A."

She crumpled the bills in her fist. "What are you trying to pull on me? Two hundred and fifty measly dollars! You'll sell the tape for a hundred times that much."

"I'm not planning to sell it."

"What are you going to do with it?"

"Hang somebody."

"You're not going to try and hang me?" Her free hand embraced her not quite classic throat. "I thought you liked me."

"I like you, and this is the proof. If I wanted to hang you, I could do it with a quick call to the Hall of Justice. Or I could simply take the damn thing away from you. Instead, I'm giving you all the ready cash I can spare."

While she stood and watched me, I rewound the tape and took it off the machine and slipped it into my jacket pocket.

"What can I do with a measly two-fifty?" she said, hugging the crumpled bills to her chest.

"You can make a down payment on two funerals. Or you can buy a ticket out of here."

"Going where?"

"I'm not a travel agent," I said from the neighborhood of the door.

She followed me to it. "You're a hard man, aren't you? But I like you, I really do. Are you married?"

"No."

"I don't know what to do with myself. I don't know where to go." She leaned towards me with a lost expression, hoping to be found. "Where can I go?"

Her body tempted my hands, in spite of the drowned one floating behind my eyes; in spite of all the old numb burnmarks which bodies like hers had left on my nerve-ends.

Try Ephesus. I was in a bad mood, but I didn't say it out loud.

chapter 28

I GOT TO TREVOR in the morning. He was sitting propped up in bed in his blinded room. His hands lay quiet on the covers.

He raised one of them in a weak salute. "Archer. How are you?"

"How are you, Trevor?"

"Surviving, it appears. I have to apologize for falling by the wayside the other night. I suppose I should apologize, too, for giving you a mistaken identification. Though it was natural enough under the circumstances. Even Homer had trouble ascertaining that the dead woman was his wife."

He was watching me with the ragged awareness of a poker

player after an all-night game. I stood at the foot of the bed and matched his look. It was a high hospital bed, so that our eyes were almost on a level.

"You made a false and deliberately misleading identification, and I know why."

He lifted his hands like twin burdens and dropped them on his shrouded thighs. "So it's like that. You've been doing some fairly deep digging, have you?"

"Digging your grave. Do you want to talk about the mess you've made?"

"Nothing would give me greater pain."

"Then I'll do the talking. The doctor didn't allow me much time with you, and we have a lot of ground to get over. In the evening of last November second you picked up a poker in Catherine Wycherly's house in Atherton and beat her fatally. I expect she was desperate and on the point of blowing the whistle on you: your motive was to silence her. But she didn't die right away. She lived long enough to tell Phoebe that her father was responsible for the crime.

"Phoebe naturally assumed that she meant Homer. She's very fond of Homer, and in the shock of the event she decided to take the blame on her own shoulders. Her obvious purpose was to protect her father. Dr. Sherrill would probably have a more complicated explanation."

"You've talked to Sherrill?"

"Yes, and I've talked to Phoebe. I also have a tape recording of a conversation in which you and Catherine Wycherly discussed the fact that Phoebe was your child. The tape was made the night Phoebe saw you and her mother together in a taxi in San Mateo. You may recall the occasion."

"I should. It was the beginning of all this. It's appropriate to have it recorded for posterity." He looked at me from eyes like rotting ice. "Does Phoebe know I'm her father?"

"No. She never will if I can help it. She has a chance for happiness, or at least a little peace, and you're not going to louse it up again. She's been living in the hell you and her mother fixed for her—two months in the hands of blackmailers, taking your rap for you. She finally broke down a few days ago and told Ben Merriman what her mother had said before she died: that her father was the guilty one.

"It meant something different to Merriman from what it meant to Phoebe. Merriman had the tape, and knew who her father was. When he got back from Sacramento he phoned your office and made an appointment with you. He was loaded with the money that he'd extorted from Phoebe, but he saw the possibility of more—an annuity for the rest of his life, or at least the rest of yours. He told you to meet him in the house where you had killed Catherine. No doubt that was part of his plan to screw up the pressure on you.

"He screwed it up too tight, and you repeated your crime. You rode a commuter's train down from the City, got off at the Atherton station, walked to the house and kept your appointment with Merriman, walked back to the Atherton station, boarded the next train and got off a few minutes later to meet your wife in Palo Alto. No wonder you were looking sick when she drove you home. You're looking sicker now."

Trevor winced against his pillows, and covered his face with his hands. He didn't seem to be overcome with emotion. He simply didn't want me looking at his naked face.

"That left Stanley Quillan. Stanley wasn't as tough as Merriman, he wasn't as smart, and he didn't know as much. He must have known your name, though, and been aware of the contents of the tape. He made it, after all. When he needed getaway money, he called you. You gave him a bullet in the head. Was it Merriman's gun you used?"

Trevor sat hidden-faced and still. He wasn't even breathing.

"Is that the way it happened, Trevor?"

He took his hands away from his face. It cost him an effort that made him gasp.

"More or less. It's strange to hear it from the outside. You make it sound so crude and senseless."

"It was really sensible and civilized?"

"Hardly. But let me ask *you* a question. What would you do if a pair of shakedown artists threatened the entire structure of your life, and you saw no way out?"

"Perhaps the same as you," I said. "Then I would have to pay for it. Better to keep your nose clean in the first place."

"You don't understand." I was hearing that from all sides. "You don't understand how a man's life can go sour. You start out with an innocent roll in the hay, and you end up having to kill people."

"Twenty-odd years is a long time to be innocently rolling in the hay."

"I see there's no use trying to explain." But he went on explaining: "I'm scarcely the bold seducer. Kitty was the only other woman in my life. I had no designs on her when she came into our house, though she was the loveliest thing I'd ever seen. So fresh, so young. She was only eighteen. I kept my hands off her."

"And that's why you're not here with her death on your hands."

He hardly seemed to hear me. "She was the one who took pity on me. Sex is a dirty word to my wife: she lost a child in the first year of our marriage: after that I never slept in her room. I was still a young man when Kitty came to stay with us. She saw my need for her, and she took pity on me. She came to my room one night and offered herself to me.

"It wasn't entirely a deed of charity. She was due to be married to Homer in a few weeks, and she was a virgin. She elected me to break her in. It doesn't sound romantic, I know, but we caught fire from each other. I learned what it is to treasure a woman's body. For a week or two of nights, I was back in Eden with the dew on the grass.

"Then Kitty missed a period, and got scared. I couldn't catch her. I wanted to, of course. But I had a way to make, and a wife. Helen would have stripped me, with Homer's willing assistance. I'd worked my way up from a twenty-dollar-a-week job in the Meadow Farms bank, and I couldn't see myself starting all over again at thirty-two. We did the best we could with the situation. Kitty let Homer have her before their wedding and convinced him when the baby came that it was slightly premature.

"The next few years were rugged ones for me. It grew on me like a disease—the realization that I'd had the one thing worth having. A little warmth and companionship in the void. I'd had it and given it up, in favor of security, I suppose you'd call it. Security. The great American substitute for love."

"But you went on seeing her."

"No, I did not, except of course in the most casual way. She wanted to give her marriage a chance, she said. I found out years later that she was deeply offended with me for not divorcing Helen and marrying her.

"She was in love with me," he said with mournful pride. "Naturally her marriage didn't work out. I doubt it would have worked out if I had never existed. She and Homer lived like enemies, fighting over the child. My child. You know what Bacon has to say about your children: that they're your hostages to fortune. It's a grinding thing to know that and feel it, as I have, and be unable to do anything much about it. I sat on the sidelines watching them make a hash of Phoebe's life as well as their own. The not so innocent bystander.

"That went on for nearly twenty years. Then, a couple of years ago, my heart went back on me. A close brush with death affects a man's thinking. When I came out of it I determined to get something more out of life—something more than going up to the city and entertaining the right people and staving off the next coronary.

"I went back to Kitty. She was willing. Her marriage, as I said, had not worked out. She felt very much as I did, that she had missed the best part of life.

"She wasn't the girl she had been. She'd aged and coarsened and lost some of her looks and most of her gentleness. There had been other men. Still we had something between us—something that was better than nothing. When we were together, at least we weren't alone.

"She got a place where we could be together two or three times a month. Unfortunately she rented it through Merriman. I suspect from something he said that he had been one of the other men. He had an ascendancy over her—"

"Something he said when?"

"The night I killed him. He talked about her as though she was a common whore. It was one of the reasons I killed him. Yes, I see the irony. I killed a man for defaming the character of a woman I had killed two months before."

"You still haven't explained why you killed her."

"I can't, really. I suppose the sheer involvement became too much for me. I tried to break away from her when Merriman and Quillan started to blackmail her. It looked as though I would be next, and the game wasn't worth the candle any more. After her divorce she went to pieces very rapidly. She seemed to expect me to pick up the pieces. I had barely enough stuff to get through the motions of everyday life. I couldn't take her on."

"I thought you already had."

"I mean in a full-scale way—divorce and remarriage and all the trimmings. I couldn't face all that, and I told her so. She got more and more desperate, and more threatening. She was going to ruin me if I didn't bail her out. The whole thing came to a head on that last day. Homer was leaving the country, rich and free; she was being swindled out of what money she had; she was under bad pressures. During the famous leavetaking in Homer's stateroom, she was on the verge of blurting everything out.

"I went to see her that night, to try and make her understand what she was doing to me, to all of us. She wouldn't listen to reason. Phoebe was coming to visit her, she said, and she intended to tell the girl the whole story. I tried to convince her that it was too late for that. When I couldn't, I took the poker and silenced her, as you said. It was an

ugly way for it to end." He might have been criticizing a
scene in a play.

"When did you undress her, and why?"

"She undressed herself. It was one of her means of per-
suasion which had worked on me in the past. But I felt no
desire for her. For some time now the only real desire I've
had is a desire for death. Darkness and silence."

He sighed. "Everything was very silent for two months. I
had no idea what had happened to Kitty's body. I wasn't
even aware that Phoebe was missing. Normally I kept in
some sort of touch with her, but I was afraid to do that now.
I was afraid to do anything that might stir up the situation.

"Then Merriman called my office the other afternoon. He
insisted I keep an appointment with him in Kitty's empty
house. You know the outcome of that. I searched Merriman's
clothes and car in the hope that he might have the tape
with him. He hadn't, but I found his gun, and the money.

"I had no intention of keeping the money for myself. If
the other fellow—Quillan—tried to carry on the blackmail
game, I thought I would use it to pay him off. I liked the
irony of that." He was making a desperate effort to hold his
style.

"Why didn't you do it if you liked it so much?"

"I tried to. I went to Quillan's shop and tried to go through
with the payoff. But he recognized the source of the money.
He said things I couldn't endure. I shot him with Merriman's gun, as you guessed. It *was* a senseless crime, and I
admit it. After I talked to Phoebe in Sacramento, I no
longer had any real hope of pulling it out. I could have
taken the money, I suppose, and left the country. But I had
no heart for it."

He heard the double meaning in the word, and touched
his rib-cage in a gingerly way, as if it held a sick animal
which might bite him.

"How did you reach Phoebe?"

"I found a bill in Merriman's pocket, a paid bill from the
Champion Hotel, made out in Kitty's name. I conceived
the wild idea that she had survived somehow, that Merriman's accusation was only a bluff. I flew to Sacramento that
night after I talked to Royal, rented a car at the airport and
drove to the Champion. When Phoebe came to the door of
her room I still believed she was Kitty. There was very
little light, and I was very willing to believe it. I thought
some miracle had saved her, and saved me.

"I took her in my arms. Then she spoke to me. She told
me who she was and what she was doing there."

"What did you tell her?"

"Nothing. There was nothing I could tell her, then or ever. I did do my best for her, though. I gave her money and got her out of that wretched room into a decent place. The Hacienda was only a temporary expedient, of course. I saw as I talked to her that she needed medical care. I was in need of it myself. I was so completely exhausted by this time that I had to lie down in the other room of her bungalow. I wasn't up to so much stress and activity."

"Like hitting people on the head with a tire-iron?"

"I'm sorry about that, Archer. I heard the two of you in her room. I had to stop you in some way. I was afraid she'd talk herself into a murder trial."

"Or talk you into one."

"There was that possibility, of course."

"Your tense is wrong, and it's more than a possibility."

My words hung between us on the air.

"Have you been to the police?"

"Not yet."

"You're planning to go to them, of course."

"I couldn't keep them out of this even if I wanted to, and I don't."

"It won't do Phoebe any good to put me on trial for murder. She's had her fill of disasters. She deserves a chance at life, as you yourself said. You don't want to saddle her with the knowledge that she's the bastard child of a murderer."

"She doesn't know you're her father. She doesn't have to."

"It's bound to come out if there's a trial."

"Who will bring it out? You and I are the only ones who know."

"But what about Catherine's dying words?"

"Phoebe can be persuaded that she misheard them."

"Yes. She actually did mishear them, in a sense, didn't she?"

Trevor sat and studied me. His eyes closed and opened from time to time, so slowly that he seemed to be alternating between death and life.

"Phoebe is my chief concern," he said. "I care nothing for myself. I'm thinking of her solely."

"You should have been thinking of her when you killed her mother."

"I *was* thinking of her. I wanted to protect her from the ugly reality. It's uglier now, and I still want to protect her. I believe I proved something when I brought her back to Dr. Sherrill. I knew the chance I was taking."

"You proved something."

"Will you do something for me, and incidentally for her? My clothes are in the closet there." He gestured towards a door on the far side of the room beside the bureau. "I have some digitalis capsules in the pocket of my coat—more than enough to kill me. I tried to get to them before you came, but I collapsed and had to be lifted back into bed." He took a breath which whistled in his nostrils. "Will you bring me my coat?"

I was still on my feet, facing him. Nothing had changed about Trevor except his eyes. They were glittering and sharp-edged like the broken blue edges of reality.

I didn't know what I was going to say until I said: "In return for a written confession. It doesn't have to be long. Do you have writing paper?"

"There's some in the bedside drawer, I think. But what can I possibly write?"

"I'll tell you what to say if you like."

I got a tablet of stationery out of the drawer and handed him my pen. He wrote on his knee to my dictation:

" 'I confess the murder of Catherine Wycherly last November second. She resisted my advances.' "

Trevor looked up. "That's rather corny."

"What do you suggest?"

"No explanation at all."

"There has to be one," I said. " 'She resisted my advances. I also killed Stanley Quillan and Ben Merriman, who were blackmailing me for her murder.' Sign it."

He wrote slowly and painfully, frowning over his penmanship. I lifted the tablet from his blue-nailed hands. He had added after his signature:

"May God have mercy on my soul."

And on mine, I thought. I tore out the page and laid it on the bureau, out of Trevor's reach. Shadows lay like sleeping dogs behind the closet door. Darkness and silence. We didn't speak again.

ABOUT THE AUTHOR

ROSS MACDONALD was born near San Francisco in 1915. He was educated in Canadian schools, traveled widely in Europe, and acquired advanced degrees and a Phi Beta Kappa key at the University of Michigan. In 1938 he married a Canadian girl who is now well known as the novelist Margaret Millar. Mr. Macdonald (Kenneth Millar in private life) taught school and later college, and served as communications officer aboard an escort carrier in the Pacific. For over twenty years he lived in Santa Barbara and wrote mystery novels about the fascinating and changing society of his native state. Among his leading interests are conservation and politics. He is a past president of the Mystery Writers of America. In 1964 his novel *The Chill* was given a Silver Dagger award by the Crime Writers' Association of Great Britain. Mr. Macdonald's *The Far Side of the Dollar* was named the best crime novel of 1965 by the same organization. Recently, he was presented with the Mystery Writers of America's Grand Master Award. *The Moving Target* was made into the highly successful movie *Harper* in 1966. *The Goodbye Look* (1969), *The Underground Man* (1971), *Sleeping Beauty* (1973) and *The Blue Hammer* (1976) were all national bestsellers. Ross Macdonald died in 1983.